Enchanting the King

Eli Donovan, E.D. Walker

Cover designed by Najla Qamber Designs

Edited by Deb Nemeth

Copy edited by the Formatting Fairies

Formatting by Eli Donovan with Atticus Software

Contact the author: writerelidonovan@gmail.com

Eli Donovan Website: www.elidonovan.wordpress.com

Contents

Dedication

*T*o Casey, because she told me she really wanted to read this book when I most needed to hear that.

And to all the other loyal fans who were hoping I might return to the world of The Beauty's Beast again: Thanks for waiting for me.

Prologue

Thomas led the last desperate charge of his men toward the nearby cliffs. They would get into the canyon up ahead and create a chokepoint. Then the sorcerous army they faced would have less of an advantage. The cliff loomed close now, high red stone streaking the ground with its immense shadow. His men were close behind him, pushing their mounts and their own strength hard. He hoped they could snatch survival at least from the jaws of this ruinous defeat.

Something collided with his horse, and hot pain flared along Thomas's leg. Spellfire. His mount screamed and reared beneath him, kicking and thrashing. Thomas gritted his teeth, trying to hold on, but the world still snapped sideways as he flew from the saddle. He saw sky, then red earth, then he slammed down hard enough to steal his breath. Pain flared bright and immediate across his head, and he tasted blood.

Thomas still dragged himself upright, even as his vision narrowed to a black tunnel. His men had run on ahead, pushing on for the canyon, he thought. A lone, twisted tree sat up against the cliff wall. He ran for it. His boots slipped in churned sand, and every movement he made created a fresh spike of agony in his head.

He at last reached the tree and hauled himself up. Rough bark scraped his palms raw, and the higher he climbed, the worse his head throbbed. Still he climbed on, because he had to see.

From the branches, the battle unfolded in terrible clarity. There was no line of soldiers anymore. No formation. Just slaughter. His knights fought in knots and pairs, backs to each other, their swords flashing uselessly as spells tore through them.

Thomas gripped the tree until his fingers cramped. His heart was crushed by this slaughter, but he couldn't–wouldn't look away.

But Fate had different plans for him. His world tilted all at once. The screams grew muffled, as if heard through water. His strength drained away, leaving only the ache and the dust and the awful certainty that this was the end.

The tree swayed. Or maybe he did. Thomas's vision narrowed to a single point of light, and then even that was gone.

Chapter One

The gentle rocking of her wagon might have been soothing once upon a time. Unfortunately, after so many weeks spent trapped inside it, Aliénor thought she might go mad if she had to travel another foot in the damn thing.

"Do you have the headache again, Princess?" one of her ladies-in-waiting asked.

"I'm all right." As they rolled over a bump in the road, Aliénor flung a hand out to steady herself. The wagon bumped again almost immediately, and she nearly collided with one of her ladies in waiting. Aliénor gritted her teeth. "I did not join this quest to be rolled across the world in a cramped wooden box."

Aliénor twisted away and snatched up one of the plush silk pillows littering the benches of her coach. She hugged it to her gut, resisting the urge to tear the stuffing out. This wagon had been a gift from her husband Prince Philippe. She knew he'd meant it as a pointed reminder of how she should conduct herself on this journey. Filmy curtains at either end of the compartment helped separate her ladies from the dust of the road *and* the stares of other men.

"Would you like to walk outside a bit, Princess?"

Aliénor shook her head, feeling her mood darken. Some grand adventure: riding along in a wagon she could probably outpace without breaking into an unladylike sweat. *Oh, Papa, your war stories were never like this.* When Aliénor had set out on this road, she'd meant to walk in the footsteps of her glorious father. See the lonely mountains of the east, smell the fresh sea air, taste the wind of the deserts. Expand her mind, stretch her horizons. Instead, her husband kept her closed up tight in her plush little box with not one but *two* lady chaperones. Instead of stretching her horizons, she'd shrunk her world to a stuffy wooden trap.

No more. Aliénor knocked smartly on the wooden roof. "Driver, stop."

Her two ladies-in-waiting blinked in surprise. Aliénor shoved the curtains away on the back to step out. Servants had already come around the sides to help her. Aliénor shook their reaching hands away and leapt down herself.

"My lady, are you all right?"

"What do you require, Princess?"

"Saddle my horse, please," she said. "I will walk for a bit while you do."

The servants exchanged a look, but finally one went off to do as she'd asked. Happy for the first time all day, Aliénor tipped her face toward the sun as she walked. She took a deep breath too but choked on road dust. Aliénor laughed at herself, and covered her mouth with a kerchief once she'd finished coughing. Servants still hovered at her elbow, but she dodged around them and began walking down the road. A flurry of activity and raised voices sounded behind as ladies and servants scurried around, some to catch up to her and some to saddle her horse like she'd asked.

In the confines of the coach, her husband's army had not been so loud, but the sound rolled over her now: thousands of feet tramping, thousands of men chatting and laughing and yelling good-naturedly at each other. Horses too, hundreds of them prancing down the road with their masters. It was a dizzying sight, impossible to take in all at once. The supply wagons were still somewhere far behind, carrying tents and mattresses and other accoutrements of camp. Her husband's army did not travel light. Behind her, down the road, the baggage train seemed at least half as long as the column of soldiers. She frowned as she contemplated that tail of carts and animals lagging behind on the long river road.

The jingle of a harness drew her attention, and she wheeled around just as her husband rode up. Her heart quailed to see he had brought his royal witch with him, Mistress Helen. The witch was a decade or so older than Aliénor. The royal witch had a cool, composed manner that never failed to make Aliénor feel like a grubby, disorderly child. And Mistress Helen's magic never failed to make Aliénor ill at ease.

Philippe dismounted with easy grace and hurried toward Aliénor. His dark hair had a fine red coating of dust, turning his hair a lighter shade of brown than usual. He crossed straight to Aliénor and caught her by the arms. "Why has your wagon stopped? Are you ill?"

She fought to keep her gaze focused on him and not the witch behind him. "I needed some air. That's all."

"Again, Aliénor? I thought we'd settled this. It is not proper for you to walk about in the open air. You are a Princess of Jerdun. You are not meant to be a spectacle for the common rabble."

"I often walked and rode at home in Jerdun. How is this different?"

"Because you are one of only three noblewomen in the camp. Indeed, you are one of only a handful of women in the camp at all. I'm doing this to protect you."

If you hadn't banished all the camp followers, my women and I wouldn't be such a curiosity. Or a temptation. She bit her tongue on that unwise remark. Discipline had been harder to maintain since Philippe's order to ban all prostitutes in camp. But a large army in a foreign land was difficult to manage at the best of times.

Isn't it? Aliénor looked away, studying that rugged line of mountains in the distance. High red peaks stood barren and harsh against the blue of the sky. The sight fired a longing in her blood, a determination. *I want more than simple comfort and privilege.* She wanted to reach those high red peaks and trail her fingers across the sky.

"Aliénor." Philippe cupped her cheek, turning her face toward him. His eyes were pinched, his mouth tight. "I have so many responsibilities on this expedition. Please do not make yourself a burden."

She flinched. "Do not treat me like a child, Philippe."

"Stop behaving like one."

"I did not come on this trip to sit in a wagon and rot."

His nostrils flared. "You shouldn't have come on this trip."

She broke away from him. Though the blood pounded in her veins, she managed to keep her voice low. "If I hadn't rallied my nobles in the south, if I hadn't spent *months* persuading and cajoling them to come along, *you* wouldn't have an army at—" All along her body, Aliénor's muscles tensed up, and her jaw clamped shut with a click of teeth that hurt. *No.* Aliénor tried to twist away, as if simple motion could stop what was happening. Her muscles refused to obey her.

Mistress Helen sauntered forward, and her eyes glowed a little. The witch's magic now held Aliénor in a grip so tight it ached. "Now, now, Princess. We discussed this. You swore to do better. To be more obedient."

An angry flush darkened the sallow skin of Philippe's face. "Helen, let her go."

"But, my prince—"

"I don't need your help to control my wife, witch."

Needles of pain stabbed all over Aliénor's limbs as she tried to throw the witch's curse off. Useless. She ground her teeth together in mingled alarm and fury.

With a flick of one hand and a grimace, Mistress Helen lifted her spell. The sudden release of tension made Aliénor gasp. She would have fallen over if Philippe hadn't tightened his arm around her waist. Every muscle she possessed prickled like a sleeping limb waking to life. "Philippe, you promised you wouldn't let her do that again."

A muscle ticked in his jaw. "If you were better behaved, she wouldn't have to. What did I do to be cursed with such a termagant for a bride?"

Aliénor opened her mouth to make a sharp reply. Then, remembering Mistress Helen's presence, she snapped her mouth shut.

"My prince, apologies if I overstepped myself," Mistress Helen murmured in her soothing alto, "but this is not seemly, to be seen quarreling on the road. Perhaps a compromise?"

Philippe smoothed a hand down the front of his neat surcoat. "You're right, Mistress Helen. Aliénor, I apologize for the spell, but you *must* do better." He let out a deep sigh. His look was sad, resigned, as he gazed at her. "If you wear a veil, you may ride. All right?"

Aliénor clenched her hands under her bosom and swallowed her anger, though it almost choked her to do so. "Thank you, Philippe."

He just shook his head and walked away.

The witch raked her gaze up and down Aliénor with a cat-like smile. "Soon, Princess. Soon I will have the ruling of you."

As the woman walked away, Aliénor glared at Mistress Helen's back, but inside Aliénor's heart felt cold. Philippe had put a stop to the spell this time, but he grew more exasperated with Aliénor by the day. How much longer before he decided to let Mistress Helen control her completely?

"My lady?"

Aliénor startled out of her reverie as her lady-in-waiting brushed her arm. "Yes?"

"Your horse is ready."

"Oh, good. Excellent. Thank you." Almost despite herself, her heart lightened. A small victory then. In these dark days, she would take what she could get. "Bring him round, please. I'll ride now."

⸺◈⸺

When Aliénor had argued for her choice to ride, she hadn't quite realized how physically draining it would be. Her rump was already sore, her shoulders stiff. Still, the view was everything she could wish for, the fresh air stimulating despite the massive dust cloud created by the army's marching.

The river gurgled and rushed happily to her right, running parallel to their road. The waters flowed a deep blue-green that looked deceptively calm, with scrubby bushes scattered along the far bank. The land on their side of the river-bank was relatively bare, stripped of its trees and bushes to accommodate the traffic of the road.

Across the flow of water, though, the riverbank was verdant with tall, round-topped trees bending their boughs toward the river. To the southwest the mountains loomed, ragged red stone looking like a potter's unfinished project.

The day was warm, but the breeze off the river was crisp and lovely. Aliénor shut her eyes and let the wind dance over her face like a caress.

Her senior lady-in-waiting, Noémi, rode at her side, placidly and without comment. Her other lady-in-waiting had stayed behind in the wagon to sew. Aliénor and Noémi were near the front of the line with some two dozen men ahead of them, but still close enough that the two ladies could see a little of the road ahead. A sluggish trail of smoke wound through the sky ahead and to the west, coming from the mountain trail.

"Captain, what is that?" Aliénor asked.

The captain of her personal complement of guards half turned in his saddle and frowned, squinting at the sky. His mouth twisted, and he called for two men to ride up from further back in the line. More guards for Aliénor.

She frowned and looked again at the gray plume in the sky. "What's amiss, Captain?"

The man let out a grumpy sigh and turned to her with a pasted-on smile. "I am only worried that is the army of Lyond, Your Highness."

Noémi let out a small puff of surprise. "Lyond? But their army left months ahead of ours."

"Perhaps they have been delayed on this road as disastrously as we have." The captain shrugged, turning away as if their conversation wearied him. Aliénor should ask Philippe for a replacement for the impudent man. Her own dear captain of the guard from home had drowned a few months back. Several of her best men had died in that accident, when Philippe had ordered the army to ford a river instead of paying a ferryman's fees. She might have suspected treachery, except so many of their soldiers had been lost in that disaster, from every faction.

She shook her head, refusing to let the captain brush her off. "Captain, why should the Lyondi army trouble you? We are no longer at war with them. They are here to reclaim their colonies the same as us." Indeed, Aliénor had passionately argued back home that their Jerdic force should ally with the army of Lyond since their mission was so similar. However, after decades of near constant war and only a few years of uneasy peace with Lyond, the men of her homeland hadn't listened. Philippe and his brother, the king, had actually laughed at the idea.

The captain let out a long, slow sigh and turned to her with another one of his false smiles. "Princess, here in this wilderness, an army of those Lyondi barbarians will not care about any peace agreement made back home. Especially not if they catch sight of you and your two pretty ladies." He made a small half-mocking bow in his saddle to her and Noémi.

Aliénor's cheeks heated with an indignant flush.

Noémi tugged gently on Aliénor's sleeve, coaxing her attention away from the ill-mannered captain. "Your husband won't want you bickering with a guard captain in the middle of the road." She kept her voice low, calm. "He'll send you back to the wagon if he hears of a fight."

Or worse. Aliénor let her breath out through her teeth. "Wise counsel, my friend."

Noémi hummed in her throat, a faint note of approval.

Aliénor flicked her a teasing smile. "I do *sometimes* listen to you."

Noémi grinned. She was a large woman, thick-boned and stout, with a pale, pretty face unfortunately marred by deep pockmarks on her cheeks. But she had clear, snapping green eyes full of animation and intelligence. She was an unmarried lady, a widow twice over and not yet forty. Aliénor and Noémi had met only a few months ago at that bit of grand theater when the High Lord Magician of their homeland Jerdun had accepted all their solemn vows to reclaim the colonies and save the deserts to the south from the Tiochene raiders.

Aliénor had come to rely on Noémi as the one note of sanity in the swirling madness that their well-intentioned campaign had become. The wealthy widow was the first woman Aliénor had asked to become one of her "Amazons." Another flashy bit of theater in an already melodramatic display. Aliénor smiled still, months later, at the memory of the stodgy High Magician's face when she had shown up with her gaggle of noblewomen all dressed in vibrant red armor, all ready to take their solemn vows and fight.

Unfortunately, only Noémi and a young noblewoman named Violette had come along with her. The other noblewomen who had taken their vows had been forced to bow out of this grand adventure. One became pregnant, one suddenly lost her husband, and another lost her nerve when it came time to take ship. Still, Aliénor was happy to have even a *small* tribe of Amazons on this trip with her.

Both her women wore faded gray riding habits now, more practical than their flashy—and *heavy*—red armor. Yet the promise of that armor, the hope she'd had when she'd first made her impulsive vow, still pulsed in the back of Aliénor's mind. *Like a rotten tooth as needs pulling*, Aliénor wryly told herself.

They would probably have to sell the armor soon enough to pay for food. That should make Philippe happy. He'd always hated her red armor. After only a few days on the road she'd realized that Philippe had only let her buy armor because he'd planned to make her stay home. He'd underestimated her stubbornness or her bravery—maybe both. He'd wanted Aliénor to help rally the men and organize the expedition, but if Philippe had had his way she never would have been allowed out of Jerdun. *Maybe he was right*. Aliénor's grand adventure had been nothing like her plan thus far.

"We should be making camp soon, Your Highness."

Aliénor chuckled and eased back in her saddle to stretch her aching muscles. "Is my weariness that obvious?"

Noémi only smiled in response, a very politic answer.

Aliénor shook her head, laughing again.

The road dipped as they entered a valley with the river flowing between two small hills. Bare white stone jutted up around them oddly, with patchy green bushes and long, oval-shaped trees lining the road.

A foul smell reached her on the air, so strong that she gagged. "What is that?" A stench like dead animals or meat left to decompose in the sun. *Surely one dead animal could not be so strong, so overpowering.*

Noémi froze beside her, and took a deep, testing sniff of the air. Her face blanched. "Your Highness, we should head to the rearguard at once."

"Why—" Aliénor scanned the road, and the words died on her lips as she saw the first dead man ahead of them. And another. Parts of many men lay scattered along the road, their blood splashed against the stark white of the valley walls. Nearby in the center of the road lay just a man's leg with the heavy boot still upon it, a dark spot of blood beneath. Some of the bodies were badly burned, and scorch marks darkened many of the stones nearby, a few very high up on the walls.

"Send word to my husband at once." Aliénor barely managed to get the words out without vomiting. The back of her throat burned.

The column halted and called the word back to those behind. Noémi dismounted and helped Aliénor down from her own horse. Wobbly, her mouth sour with bile, Aliénor clung to her friend's arms. "I'm all right." A lie, and Noémi obviously knew it, for she settled a steadying arm around Aliénor's waist.

Noémi frowned at the gory scene ahead of them before looking away. "They appear to be men of the north like us."

"Could they be our men?" The more she talked, the easier it was to concentrate on something besides the overwhelming smell of death all around.

"These men could be deserters, or they might be men from one of the colonies. Soldiers your cousin sent out to meet us."

"How can you tell what race they are just from...from what's left?"

"Their clothes. Their boots. The local tribes around here favor lighter fabric, longer tunics, lighter armor. Sandals too, usually. These men are all wearing boots like us. They look like soldiers, not poor farmers murdered on the way to market."

Aliénor hadn't looked that closely. Hadn't been able to. Her stomach clenched again. "Does nothing faze you, my iron Amazon?"

"I held my first husband's castle during a siege in the last war with Lyond. We ate the horses before my husband's forces could come to relieve us."

Aliénor's stomach roiled again, but she swallowed her gorge and took a small breath in through her teeth.

Noémi flinched. "Apologies, my lady."

"No, no. It's fine." She stepped away from Noémi's supporting arm to prove it. "My father was a warrior, but my little island was always isolated, safe from the turmoil of the wars with Lyond. Papa told me war stories, of course, sang the ballads. But he never spoke of anything like...this." Aliénor disguised her first unsteady stumble forward as a confident step toward her guard captain. "Captain."

He looked up, his unguarded glance full of annoyance, which he quickly smoothed away. "Yes, Your Highness?"

"Have you assembled a party to look for survivors yet?"

He hesitated, a muscle ticking in his jaw. "Ah, no. Your Highness."

"Why not?"

"Begging your pardon, but there doesn't seem to be much point."

The image of the severed leg flashed through her mind's eye, sending her uncertain stomach swooping again. She stared at the clear, unblemished sky, focusing on that to blank her mind out. Soon enough her gut settled. She regarded the guard captain with her most imperious glare. "It is our pious duty to look for survivors of this battle."

"This looks like it was a slaughter, my lady. Not a battle."

Aliénor felt her grip on her temper slipping again, as if her moods were an unbroken horse she had yet to tame. However, she would get nothing from this man if she threw a tantrum. Instead, she offered him her most solicitous smile. "My Amazons will undertake a search, Captain. If your men cannot be spared from their other duties." She let her gaze flick to the two soldiers who had already dismounted and begun a game of dice on the trail.

The guard captain let out a low, exasperated sigh, then swung back onto his own horse. He pointed to some dozen of the various men-at-arms milling about. "You lot, with me. Her Highness"—he swept her a bow just short of outright mockery—"wishes us to search for survivors until such time as the prince arrives." *We're only doing this idiotic hunt until Prince Philippe gets here and puts his uppity wife in her place*, he left unsaid, but his meaning was clear.

She set her teeth and waved the captain on his way. She leaned close to Noémi and whispered, "Perhaps I shall get the good captain assigned to digging the latrine pits when we break for camp tonight."

Noémi snickered. "You handled him all right, my lady."

"Hmm. The captain's correct, though. My power will last only as long as it takes for my husband to ride to the front." A galling truth that her power was so slight and temporary, borrowed only from her husband, and that begrudgingly. "Will they find any survivors, do you think?"

"Perhaps." Noémi squeezed her hand. "I will go with you now to look. If you like."

Aliénor swallowed, flinching at the thought. Yet should she command her men to do that which she would not do herself? What sort of leader would she be if she did that?

The sort like my husband.

A spiteful thought. Aliénor sighed in frustration with herself. What was it about Philippe and her together that always seemed to bring out the worst in both of them? She gave Noémi a nod and swung herself into her saddle again, groaning only a little bit as her aching limbs shrieked in protest.

Noémi summoned two more of the soldiers to ride with them as guards. The young men followed the formidable Noémi's lead when they might have hemmed and hawed at Aliénor's authority. Perhaps that was Aliénor's lack, not in power itself but in her confidence in exercising it. Or perhaps she still looked too young for grown men to trust her wits.

She let Noémi lead the way with one of the soldiers beside her. The other fell in so close to Aliénor's horse that her little palfrey started and sidled away with nerves. "Careful," Aliénor snapped to the boy.

He nodded apology but stayed close nonetheless. "Beg pardon, Your Highness, but there might still be raiders about. Stay close to me, eh?" He drew his sword as he said it.

Aliénor shivered at the sight of the naked steel. The army had been marching to battle for months but had not seen any action as yet. One could almost forget they were riding to war. Until something like this happened.

She nodded to her guard and turned her gaze away to follow Noémi's progress. Her handmaiden had led them farther away down the road from the captain and her men, closer to the cliffs, while still staying in sight of the column. Perhaps Noémi knew if they came within calling distance of the captain he would order them back. Or perhaps she was just trying to keep Aliénor from seeing more bodies.

I am coddled from every side. Was she anything other than a silly, useless woman if even her friend refused to let her help in this small way? *If I am just a burden to be protected then I might as well turn back for home now and get out of everyone's way.*

She scanned the horizon and let her horse pick his way where he would, for they were in rocky terrain close to the mountains now. Scrubby brush and gray-trunked trees with tight, prickling foliage dotted the landscape. Her eye caught on one the trees where it grew practically against the foot of the hill. A bright flash of pale blue fluttered in the branches. A bird? She had seen no bright-plumed birds like that this far south.

Her pulse kicked up as she turned her mount toward the tree. Behind her, she heard her guard follow her with a small muttered oath.

The closer she came to that bright blue cloth, the harder her pulse beat until it was a veritable drum in her ears. Aliénor stopped short of the tree and slid off her horse.

When she saw the man tangled in the branches of the tree, her blood jumped all at once inside her like a bright flash of heat. Bile burned the back of her throat, but she forced herself forward one unsteady step at a time.

The man's chest rose and fell. Alive. *Thank Merciful Fate.* He voiced a low groan, and she hopped back a step in surprise. She wet her dry mouth and wheeled toward the guard riding toward her. "Help! Bring help."

She rushed forward to the tree and reached to lift the man down. He was braced against the branches, and a sword—stained red and nicked from battle—lay among the roots of the tree. Blood had also splashed the tree all around, as if the plant needed human sacrifice instead of wholesome water to live.

Together, Aliénor and her guard lifted the man down from the tree and laid him out on the ground to check for injuries. "Bring water from my saddle," she told her man. Flustered, the soldier rushed back to their horses.

The stranger stirred again, and his eyes fluttered open—a startling gray-blue color. "*Getfalen hwaa?*"

Aliénor's breath caught.

He tried to shift in her arms and look at her, but the movement seemed to overwhelm his strength, and his eyes rolled back into his head. He'd lapsed into unconsciousness by the time the soldier had returned with a canteen.

"What did he say?" her guard asked as he took a deep drink of water for himself.

Aliénor cleared her throat. "Gibberish. He's disoriented, I think." A lie. She'd understood his words perfectly well. The problem was, he had been speaking the language of Lyond—the language of her nation's greatest enemy.

Chapter Two

The wounded man did not awaken before the army stopped to make camp that night.

Noémi tried to distract Aliénor as she waited for the rest of the army to arrive at camp, but it was no use. Aliénor had only half an ear for anything said to her. As they walked to her tent, her belly went tight from anxiety, anticipating her husband's arrival.

Her other lady-in-waiting, Violette, was already at the tent when they arrived. Violette was a pretty child of fifteen or so, thin and delicate-boned with dark, copper-colored skin. Her tightly curled black hair was still in a neat coronet braid atop her head despite the trials of the road. Aliénor's own hair was a disordered mess atop her head, her braids slipping down as the hairpins fell loose from her baby-thin hair.

Violette smiled a greeting at them and continued to direct a few of the male servants as they bustled about, arranging the two feather mattresses Aliénor slept on each night. The mattresses were a ridiculous extravagance, of course, and every time Aliénor looked at them, she felt a fresh flush of mortification. She'd been so naïve when she'd left home. *Feather mattresses in this wilderness.* Yet Philippe had not forbidden them. Indeed, Philippe and his closest officers slept on feather mattresses of their own.

Noémi persuaded Aliénor to sit beside her on a camp stool, apart from the activity of Violette and the servants. "The prince might be impressed by your initiative, my lady. He might be pleased."

Aliénor snorted.

"He was pleased when you helped him organize this expedition. He doesn't always mind when you take charge of things."

Aliénor twisted her mouth into a smile that had nothing at all to do with happiness. "Those efforts pleased my husband because they served his ambitions. He needed my treasury to fund this adventure, and he needed my influence to convince the other lords to follow him. Without the lords loyal to me, there would not have been enough men to undertake this campaign." Once she'd accomplished those tasks for him, raising the money and the men, Aliénor was supposed to have stayed at home, waiting for Philippe's triumphant return.

Aliénor rose to begin her restless pacing once more, but both ladies jumped as someone yanked the tent flap back. Philippe stormed inside, his pale skin flushed with anger. He was a slight man, slender, but the anger on his face made Aliénor recoil from him. Noémi shifted in her chair but seemed to restrain her first protective impulse to leap in front of Aliénor.

"You, *out*." He flung a hand behind him, and Noémi hustled out with a quick, worried look at Aliénor. Violette and the servants scattered as well, abandoning the mattresses in a lopsided heap for the moment.

Philippe circled Aliénor and glowered. "You should not have risked yourself. There might have been Tiochene soldiers still about."

"Husband—"

"You are meddling where you are not needed, are not *wanted*."

She folded her hands together behind her back to hide how they shook. "I found the injured man myself. My guard captain was not—"

"*Bah.* One injured soldier? Is that worth the life of a princess of Jerdun? *No.*"

She gritted her back teeth, feeling again like she rode an unsteady mount, and at any moment she might lose control of her wild temper. "I thought the soldier might tell us what happened, how the raiders attacked. Then we could take better precautions for ourselves on the road ahead."

Philippe blew his breath out through his teeth, looking deflated at this sound reasoning. But then he straightened and waggled his finger in her face. "You should not even have been riding at the front. I knew I should have made you stay in the wagon."

She fought to maintain her composure, but the wild stallion of her temper broke from her control. "I did not go on this quest to ride around like some fragile pearl in a jewelry box—"

"*Always* you put yourself forward. *Always* you seek more than is proper. You are my wife. You belong to me, and you should damn well start learning to obey me."

Ever the same argument, ever the same problems between us. She scrubbed both hands over her face, trying to rub the fatigue away. Her efforts were in vain. This weariness went bone-deep, an infection in her blood, her very spirit, which seemed impossible to overcome.

"Aliénor." He must have sensed how near she was to breaking entirely, for his tone had gentled. She heard him approach but could not make herself face him. He caught her hand and gave it a gentle squeeze. "I'm sorry, my dear. I was just so worried for your safety when I heard what you had done." He planted a chaste kiss on the back of her hand. "Join me for dinner tonight?"

He framed it as a question, but Aliénor knew she had little choice. He was right: she was his wife. Her movements and every last detail of her life could be dictated by him should he choose to exercise that power. "Of course, my lord."

"No more madcap adventures, my girl." He patted her cheek as he said it but hurried out of the tent before she could make any reply to him.

She folded herself back into her camp stool and massaged her throbbing temples. At a rustle of cloth, she looked up. Noémi returning.

"Well?" her handmaiden asked.

Aliénor puffed out a mirthless laugh. "I know how thin the walls of this tent are. Don't pretend ignorance. You know how it went."

"*Hmm.* It's not...entirely unreasonable of him, you know."

"To expect better obedience from me? I know. As a loyal subject I owe that to him, and how much more so as his wife? Did you have such problems with your husbands?"

Noémi tilted her hand in a *so-so* gesture. "The first one, I suppose. At first. But then he broke me to bridle. Or I broke him." Her teeth flashed in a smile. "Or perhaps better to say we learned to work in tandem, like the horses that pull your wagon. To aim ourselves and work together rather than trying to run away in opposite directions. You only end up with a mess of tangled reins and broken legs that way, my lady."

"I know it."

"My second man, well. I married him for his looks, and we didn't much leave the bedroom. We worked well enough together *there.*"

Aliénor flopped back in her chair, combing her fingers through her hair and mussing her braid. "So perhaps it's me. Perhaps I'm not made for marriage. Perhaps I lack that womanly trait, that ability to combine my will with another's to make us both better."

"Yes, or—" Noémi bit the word off and pinched her lips tightly closed, as if the words might fight their way free despite her.

"Or what?"

Noémi shook her head, but Aliénor knew well enough what she would have said. What they were both thinking: *Or perhaps you and Philippe are simply not well suited.* But neither of them could say that aloud. Jerdic women married for life. To contemplate leaving Philippe, being free of him...

Noémi touched her hand. "For both your sakes, my lady, perhaps you should try harder?"

Aliénor flinched. *Marriage is for life. I took this vow for life.* However ill-considered it was, however young she'd been— *This is no good. Sitting here wallowing will accomplish nothing.* "Noémi, let us see if that wounded soldier is awake."

"An excellent idea, Your Highness."

Thomas awoke in pain, disoriented. When he opened his eyes and looked around, he recognized neither his surroundings nor his caretakers.

"Easy, easy. You're safe." The lady had a pleasant voice, young and clear, so it took him a moment to understand the spike of alarm that arose inside him at the words. It wasn't until she spoke again—"How are you feeling?"—that he understood his instinctive fear.

The woman was speaking Jerdic, the language of Jerdun. Thomas eased onto his elbows and smoothed the lines of his face to stillness. When he answered her, he answered her in perfect Court Jerdic. "Where are the rest of my men?" There were a few other injured men laid out on pallets on the ground in this tent as he was, but none that he recognized.

She tilted her head, looking surprised as her large brown eyes widened. She had a lovely face with strong cheekbones and a determined chin. Her skin was ivory pale but dotted with freckles, and her hair was a light red-gold braided in a somewhat mussed coronet atop her head after the Jerdic fashion. A married woman most likely and, judging by her cultured accent, a lady. *No matter. Too young for you, old soldier.* She couldn't have been more than twenty, nearly half his age. Still, she was exceedingly pleasant to look at.

She stared at him from narrowed eyes for a long moment and cleared her throat. "I'm so sorry. You are the only...the only survivor we've found so far."

Thomas gritted his teeth, tamping down the wave of despair that threatened to swamp him.

"I'm sorry." She made a small flinch of movement, as if she would have touched his hand, but then her eyes fluttered downward again. She kept her hands tightly folded in her lap.

He wet his lips. "I think I owe my salvation to you, fair lady. It was you who found me, yes?" He thought he remembered her face now, hovering over his before he'd blacked out. "May I know my rescuer's name?"

"I am Princess Aliénor. Of Jerdun." Her gaze flicked to his face, avidly studying him for some reaction.

So this is young Philippe's bride. Thomas knew of her husband by reputation—a weak, petulant child—but Thomas knew nothing of this woman. A duke's daughter, perhaps? Was he remembering right? A particularly insistent thread of pain uncoiled in his forehead, but he still smiled pleasantly for this woman. A soldier never shows weakness in front of his enemies.

"And you?" the Princess Aliénor asked, and there was more than a bit of challenge in the question.

"I'm called Thomas." True enough, if incomplete information. He should have invented a minor barony or claimed residence in the colonies here, but some foolish whim inside him disliked the idea of lying to this good lady. She had saved his life, after all. Falsehoods and trickery seemed a poor repayment for that.

"Can you tell us what happened?"

He scrubbed the back of his hand over his brow. The clang of swords rang in his ears. The smells of piss and offal and blood prickled in his nostrils. If he closed his eyes he would be back on that pass through the valley, under attack, watching his men die... "We were attacked, my lady. A pack of raiders swooped down on us in the mountain pass. They had magic users, more than I've ever seen together at one time. Their bows rained arrows on us from all sides so that the sun was entirely blacked out, and each bolt found its target with deadly aim. They struck fast and hard, cutting the rest of my men down with fire spells. Failing that, they used their hatchets and swords."

He and his men might have been able to fight them off but for the alarming amount of magic at the raiders' disposal. Magicians were rare in Lyond and Jerdun, and the practice of even simple magic outside the nobility was frowned upon in both nations. He'd assumed that to be the case everywhere. How could the Tiochene raiders here possibly have so many magicians? Nearly one in three among the Tiochene fighters seemed to have had a least a small amount of Talent. "I led— Our army retreated, fleeing for our lives, but the Tiochene caught up to us here on the river road. They...they showed no mercy." His eyes stung.

"Here, have some water." Princess Aliénor lifted a flask toward him, and she held it to his lips when his hands proved too unsteady for him to do it himself. He sipped a moment, then nodded his thanks.

Behind Princess Aliénor's shoulder, her stout lady companion pursed her lips in disapproval. "How did *you* survive?"

"I was knocked off my horse and separated from my men—from the others. I climbed that tree you found me in and kept my back to the mountain. I must have passed out after that. It's a miracle no one found me before you—"

Before he could finish, a young man threw back the flap to the infirmary. The boy swept into the room like he owned the place. He had a mass of waving dark hair and heavy-lidded brown eyes that gave him a sleepy appearance. Prince Philippe, Thomas guessed. He'd never met the prince, but the lad had the look of the late King Bernard about him. Philippe's face was narrow and thin with delicate, somehow fragile features. His eyes bulged with anger as he stepped closer and saw the Princess Aliénor by Thomas's bed.

The lady, for her part, rose to her feet and stared the prince down with calm composure. "My lord, I was just checking on this survivor."

The boy let out a low, quick huff and whipped his gaze away from her to glare at Thomas. "You, soldier. More survivors from your party have wandered into our camp. Shall I take you to them?"

Princess Aliénor held her hand out, palm down in a flat gesture of denial. "He is not well enough—"

"No, no, I will come. Show me." Thomas shot her an apologetic glance as he pushed slowly to his feet. He was dizzy and weak, but damned if he'd let this arrogant princeling see it.

Princess Aliénor flicked a glance at her handmaiden. The larger woman immediately stepped in to catch Thomas's elbow and let him lean his weight on her side. He gave his helper a quick, thankful nod. She returned him a brief, irritated grimace in return. The handmaid clearly did not like him.

"This way." Prince Philippe turned and started to go. When he realized Princess Aliénor was not immediately at his side, he grabbed her by the arm, towing her out beside him as he whispered angrily in her ear.

"Her husband," the handmaiden explained. "Prince Philippe of Jerdun."

Thomas flashed the handmaiden a wide grin. "Remarkable. Me, rescued by royalty. That'll be a story to take home to the lads in my village."

She snorted, sizing him up from the corner of her eye. A worldly woman, and a suspicious one it seemed.

Suspicious of me, *at least.* "And you, my lady? What is your name?"

"I am Lady Noémi of Orullion, *Thomas.*"

"Lords and ladies all about the place then?"

She swallowed a small sound of amusement and shook her head at him as they walked along behind the prince and his...princess. His wife. He watched Philippe jerk on her arm and scold her as they marched forward. How could the fair Princess Aliénor be married to that pompous little twit?

"They were married when they were quite young," the handmaiden murmured.

And that explained everything. A state marriage. A wholly arranged marriage, no doubt. *Fate spare me from the same.*

They had reached the outer edge of the camp now, and Thomas caught his breath at seeing a line of nearly two dozen men on their knees on the ground with their hands tied behind their backs. They were alive. Not all of his men, not even that many, but— As he scanned the line of faces, his breath caught, his heart beating hard, hoping, hoping...

One prisoner with blond hair so pale as to be almost white had looked up at their approach. His gaze had been scanning the line of faces just as Thomas's was. Their glances locked, and the blond man's shoulders rolled down in a release of tension so great he almost collapsed with it. When he looked again, he was smiling fit to crack his face. Thomas smiled back at his friend. *Llewellyn's alive.*

Having established that fact, Thomas let himself tally the rest of his men. Mostly these were his own personal knights, with two of his barons as well. Men who would have been close to Llewellyn in the melee, no doubt. None of them seemed to have very serious wounds, although a few were sporting cut lips and black eyes. *How—*

Princess Aliénor turned one man's face gently toward herself and examined the signs of a fresh beating. She wheeled on her husband, her face pinched with anger. "Couldn't you control the soldiers?"

Young Philippe dropped his gaze and scuffed one toe in the dirt, looking every inch a sullen boy. Come to think of it, he couldn't have been much more than twenty, by the look of him. *What is this child doing leading an army over dangerous ground like this?*

"These men resisted being bound," Philippe said, making his voice pompous. "What was I supposed to do?"

Thomas snorted. Meaning *no*, Philippe could not control his soldiers.

Philippe crossed to one of the soldiers and pointed at the man's pale blue surcoat with its three black wolves rampant against a gold-and-gray shield. The Jerdic prince locked eyes with Thomas and raised one eyebrow. "This is the crest of the King of Lyond, and I know the king himself led a force of men down this way. Where is your king, soldier?"

Thomas let his gaze drop as if in sorrow. "He was killed. I saw him fall."

"Is that right?" Philippe all but purred the word out.

Not entirely stupid then, this one. Thomas kept his gaze sadly lowered, his voice firm. "Yes. Our king was yanked off his horse, and then the raiders killed him."

"If I were to ask each one of your men here the same question—"

"They would give you the same answer, Prince Philippe."

Philippe's eyes fluttered at the honorific, as if he hadn't wanted Thomas to know who he was just yet. He tilted his chin and eyed Thomas head to foot. "I wonder."

"I am here, my prince. Apologies for my tardiness." A woman bustled up. She was thirty or so, with dark eyes and long, waving black hair falling loose around her shoulders, sleek as a raven's wing. All the other women in camp he'd seen wore gowns with skirts split for riding, but this woman was dressed almost as a man with a thick, high-collared red tunic, a long cape, and black hose on her shapely legs. A small, wickedly sharp dagger was belted to her waist, another oddity for a woman. She was clearly a woman, though, with a voluptuous figure and a delicate, pretty face. She had a low, throaty voice that was entirely pleasing to the ear. *The prince's lover, perhaps?*

Philippe smiled, but there was an edge of malice to it. "Mistress Helen. Just in time."

Princess Aliénor's shoulders inched up with tension. Her husband, distracted by the older woman's arrival, had released his wife's arm. The princess sidled away from him and eased close to Thomas. "Noémi"—she murmured the name quickly, urgently—"get back to the infirmary. You know what to do?"

Lady Noémi nodded once, then wandered away, moving in a leisurely manner so as not to draw either the prince's or Mistress Helen's attention. Thomas swayed at the sudden loss of support. Princess Aliénor, eyes wide, flung out a hand to brace him.

Thomas shook his head, blinking his eyes to clear them. "What is happening?"

Philippe conferred with the strange Mistress Helen in a low voice.

"She is my husband's spell-caster."

That explained the odd attire, and the voice. Spell-casters, whether through breeding or practice, always had the loveliest voices. Female spell-casters at royal courts were rare but not unheard-of. Usually women with magic stifled it or became midwives, but an ambitious woman could climb high if she'd a mind to.

Princess Aliénor wet her lips, watching her husband. "Be wary of Mistress Helen, soldier. She is a blood witch." The hair prickled on the back of Thomas's neck. He took one impulsive step forward, but Princess Aliénor held hard to his arm. "You are outnumbered, good sir."

He tensed his back teeth, his blood popping with the need for action as he watched Mistress Helen approach his men.

The witch paced down the line, looking all of the soldiers over. "You say your king is dead." She whipped her small dagger out, and the sharp stiletto blade gleamed in the sun. Each of the prisoners bravely raised his eyes and stared her down, unwilling to be intimidated by a woman.

Thomas put himself forward, gently disengaging from Princess Aliénor's hold. He pitched his voice to carry. "I say the king is dead. I saw him fall."

Mistress Helen waved her hand, rolling her eyes at him. "Yes, yes. But what if I were to ask...oh, *you*." She stopped in front of Thomas's friend Llewellyn, and swung her blade in a wide loop so the point came to rest just under his chin. Using the pressure of the knife's blade, she forced Llewellyn to tilt his head back at an uncomfortable angle to meet her eyes.

Ever the brilliant actor, Llewellyn let his voice throb with emotion. "My king is dead, lady. One of the fire spells knocked him off his horse, and the raiders slit his throat, to be sure."

Thomas just hoped the men marked that comment well so they would keep this same story straight as they were questioned.

"Hmm." Mistress Helen pursed her lips in displeasure and moved on to the next man in line. This was one of Thomas's knights, a tall, beefy man named Godric. She held the knife to Godric's throat and asked him the same question. "And you? Did you see the king fall?"

"Yes. The fire spell killed his poor horse, and they yanked the king out from under the dead beast by his surcoat."

"*Hmm hmm hmm*," Mistress Helen hummed in apparent thought. Suddenly her blade flicked out, and a line of blood rose on Godric's cheek. Thomas flinched. The witch lifted her blade carefully to her mouth and licked a single drop of Godric's blood off the tip. She smacked her lips afterward and closed her eyes.

Princess Aliénor shifted beside Thomas, and he noticed the hand she used to brace his arm had begun to tremble. Without thinking, Thomas reached up to cover her hand with his own.

The witch let out a low, almost sexual groan, and opened her eyes again. Thomas let out a startled oath. The witch's eyes had turned red and faintly glowed as if she were on fire from within. "I ask again, Sir Godric of Lyond, is your king dead?" Her voice had changed, grown deeper, more masculine. It almost sounded like Godric's own voice speaking back to him.

Godric stood taut as a cord stretched between two posts. All the veins in his neck stood out in sharp relief as his mouth worked, as he strained to fight the evil spell she'd cast on him.

"Stop." Thomas tried to disengage from Princess Aliénor.

She held on to him with a small, scared, "*Don't.*"

The blood witch knelt before her victim and tilted his chin up with her bloodied dagger. "You are strong, sir, but I am stronger. Is your king dead?"

Godric's throat worked, and he breathed hard as if pushing against a crushing weight. "*No.*" The word burst from him with great effort, yet his face still fell with shame after he had spoken.

Thomas winced.

The witch whirled around and leveled a cool glare at Thomas. "You lied, soldier." She took a step sideways to stand before Llewellyn. "You, also, have lied." She lowered her dagger to cut Llewellyn next.

"Stop." Thomas tore himself free of Princess Aliénor's protective grasp and stood straight and tall before the witch. "Stop this."

She raised an eyebrow. "Why?"

He drew in a deep breath, praying he would not regret this. "I will tell you where the king is."

"All right. Where is he?"

Thomas gave her a small lopsided smile. "Right here. I am the King of Lyond."

Chapter Three

The witch gave Thomas a frankly dubious look. "You?" She turned back to poor Godric and brandished her dagger. "Does he speak truth?"

Godric flicked a glance at Thomas, asking for permission, and even that small hesitation cost him as the veins in his neck bulged with the effort of resisting. Thomas gently nodded. Godric let out a low, pained sigh. "Yes, yes. He is our king. He is."

Thomas's gaze briefly caught with Llewellyn's as his friend shot him a very exasperated look indeed. Thomas gave a small shrug back.

Philippe sauntered forward with his chest puffed up, trying to look strong, trying to look authoritative. Thomas kept his face straight to spare the young man his dignity.

"King Thomas."

Thomas made a small acknowledging nod. "I am he, Prince Philippe. I'm sorry I didn't greet you formally before, but I wasn't sure what my reception might be." He flicked a wry look at his cut-up knight.

Philippe cleared his throat uncomfortably.

"The King of Lyond." The witch's eyes had returned to normal now the blood magic had faded, but they gleamed all the same with a dark, avaricious light. She lifted her knife in an almost instinctual move to take some of Thomas's blood.

Princess Aliénor flung herself between Thomas and the witch. "*No*. Husband, are you so lost to good sense that you would knowingly let your witch attack a fellow royal?"

"Uh..." Philippe's mouth hung open as he flicked an uncertain glance between his witch and his wife. "Um."

Princess Aliénor, with an uneasy glance at Thomas, gently drew her husband out of Thomas's earshot. The witch followed at once, her strides stiff and angry, picking deep divots into the sand as she walked.

Thomas eased closer to his men and bent to check the cut on Godric's face.

"I'm sorry, my lord," the knight whispered in a broken voice.

"You were bespelled, Sir Godric. No shame in it."

Beside them, Llewellyn let out a snort. "You should not have come forward, my king. These men are here to protect you, not the other way around."

Thomas shook his head. "She was going to cut you next, Llewellyn. Should I have let her?"

Llewellyn grimaced but made no reply. He watched the witch with uneasy eyes. "I wonder."

"I didn't like to test your strength, old friend. Better to let some of us keep our secrets from that beldam, eh?"

"Hmm." Llewellyn still looked unhappy. "She may get her chance. That prince believes he has the witch on his leash, but I think it is the other way round."

Thomas glanced back to watch the low-voiced argument continue. "Can you get your hands free? If there is a need."

"My king, what makes you think I need my hands free to deal with that witch?"

"Don't underestimate her."

"Who is the other woman? The girl who leaped to your defense?"

Thomas turned his attention to dabbing at the cut on Godric's face. "She is Philippe's wife, the Princess Aliénor."

Aliénor tossed her head in exasperation as she dragged her husband away from the prisoners. "If you let the witch have her way, then you will have to kill King Thomas, for I'm sure he could never forgive such a breach of diplomacy."

She had not wished for the witch to follow, but of course that damned Mistress Helen had. The witch toyed with her dagger, watching the blade flash in the sun. "The King of Lyond is a great prize, my lord."

At the witch's words, Aliénor's skin went cold. "You cannot be serious."

The witch eased closer, trying to push Aliénor out of the way as they jostled for Philippe's attention. "Think, my prince. Let me bleed King Thomas just a little every day and I—you can control his every action, every move. You can return home not just having reclaimed the colonies but having taken Lyond."

Aliénor's heart hammered. "These Lyondi men saw her power, Philippe. They will know what is happening."

"So we kill them." Helen shrugged. "We can make up any story we like after that. A daring rescue from barbarians. You saved King Thomas with your own sword. Anything."

Philippe caught his lower lip between his teeth. His eyes warmed a little at the witch's suggestion. A desperate, tearing fear gripped Aliénor, and she grabbed her husband by both arms, forcing him to look her in the eye. "Philippe, if you follow Mistress Helen's plan, all you will do is start another war with Lyond."

"Do you doubt my power, Princess?" the witch asked.

"I doubt the Lyondi will let themselves be ruled by a man who's clearly a puppet to foreign powers."

Philippe's gaze flicked back and forth as he studied the ground, but she knew he was thinking, weighing his options.

Aliénor pressed on. "We are in neutral territory, Philippe. I do not think the Prince of Anutitum will thank you for this offense. Your brother the king sent you down here to defend our territories. He did not send you to start a war with Lyond."

Philippe's mouth pinched, but still he made no reply. The witch's smile widened.

Aliénor shook Philippe as hard as she could, and at last his gaze met hers in shocked offense. "Husband, you cannot murder these soldiers in cold blood. Is *that* the kind of prince you want to be? The kind of man? Why did you even go on this holy mission if this is what you would do? Will this be like that destroyed village in Jerdun all over again?" Her voice broke at the end, remembering the tragedy of Philippe's first military effort.

Philippe's eyes swam with sudden tears, and he grasped her hand tight, mashing the bones together in his own remembered pain. "No, no, you're right, my love. We must not become like the barbarians we were sent to fight." He flicked a glare at Mistress Helen, and stepped away to approach the Lyondi prisoners.

Mistress Helen accepted the snub with a small bow. As soon as Philippe's back was turned, she glared at Aliénor. Aliénor shivered. With a grunt of disgust, Mistress Helen stomped away into the bustle of camp. No doubt looking for someone else to torment.

King Thomas—*how strange to think him a king*—stood at Philippe's approach, and how strange to think the two men were both royalty, for they could not have been more dissimilar to Aliénor's eyes. Philippe was slim and slight where King Thomas was broad-shouldered and tall. The foreign king was older than her, but he moved with the sureness and strength of a soldier despite his recent wounds. He had the face of a soldier too, stern and rugged, yet still handsome for all that with a regal, leonine nose.

Philippe made a small nod of conciliation. "King Thomas, forgive us our rough and ready methods, but this is a dangerous land. We needed to know how matters stood. Please, accept my hospitality. You and your men are welcome to travel with us as long as you care to. We are on our way to Anutitum, but there will be a port before then that I'm sure can convey you and your men safely home to Lyond."

Thomas—*King* Thomas—narrowed his eyes in brief assessment and held his hand out to shake on the bargain. "I accept your hospitality, Prince Philippe." A formal declaration, and Philippe understood it as such, for he gave a formal half bow in return. When the two royals shook, the king's massive paw almost swallowed Philippe's delicate hand.

Philippe smiled. "Come, let us seal our accord and share the Kiss of Peace."

King Thomas's mouth gave a small, wry twist, but he allowed Philippe to kiss the back of his hand and returned the kiss himself. "I thank you again, kind prince. I have your permission to cut my men free, I assume."

Aliénor bit her lip to keep back an unwise chuckle.

Philippe flushed. "Of course, of course. Apologies. We will find somewhere in camp for you and your men. I will send my healers to you."

"I have a healer among my own men, but if you could arrange for supplies to be brought, that would be appreciated."

Aliénor did not blame King Thomas for not wanting their Jerdic healers among his men. After witnessing Mistress Helen's blood magic, she knew it to be a wise precaution on the king's part. She stepped forward and touched Philippe's sleeve to get his attention. "If it please you, husband, I can make arrangements for King Thomas."

Philippe flicked her a grateful glance. "It is well. See to it, my love."

Noémi had returned, and she fell easily in step with Aliénor as they moved away from the soldiers. Aliénor cast one quick glance at King Thomas. He gave a small nod of thanks. She felt her cheeks heat and hurriedly looked away. "Has the gossip made its way through the camp?"

"That he's the King of Lyond?" Noémi muttered dryly.

Aliénor flinched. "I'll take that as a 'yes the rumor has spread'." Aliénor turned to Noémi as they moved through the camp together. "Did you do as I asked?"

"I sent the king's chain mail to be cleaned by one of your servants, and I had all the bandages, sheets, and other detritus burned by the physician while I watched. He grumbled at the waste, but I thought boiling wouldn't be good enough. Mistress Helen wasn't pleased when she came sniffing around a few minutes ago."

"Good."

The camp was all a-bustle with people setting up the tents and fire pits for the night. A stream of stragglers was still riding in from the rearguard. The vanguard always had to stop at midday just to give the soldiers at the tail end time to catch up before nightfall.

Noémi pointed ahead. "The servants have finished readying your tents."

"Good." Aliénor continued in a straight line to her own tent. She let out a sigh of relief when she stepped inside its coolness. Violette was already there with wash water prepared, and the gossip about the Lyondi soldiers did seem to be spreading, for she had already heard all of it.

Her two ladies chatted and gossiped as they helped Aliénor to remove her travel-stained dress. That accomplished, Aliénor went to the wash basin to sponge away the day's coating of dirt and blood.

Noémi crossed to sit in one of the four camp chairs in Aliénor's tent and sank her pudgy chin into one hand, her brow furrowed.

Aliénor raised an eyebrow. "What troubles you, Noémi?"

"Did you know when you rescued him?"

Aliénor flinched. "Yes, I knew he was Lyondi when I had him brought back. He said something in Lyondi when he woke up."

Violette's eyes went wide, and she lowered her voice to a scandalized whisper. "Why didn't you say anything? Tell someone when you brought him into the camp?"

"He was injured, barely able to stand. We are not at war with Lyond any longer." Aliénor sighed. "We're all so far from home. The Lyondi are here to defend their territories from the Tiochene raiders as well. In this strange land, doesn't it make more sense that we be allies with them?"

Violette opened her mouth, then closed it with a small snap, her uncertain gaze darting to Noémi.

Aliénor knelt in front of Noémi, reaching to press her dear friend's hand. "Noémi?"

"A wise and practical thought, Your Grace." Noémi's voice was utterly flat.

"Noémi, please, how do you really feel about this?"

Her handmaiden was silent for so long that Aliénor thought she wouldn't answer, but at last Noémi wet her lips and gave Aliénor a level stare. "Sometimes when I forget myself, I can still remember the taste of my favorite horse, still smell my old home burning from the flaming arrows the Lyondi shot over our walls."

Gut churning, Aliénor rose to her feet. "Noémi—"

Noémi waved her hands to ward Aliénor off, and her face was calm as she spoke. "I'm a practical woman like you, and we are far from home. The raiders that killed the Lyondi force still roam these mountains. I think by the end of this road we shall be grateful for all the help we can get. Even from our enemies."

Chapter Four

Dinner was an awkward affair, with poor Philippe trying to make stilted conversation with King Thomas. A difficult transition that, to go from torturing Thomas's men in the afternoon to fêting them with the sunset. Aliénor could have helped, perhaps, except Philippe had set out a table just for her and her ladies, "so you are not bored by all our military talk." Rather so she would not speak too much with King Thomas. She noticed Mistress Helen still sat with Philippe, which seemed to Aliénor a social faux pas at best and, at worst, a grave insult to King Thomas.

As dinner finished, Aliénor gazed at the darkening sky and studied its ominous blanket of clouds. The army had made camp on the slopes by the river, and now the whole shore seemed transformed into a jolly little city with tents and banners arranged on one side. The horses had been turned out to pasture in meadows nearby, and all her husband's fearsome soldiers seemed transformed to country lads as they laughed and splashed each other on the river's shore. Aliénor longed to take a swim in that cool water herself, but there was nowhere private enough for her and her ladies to bathe. For a moment she missed the warm waters of her island home with an almost physical ache.

A chill wind kicked up and blew a tendril of Aliénor's hair into her face. The tents whistled and flapped all about them. The air blew heavy and cold, damp with a promise of coming rain. Dinner had been concluding anyway, but with these ominous signs from the weather, Philippe rose and formally took his leave to return to his own tent.

"Prince Philippe, a word?" He kept his voice low, but King Thomas caught up to Philippe very near Aliénor's own table, so she could not help but hear their murmured conference.

Philippe raised an eyebrow. "Yes, King Thomas? Is there something I might assist you with?"

"I wanted to drop a word of advice into your ear."

"Oh?"

Aliénor winced, hearing that chill tone. Philippe did not like advice. He did not like anything that might call his authority or knowledge into question.

King Thomas, either oblivious to the uninviting tone or determined despite it, shifted closer to her husband. "I don't think you should let your men camp so close to the river. It looks like rain is coming on, and the water—"

"King Thomas, I thank you for your kindly meant counsel, but I'm sure my men know what is best. They are experienced campaigners."

Aliénor bit her lip to stop herself from joining in the argument. She looked down to the river again, seeing it with new eyes. Were it a fine summer evening, it might have been appropriate to have men and horses camped so close to the water's edge, but this was winter with a storm coming on. The scene no longer appeared cheerful to her eyes—now it seemed a disaster waiting to happen. She glanced again at the misty gray sky and felt her stomach drop.

Violette had already finished her dinner, so Aliénor touched her hand to get her attention. "Violette, go to Lord Ysen and ask him to order the men to move back from the river's edge." She kept her voice low so Philippe would not hear.

Violette rose from her seat, her face troubled. "Most of the men down there are not from Ysen's force, though. They might not listen."

"Have Lord Ysen try."

Violette gave a determined nod and took herself off, one of the servants following behind as escort.

Aliénor forced herself to finish her portion of dinner before rising. She knew how precious these supplies were, and she had learned over the long hard months not to waste food when it sat before her. She was still chewing the last piece of dried meat as she pushed to her feet to leave the table.

"Princess Aliénor?"

She whirled at the sound of King Thomas's baritone, a pleasant prickling starting along her scalp. She swallowed and dropped a small curtsy. "King Thomas."

"I wanted to apologize for my deception earlier. Not telling you my name. I would not have willingly lied to you, especially after you saved my life."

"No, I understand why you did so." She hesitated, wondering whether to speak to him about the dangers of the river, and then decided against it. She had already taken steps to avert potential disaster, and she did not want to be accused of scheming with the Lyondi king.

"May I walk with you awhile?" he asked.

A little thrill of feeling burst inside her, which she did not understand. She should have been wary of the attentions of this Lyondi soldier, not flattered. More evidence of the perversity of her nature, she supposed. She cleared her throat, then said to him in her best Court Lyondi, "I should be delighted to show you the way to Lord Ysen's tents where you will be sleeping."

He blinked, startled, and a spontaneous smile broke over his face before he smoothed it away. "I thank you, Princess," he answered her in the same tongue.

They moved forward together in step, and Noémi fell back to walk beside the tall blond man from this afternoon, one of the king's men. The Lyondi king clasped his hands behind his back and shortened his stride to match Aliénor's. "How is it you speak my language so well?"

Aliénor waved a dismissive hand. "Oh, my nursemaid was Lyondi. An old village woman who married a Jerdic soldier long, long before the wars started in your father's time." The memory of her old nursemaid was probably why Aliénor could never find it in her heart to hate the Lyondi as so many of her countrymen did.

"How many of your cities are threatened by the Tiochene, Princess?"

"My cousin, the Prince of Anutitum, first requested our aid. But two of our other cities further south will be in danger if Anutitum is taken."

"Yes. Four of our colony-cities were imperiled when we first left, and the damned Tiochene have already taken one of those since. Without much bloodshed, thank goodness."

"Really?"

He shot her a wry smile. "These places have been our cities for only a generation or so. Most of the people in them are, shall we say, *sympathetic* to the Tiochene cause."

"I see." Aliénor gnawed on her lower lip. *What a complicated mess of politics. What a silly girl I was to throw myself into this without better knowledge.*

"I was a little surprised at our early dispersal from dinner." King Thomas's voice had gentled, as if sensing her inner doubt. Indeed, this subject change was a mercy. "Do the Jerdic nobility enjoy no music or poetry in the evenings? Surely the nights grow long without something to while the evening hours away."

Aliénor restrained a sigh. King Thomas did not know he prodded an older wound of hers. "My husband views this mission as a sacred crusade to reclaim Jerdun's rightful lands. He thought it impious to bring along troubadours and bards on what should be a most solemn mission."

King Thomas's mouth worked as he fought back some small sound, either of contempt or frustration. "Prince Philippe has led many military campaigns?"

"This is his first."

"Ah."

"What?"

King Thomas hesitated, then looked at her with a pleat between his brows. "On a military campaign, your greatest enemy is not necessarily the one you move to fight. It is boredom. The soldiers need some distraction, entertainment as they make the long march to war. If you do not provide it, they will find their own."

Aliénor opened her mouth, then swallowed the words down. *I must not be disloyal. I must not speak ill of my husband.* Especially not to this man. Yet she could not help but remember the chaos that had followed her husband's army like a poisonous cloud. They had been forced to hang three of their soldiers in the last two weeks for brawling and stealing. In every town they had passed through, they paid heavy fines and penalties because of the rowdiness of their soldiers. The last town had even refused them entry, barring their gates and only lowering supplies down to them in baskets from behind the city walls. She had thought the townsfolk overly cautious because of the Tiochene raids, but now she wondered.

Wetness dripped onto her nose, and a wet plop hit her sleeve. "Oh dear. We had better hurry you to your tent, King Thomas." When she looked over, he was watching her, a warmth in his eyes that kindled an answering heat deep in her own belly.

"I do not fear a little rain, Princess."

"Nor I, but it will give us a good excuse to run. This way." She lifted her skirts a little and took off running, laughing as the rain kissed her head and shoulders. She heard the king chuckle behind her and the sound of his breath puffing out as he too began to race through the rain.

When she recognized the blue stripes of Lord Ysen's tents, she tried to slow to a stop, but the treacherous rain had wet the ground to a deep wet muck already. She slipped and slid in the gooey stuff. King Thomas caught her elbow but was too imbalanced himself. They crashed together and fell with a splat into the mud.

On his knees now, the king lifted her by her arms. "Princess Aliénor?" Mud had splattered a trail of dots across his long aquiline nose. Seeing that, she choked on a laugh, and he grinned at her. "The dignity of kings, eh?" Chuckling, he smeared some mud away from her cheekbone with his thumb.

Her skin tingled at the touch, and the laugh died on her lips. He hissed a quick breath out and jerked his hand back as if her skin burned him. Aliénor eased away from him and pushed onto her feet, sliding and slipping in the mud. King Thomas, unhampered by wet skirts, rose to his feet with better ease. He offered his hand down to help her stand.

She hesitated, but when her foot slid out from under her again in the goopy mud, she let out a weary sigh and gripped the king's hand. That awareness, that kindling heat, flared between them again where palm touched palm, and a dull ache started in Aliénor's chest. As soon as she was on her feet, she pulled her hand free and stumbled away from the king as if he were an unruly dog she feared might bite her. "Good night, King Thomas."

"Good night, Princess Aliénor." His voice was hoarse and low.

Without another word, without even checking to see if Noémi still followed her, Aliénor hurried for her own tent. The rain grew worse, and it pounded upon her like cold beads thrown at her head.

As soon as he figured out which tent was his in the dark and rainy muck, Thomas stomped toward it and flung the flap back. The good Lord Ysen had been generous and fitted the tent out with a feather mattress, chairs, towels, and a sturdy basin to wash in. Thomas grabbed one fine linen towel from the side of the basin and scrubbed it over his hair and face. He looked over as Llewellyn entered the tent and threw himself into one of the camp chairs.

"The Jerdic princess is quite lovely." Llewellyn studied his nails as he said it.

She was at that. Taller than average with long limbs and graceful hands. A pretty face with a ready smile, sweet and kind. Clever too, it seemed. And her hair, such a beautiful red-gold color—

Llewellyn cleared his throat. "I've never known you to tryst with married women, my king."

Thomas bared his teeth at his friend and tossed the towel away. "She is the only one in this whole bloody camp who seems kindly disposed toward us. If I cultivate her friendship, it is only to keep your worthless carcass from starving in the desert." He kicked the bottom of Llewellyn's boot as he passed by him.

Llewellyn crossed his arms on his chest and brushed a hand over his pale beard. "This army seems monstrously ill-run."

"Oh yes?"

"Yes, they have a sort of rolling system by which each baron is in charge of operations for a day, and it passes from man to man. Everyone takes a turn at being in charge."

"Which means no one is. No wonder they had men practically camping *in* the river."

"Hmm. Yes. They have constant problems with discipline too, so I'm told. Thieving and brawling. The soldiers have killed more of their comrades than the enemy thus far."

"I'm not surprised." Thomas lowered his voice. "And their prince?"

"An uncommonly pious lad, they say. Not puffed up either. Although, he does sleep on a feather mattress. Still, he's liked well enough."

"But not respected."

"Ah, no. I gather his mission is a convenient excuse to travel south. Not to the prince, of course, but to his men. Most of these men—soldiers and nobles alike—are here to grab everything they can get. Treasure. Land."

"Younger sons of younger brothers who think this is their path to glory."

"Yes."

"Well, we are only bound to this rabble as long as it takes to reach the next friendly port. Then we will return home." Heaviness descended on Thomas as he said it, a sort of crushing weight that bowed his shoulders.

"You've abandoned your plan, then?"

Thomas tossed a wry smile at his friend. "I should have listened to you and never come at all. My place is at home."

Llewellyn's eyelids drooped, veiling his eyes for a moment, not disagreeing, but he shook his head. "You had to try. The war hawks at home, like de Troumper, they would have kept howling until you did."

"I noticed when the time came, de Troumper didn't volunteer to accompany us."

"Funny that."

"And these colony cities were never much ours to begin with. They were held by the Tiochene not so long ago. I must trust that the people will weather this new change of fortune all right."

"We have no army with which to reclaim them anyway."

"Not anymore."

Thomas scrubbed his fingernails through his hair, his gut churning with despair and indecision. "All those men. I led them to their deaths, Llewellyn. For nothing."

Llewellyn sat forward in his chair and planted his feet on the ground as he frowned at Thomas. "How were we to know the Tiochene had so many spell-casters? In a fight of steel against steel we would have won. This is not like the courteous fighting we've had with Jerdun in which we each know the rules, the protocols. Our wars with Jerdun have become almost as genteel as a dance. No, my king, this was an ambush. None of us have had to fight like this before." Llewellyn swallowed, and his face paled at the remembered slaughter.

"We did not know what we would face. We should have waited, studied the terrain more, the people... My pride led us to this."

"Perhaps, but your wisdom will get the rest of us out of it and back home."

"I've made the right choice then. To give up? Go back?"

"We no longer have the men to mount any kind of attack. We certainly don't have the magic." He sighed. "What would our other option be?"

"I could offer an alliance to Prince Philippe." Thomas's gut roiled at just the thought. "Unite our forces and take back *all* the colony-cities here, Jerdic and Lyondi. That might even help the peace at home."

"Are you truly contemplating such a thing?"

"The thought had occurred, but no. I want to get home and see how the kingdom has fared without its king. If only my nephew hadn't..." The grief was too sharp for him to continue.

Llewellyn gripped his shoulder. "Young Gabriel may return someday."

"If I believed that, I never would have left home."

"My king—"

But Thomas did not want the gentle sympathy in his friend's eyes. He waved a hand in the air. "Perhaps I should stay here and let the war hawks take Lyond." Thomas fell into one of the camp chairs, dropping his face into his hands.

"You're tired. That's all this is."

Thomas did not argue. His body was chilled. From the wet clothes, yes, but somehow this coldness ran deeper, as if his body were slowly freezing, turning itself to ice. Ending the generations-long war with Jerdun had been a great triumph, but it had also left Thomas adrift, aimless. His only family, his nephew Gabriel, had disappeared. Left him, rejected his place in society and in Thomas's affection. Thomas had no heirs now. No legacy left but loss and failure.

Llewellyn slapped his shoulder. "We just need to get home. The sooner, the better."

"Yes." Outside the rain continued, and the tents swayed in the wind, promising a dark and dreary night for all in the Jerdic camp. Thomas dismissed Llewellyn to his own tent and readied himself for bed. The mattress was soft and down-filled, charming on a cold night, but still a ridiculous luxury to bring on such a campaign as this. *How on earth do they cart the heavy thing around when they march?*

Thomas tossed and turned on his feather bed, his wounds aching now he had nothing to distract him from their presence. He should summon Llewellyn and ask him for a healing draught. Yet something forewarned the king that on a wild, stormy night like this, it was probably best he have his wits about him. Still, because of his exhaustion he was able to fall into a light, fretful drowse soon enough.

Unfortunately for Thomas, almost as soon as his eyes had fluttered closed, a shrill scream pierced the night.

Chapter Five

After changing out of her muddy clothes, Aliénor stayed up late chatting with Noémi, listening to the winds rage. Violette's elderly husband, Lord John, sent one of his men-at-arms to fetch his young wife back to his tent almost as soon as the storm started. After that, Noémi entertained Aliénor with a lovely reading from their precious store of books—one of the few pleasures that Philippe had not yet denied his wife. Meanwhile, the storm grew steadily worse as the night rolled on, the sides of Aliénor's tent flapping and swaying with the winds.

Her rugs were soaked through with muddy water, and a small trickle of water flowed downhill over the ground. "I do not think I should undress for bed just yet." They had abandoned their reading, and she had to yell to make herself heard over the raging wind as it whipped through their camp. Noémi simply nodded—she also had not yet removed her gown for bed, either. They wrapped the blankets around their shoulders as the wind howled through the tent and made the canvas swell wide like a sail.

A great crash and the sound of gushing water startled them both. The screams of horses split the air, piercing even the horrid wail of the wind. Men cried out. The wind, like a punishing demon, blasted over her tent, and the sides billowed away from the ground. Aliénor flung herself down, and the canvas whipped at her head and body. The wind lifted the tent and tossed it away with the sound of tearing. Chill rain lashed at her body, soaking her clothes to her skin.

Noémi groaned beside her. Aliénor flung the blanket back. Blood covered Noémi's face from a cut on her head. "*Noémi*."

Her handmaid shook her head and mumbled something, but Aliénor could not make out her words over the sounds of the storm. More voices cried out. Aliénor heaved Noémi off the now-ruined mattresses and slung an arm around her friend's waist. Noémi listed heavily to the side, swaying, and nearly knocked Aliénor down.

Aliénor stumbled through the camp, half-carrying her friend, unsure where she should go. Panicking soldiers rushed past them. One frantic man clipped Aliénor on the shoulder, sending her and Noémi off-balance and spinning to the ground. Aliénor shivered as the rain beat down. She tensed her muscles, drawing strength to stand again.

Another tearing sound filled the air as the tent beside hers was blown free of its poles. The wind flung the structure atop them, and Aliénor screamed as the soaked fabric plowed into her and pressed her down. The ground was muddy and slick. She punched and kicked to try to free herself from the heavy cloth as it flattened her into the sucking mud.

Suddenly the broken tent was lifted away and the icy rain pounded upon her once again.

"Are you all right?"

Aliénor's heart leapt with gladness as she stared into the face of King Thomas. He wore only a light shirt and hose, and his feet were bare in the mud beside her.

"My lady-in-waiting. She's hurt." She bellowed the words and he must have understood her, because he moved to Noémi's other side and lifted the dazed handmaiden to her feet.

"Allow me." That tall blond man was with him again, and he helped the king half-carry Noémi into the nearest tent that was still standing. This proved to be Lord Ysen's, but the baron was not about. *Probably running around tending to the flood.*

"This is Llewellyn, my second in command," the king explained.

Llewellyn made a small bow as he tossed through Lord Ysen's things with businesslike efficiency, turning the trunks out until at last he found a small towel. He carried Ysen's washbasin into the rain, then came in with a full bowl almost at once. Llewellyn dabbed his towel in the wash water and proceeded to clear away the mix of mud and blood on her wound.

"Is she all right?" Aliénor swabbed at her own face, her sleeve coming away muddy.

"I'm fine, Your Highness." Noémi's voice had a vague, slurred quality that worried Aliénor.

"Llewellyn is a healer. All will be well." Even as the king said it, another great roar and crash boomed over the small valley. King Thomas rushed outside, and Aliénor instinctively followed him.

"The river!"

The charming stream, gorged now by storm water and snow melt from the mountains, had overflowed its banks, rushing and crashing against those who made their camps too close to the shore's edge. A line of horses were still tied too near, and several men were frantically wrestling with their knots, trying to get the precious animals free before the water swept them away. They carried glow-spells, small balls of blue light. At least the witch Helen was doing her part to help.

The water crashed against the horses' legs, and the poor beasts were hindering their own rescue as they kicked and bucked with fear. A familiar dark face holding a glow-spell caught Aliénor's eye as she moved amongst those trying to free the horses. "Oh no." Aliénor started forward, slipping and sliding down the muddy bank toward the water. "*Violette*, get back. Leave them." She yelled until her throat was raw with the effort, but Aliénor's impulsive little Amazon did not seem to hear.

Another swell reached the narrow section of the river. The cruel tide swamped rescuers and horses alike, tugging them into the river's flow.

"*No.*" Aliénor watched with sick grief as the men's and horses' bobbing heads tumbled away downstream, almost too fast for her gaze to follow, let alone to attempt a rescue. Spell lights bobbed away down the river like drowned fireflies. The lights began flickering out one by one in the water and plunging all into darkness. Her eyes stung, and her gut twisted with nausea.

"*Help.*" One small voice seemed to rise above the clamor of the storm.

Aliénor's nerves jumped, and she scanned the shore. Her heart squeezed to see one small glow-spell caught in a pocket of debris, and a scared, dark face lit by the blue light. *There.* "Praise be," Aliénor whispered. A clump of debris was pinned against the store for the moment by the curve of the bank and the current's push. Young Violette clung to the mass, fighting the river's murderous drag.

Violette's glow-spell flickered but didn't entirely go out, and Aliénor's breath caught. *It's the water. Magic doesn't work over running water.* "Hold on!" Aliénor called even though Violette probably could not hear her.

"*Aliénor.* My lady, wait." Aliénor whirled at the sound of the king's voice. He slid to a stop next to her and gripped her by the arm. Water dripped off his chin and into his eyes.

She dashed water from her own face so she could see him. "One of my ladies is down there."

"I'm no swimmer, Princess, but let me find—"

"*I* am the best swimmer in this camp. I grew up on an island. *Let me go.*" She yanked her arm free, then staggered her way down the loose and muddy bank. At the water's edge she hesitated. The river's swollen banks crashed ahead of her, water lapping against her ankles and tugging on them.

"Aliénor."

She whipped around as the king skip-hop-stumbled the last bit down the bank. He held a rope aloft in triumph and didn't even wait for her permission before he slung it around her waist and tossed off a sailor's knot. He tugged on the rope to test, pulling her toward him by the rope.

"That should hold." His teeth flashed at her in the darkness. "Try to get to the other shore and get to her that way. Don't try to swim straight across."

"I know."

He squeezed her arm. "You can do this."

"I know." Something surged in Aliénor then, a burst of feeling in her chest that left her nearly breathless. *No time.* She seized her skirts, dragging the hemline between her legs, then tucking her skirts into the knot the king had tied, creating rudimentary hose and leaving her legs free—and immodestly bared. *Some things are more important than propriety.* "Hold me tight."

"I will."

She scanned the debris pile. Poor Violette still determinedly, miserably clung to her pile of twigs and logs on the opposite shore. The glow-spell was dim and flickering still. Violette's eyes were wide. The skin around her mouth showed nearly white with fear in the sickly blue spell-light.

Hold on, Violette. Aliénor flung herself into the river, the icy water like a punch to the gut that left her trembling and gasping. She tipped her head up, spitting water out the side of her mouth. A wave crashed over her and she ducked, then inhaled as she bobbed to the surface again. Something smashed into her from behind, pushing her under and leaving a stinging bruise across her back. She squeezed her eyes tight, her chest hurting, and kicked back to the surface. She sucked in another breath before a wave crashed over her again. Her arms and legs burned. Her linen dress dragged in the water, slowing her down. Her body felt sluggish, almost frozen. These waters were very different from those of the warm summer beaches of her home. *I should have known that.*

The other shore beckoned. *So close.* Aliénor clawed for the muddy bank, digging her fingers in and scrambling like a landed fish. Once she felt secure on the shore, Aliénor tugged on the rope at her waist. A signal to King Thomas.

The pounding rain had slowed to a misting drizzle. Legs heavy, Aliénor followed the riverbank down, staggering toward Violette's debris pile.

"Princess! My lady, I—" Violette's voice broke and she let out a small, broken sob.

The spell-light was caught in the tangle of twigs, and poor Violette was also pinned among the sharp branches. The pile was too big for Aliénor to reach Violette from the shore. Aliénor's stomach clenched, but she saw another way. Bracing herself for the cold shock, she eased into the water beside the debris pile. The current took her at once, pushing her with alarming speed toward that knotted mass of broken wood.

Aliénor gritted her teeth and gripped at branches in the debris pile, flapping her cold-clumsy hand back and forth, trying to catch hold of Violette. Something cracked beneath her, and water rushed over her head.

Violette was screaming when Aliénor surfaced again. Aliénor flung an arm out, and the girl caught hold of her wrist, gripping it painfully. Aliénor grasped Violette's other wrist and tugged her forward, fighting against the river. When she was close enough, the girl wrapped both arms around Aliénor's neck, sobbing into her shoulder.

The angle was awkward, water rushing over the both of them so they were coughing and gagging. Aliénor yanked hard on the rope around her waist and felt an answering pull. They were jerked free of the debris pile, and Violette shrieked again, startled by the sudden movement into open water.

Aliénor squeezed her friend's waist. "No, it's all right. We're almost out."

Something caught at the billowing skirts of Aliénor's dress below the water, and she jerked downward. She managed, barely, to turn her scream into a gasp as her head disappeared beneath the water.

Chapter Six

Aliénor held hard to Violette with one hand as the girl thrashed and tried to fight free. The roiling waves of the river trapped them, but the rope around Aliénor's waist still drew them toward the bank. *If only I can get my skirt free of this blasted*— Aliénor kicked and kicked again, her eyes stinging, her chest on fire with the need for air. She tugged on her skirt and felt the fabric give. Suddenly their rate of motion increased, and she kicked toward the surface, gripping Violette desperately tight in her arms as King Thomas dragged them back.

When the other shore came into sight, Aliénor made a feeble kick toward safety, but her arms and legs were tired, her body chilled. She and Violette scraped against the other shore, mud sliding down the neck of Aliénor's gown.

"*My lady.*" King Thomas splashed toward her, more men following behind, and they dragged her and poor crying Violette higher onto land. Aliénor found she could barely move. Her frozen limbs might as well have been stone for all that they obeyed her. Men brought blankets and threw them around her, even though the rain still beat down upon everyone. The king's arms slid beneath her knees and shoulders, and she bounced a little as he lifted her high into his arms.

He was as cold as her, his skin clammy and wet, but she leaned against his chest. The sound of his heartbeat pounded fast and steady beneath her ear. "Brave girl," he muttered as he ran with her up the hill from the riverbank. "Brave, *foolish* girl."

"But I am a good swimmer, am I not?"

He sent an incredulous glance down at her face but then burst out laughing the next moment. "You are at that, my lady." He ducked inside a tent and deposited her into one of the small camp chairs.

"Bed," she protested, feeling light-headed, her joints aching with cold.

"Your women have to get you out of your wet things first, my lady."

"*Hmm.*"

His hands traced her face, smoothing the water away from her cheek, and she was tired enough that she leaned into the touch with a hum of pleasure. His hand was calloused and rough against her skin but gentle for all that.

"Violette? Is she all right?" she murmured.

"She's been taken to her husband's tent. She'll be tended well."

"Noémi?"

"Here, my lady." Her handmaiden's round, kind face swam into focus over Aliénor's, a heavy bandage wrapped around Noémi's brow. "We must get you out of these wet things. Thank you, King Thomas." It was a dismissal, and a rather curt one at that.

Aliénor forced her weary eyes open and caught his hand when he would have left. He turned toward her, but stiff formality had replaced the warmth on his face. Yet when she glanced down he was still barefoot. He had wiry black hairs on his toes. She bit her lip to restrain a giggle and met his gaze again. "Thank you for your help tonight, King Thomas."

His expression softened, just a little, his eyes crinkling at the corners.

So handsome. Her cheeks warmed, the only part of her body that felt so at that moment, and she dropped his hand.

Noémi stepped forward and blocked Aliénor's vision so she did not see the king leave. With brisk efficiency, her handmaiden stripped Aliénor's wet clothes off and bundled her into several warm and wonderfully dry blankets.

"I've sent for a healer. You're scratched and bruised all over." Noémi began smoothing the discarded garments and straightening the linens on the bed. Her mouth was pinched, her jaw working. "You should *not* have gone charging off like that, Your Highness."

Aliénor felt her head drooping with sleep. She tried to nod, to pay attention, but she was so *tired*...

Noémi's voice seemed distant and far away as she continued, "Your husband will be very angry when he hears of this."

Aliénor could only manage a small, sleepy sound of inquiry before her head slumped to her chest with exhaustion, and she fell asleep in the awkward camp chair.

———————◆———————

"Aliénor." A male voice, impatient, angry.

She frowned in her sleep and rolled away.

"*Aliénor.*" Fingers dug into the flesh of her arm, yanking her onto her back.

She startled awake, gasping, heart racing. Philippe's face swam into view above her. She swallowed, but her frantic heart slowed only a little. "Husband." She sat up and knuckled sleep from her tired eyes. Someone must have moved her from the chair to the bed last night. The blankets slipped from her chest as she moved, revealing her shift to the chill morning air.

Philippe averted his eyes, a flush staining his cheeks. They'd been married nearly five years, and the sight of her half dressed still flustered him. Offended him. How she wished sometimes that his father had let Philippe become one of the chaste Oracles of Fate as he'd always wanted. Aliénor gathered her blankets around her shoulders as she tucked her feet beneath her to sit upright on the mattress.

"Good morning, Your Highness." Mistress Helen chirruped from one of the camp chairs.

Aliénor's hand twitched with fear, and she gathered the blankets more tightly around herself. "Good morning, Mistress Helen. Husband, what brings you here so early?" For he clearly had no wish to exercise his marital rights upon Aliénor's person.

Philippe paced the tent, back and forth, but he whipped around now, and his eyes blazed with wrath. "How *dared* you, Aliénor? Throwing yourself in the river, flaunting your legs like a common whore."

She recoiled, and inadvertently her glance caught on Mistress Helen, who sat smiling and twirling her little knife in the corner. Aliénor wet her lips and weighed her words carefully. "All was in chaos last night, my prince. One of my own ladies fell in. I knew I could help, so I did."

Philippe gripped his hands into fists of frustration before his face. "That is not your place." He dropped his hands and raked his gaze over her with disgust. "And to help in such a brazen, unwomanly manner. Better you had died than expose yourself so."

The breath puffed out of Aliénor in a small, pained gasp. "If that is how you feel, then perhaps we should discuss an annulment again."

"*Never.* You are my wife. You *belong* to me—"

"I do not please you." A wild, tearing flurry of emotions battered away inside Aliénor's breast. "You tell me I bring shame upon you with every move I make. Why do you want to stay married to me if you believe these things about me?"

"I only want you to behave yourself. I want you to be a wife I can be proud of."

Wild, frantic fear tightened her throat with tears. "I will not break myself in half just so I can fit in your shadow, Philippe."

"You do not even *try*." Tears glittered in his eyes and his lips trembled, flecked with spit. His eyelids lowered, and his gaze flicked sideways toward Mistress Helen. "You *must* try, Aliénor."

Against her will, Aliénor felt her own gaze drawn to Mistress Helen as if she had a leash around her neck already. The witch met her gaze unflinching and flashed her teeth at Aliénor in a predatory smile. Helen tightened her grip on her knife.

Aliénor scuttled sideways on the bed, ready to scream, to run. But what good would that do? This was Philippe's army, his camp. She was his wife. Even if she got safely out of the tent, she would not get much farther.

She reached out with shaking hands to clasp Philippe's sleeve. She kept all her focus on him, bent her will toward him. "Philippe, I will do better. I will. I promise. Send Mistress Helen away. You don't need her."

Mistress Helen quirked an eyebrow in patent disbelief.

Aliénor tamped down her own revulsion, swallowed her anger though her stomach clenched and roiled with the effort of it. *Meek. Mild. Docile.* She softened her voice, her features, leached the steel out of her spine until she felt exactly like the crawling worm Philippe wanted her to be. "I will do as you wish, husband. You don't need her magic. *Philippe*," her voice broke. "Please don't do this."

His features were still hard, his eyes cold. Cold enough that she shivered. "This is your last chance, wife. You will behave yourself or I *will* let Mistress Helen have the keeping of you." He jerked his arm free of Aliénor's grip and swept out of the tent, the flaps waving a little from the force of his passing.

Mistress Helen followed behind him, a smug smile curling on her lips.

Aliénor waited a moment for them to go, then hurled a pillow at the floor with a choked scream of fury. Her breath was coming so fast that her vision swam. She closed her eyes and forced herself to breathe more slowly.

How dare he? How dare he threaten her with blood magic and mind control? She threaded her fingers into her hair and pulled, trying to force her mind to work.

I must get free of him. Proper Jerdic women did not leave their husbands, and yet...*I had rather be the common strumpet he accused me of being than stay married to one such as him.* The thought was chilling, terrifying—

Exhilarating. A life free of Philippe. Free of his expectations, his disappointment, his cloying, adoring love that sought to control her instead of know her.

Her mind spun, weighing her options and assets with cold calculation. She was still Duchess of Catarlia in her own right, the title passed down to her from her father. If only she could get herself free of Philippe's physical hold and back to her island, then she would have allies enough to break free of her marriage too. Enough men would be eager to marry her themselves that they would help her get free. She could play any suitors off against each other. Then, once free of her husband, she would never need to marry again.

But how *to get free of Philippe?*

No way to do it in this wilderness. The noblemen who were loyal to her might help, but what then? A civil war in the army? Jerdic soldiers fighting each other over her?

His men would likely catch her first, and Philippe would immediately put her under Mistress Helen's control. And if not caught, Aliénor would only lose her way to starve in the desert.

But soon enough they would reach Anutitum, a city controlled by Aliénor's own cousin, Guillaume. She hadn't seen him in years, but he had been a charming boy and fond of her when they were children. He was prince in his own city. If she sought her cousin's protection, Philippe would not be able to reclaim her. She only had to bend herself to Philippe's will for the next week or so. Just until she could reach her cousin's city.

Soon. She wrapped the thought tight around herself like a blanket to ward off the chill. *Soon.*

Chapter Seven

Thomas had been awake all night, helping with the cleanup of the camp, chasing down horses, chasing down bodies of those men who had been washed away. It was dirty, exhausting, disheartening work. He'd finally stolen back to his own tent to clean off some of the clinging muck and to break his fast before he returned. The column would not move again today, and not for some days yet if this disarray continued. He was the closest thing to a leader at the chaos down by the river. Princess Aliénor's man, Lord Ysen, had been injured when the river was flooding. Still, the man was working through his head injury to salvage what supplies they could from the wreck of the baggage train. The Jerdic prince had yet to show his face.

He probably slept through the whole thing. Or perhaps Philippe felt too much shame that he had allowed his men to camp so close to the river. Many men and horses had drowned last night, and many valuable supplies and tents had been washed away. *If only the pompous little fool had listened.* Of course, the rain had come on so soon after dinner, there might not have been time anyway to get everyone clear. Nevertheless, if the Jerdic prince had bestirred himself they might have saved more men.

Thomas shook his head and ducked inside his borrowed tent. *No good going over* what ifs.

Thomas's page, Ned, waited for him in his tent, sleeping heavily on the mattress. The room smelled of mildew and damp, and the rugs still squished with water as Thomas strode across them. Yet another reason not to bring all this finery on campaign. Young Ned snored, one hand cupped under his ruddy cheek. Thomas hated to disturb the lad, for he'd been up all night too, running errands about camp. But Llewellyn was off somewhere tending to the wounded, and Thomas needed to speak with his second. He shook the page awake and sent him off to find Llewellyn.

Before Thomas had done more than splash his face with the icy water in his basin, a heavily freckled page dressed in the Jerdic colors entered his tent. "My Lord the Prince begs conference with you, King Thomas."

Thomas eyed the piled mattresses with longing. "All right. I come."

Prince Philippe was dressed in a simple surcoat and chain mail, just as Thomas was, but the prince's outfit was spotless, fresh. Only his boots were muddied, and those but little.

Thomas fought not to show his outrage. Had the prince even gone to look at the scene by the riverside? At the deaths that his arrogance and ignorance had wrought? No. Apparently not.

Philippe sat on a simple camp chair, but the effect was spoiled by the billowing silk awning around him, and the small table laden with fruit and drink at his elbow. One of his barons stood to his left, hand on the hilt of his sword. That damned witch stood to the prince's right, her hand lightly cupped around her dagger's hilt.

Thomas gave a small nod of greeting. "You wished to see me, Prince Philippe?"

"I did. Please sit, King Thomas."

The baron leapt to set a second camp chair in the shade under the awning. Thomas sat, leaning back to survey the prince—and to keep that damned witch well in his sight. Thomas had thought this an informal meeting to discuss the fallout from the flooding. If he had known that he came to a formal audience, he would have waited at least for Llewellyn. Thomas might also have paused to change his garb to something fresher. Llewellyn would probably scold him for this oversight later.

Philippe leaned forward, his voice low and confiding. "First, I wanted to apologize for the behavior of my wife. I hope you were not overly offended."

Thomas frowned. "I am not sure what you mean. She has been nothing but courteous and kind. Her bravery last night was remarkable. She's a credit to you, lad—your lordship." Thomas bit hard on his tongue and cursed himself. This arrogant pup couldn't be more than twenty, half Thomas's age. Nevertheless, Philippe clearly expected Thomas to treat with him as if they were equal in knowledge and experience. Thomas had to play along and swallow that insolence or let Philippe turn the Lyondi knights out to starve. *Or worse.* Philippe, after all, still had an army at his beck and call.

Philippe's eyes narrowed as he surveyed Thomas, but he seemed content to let the matter of the princess drop. He pressed his palms together, resting the points of his fingers under his chin in a pose of grave thought. "I asked you here because I want to offer you a formal alliance. You have lost the better part of your army. I will pledge my men to your cause if you will pledge yours to mine."

Hell. Thomas worked his mouth, his mind furiously turning over. *Dammit, I should have waited for Llewellyn.* Thomas was a soldier. He had no head for diplomacy.

At last, when inspiration did not strike, Thomas spread his empty hands. "I cannot, Prince Philippe." He wet his lips, knowing he should say no more, but the heavy guilt in his gut made his tongue unwise. "In fact, I advise you to turn back before the mountains. Or go the long way round the mountains and head home at the next port."

Philippe blinked for a moment in shock. "What can you mean, King Thomas?"

"I lost many men because I was too arrogant to admit I was out of my depth. The Tiochene raiders have more spell-casters than you can imagine and better knowledge of this terrain." Thomas fisted one hand against his thigh, remembered screams echoing hollowly in his ears. "We did not know what we were doing when we came here. What we would face. We are not prepared."

Philippe's lip curled with a contempt he did not even try to hide. "Perhaps *you* were not prepared. You'll notice I still have *my* army."

Thomas tensed his hands on his thighs to keep from throttling the arrogant little whelp. "Have you met any of the local Tiochene raiders in battle yet?"

"Not...as yet."

"Then we do not know how your army may fare, do we? As yet."

A great clatter sounded behind, and Thomas half glanced over his shoulder to see Llewellyn dash up, huffing and puffing, his sunburned cheeks even more flushed with exertion. Llewellyn tossed an exasperated glare at Thomas and came to stand behind his shoulder.

Philippe waved his hand as if to wipe away Thomas's warnings and raised his chin. "You will not join with me then, King Thomas?"

Llewellyn made a small sound of shock. Thomas did not glance back, and he did not bother to soften his answer or prevaricate. "No, I will not commit my men to any further military campaigns in this thrice-damned wilderness."

A tart sneer twisted the young prince's lips. "But you will travel with us. Use our medical supplies. Eat our food. Leer at our women."

Thomas pushed to his feet, towering so that the prince had to crane his head back. "Have I given offense, Prince? It was not my intent."

Philippe belatedly clattered to his feet too. The camp chair fell over behind him as he stood toe-to-toe with Thomas. Thomas was rather pettily pleased to see that he stood a full head higher than Prince Philippe.

Philippe's eyelids flickered, assessing his chances, glancing behind to Llewellyn, who stood now at the king's shoulder, hand oh-so-casually resting on his sword hilt. Philippe retreated and lifted his hands with a small tossing gesture. "No. All is peace between us." His lips twisted with distaste, and he half turned his shoulder, apparently ready for this interview to be at an end.

Thomas was happy to oblige and yet—he stepped close to the prince one last time and lowered his voice. "Your wife is a fine woman. Beyond reproach. You do wrong even to think such things about her."

"Perhaps less is expected of women in Lyond," Philippe scoffed.

"Or perhaps Jerdic men should learn to trust their women better."

"My king?" Llewellyn stepped forward, all but thrusting his body between Thomas and the prince. "You wanted to meet with the baron before the sun was too high."

"Of course." Thomas offered Philippe the shallowest bow that courtesy allowed. "Well, Prince Philippe, I thank you for your aid in this desperate hour, and I wish you good luck with your quest. My men and I will encroach on your hospitality no longer. We will take what we came with and depart."

"No, no, King Thomas. I will not be so ungenerous as that. Take some food and other supplies if you need them. I will not turn you out to starve."

"You are too kind."

Philippe snapped his fingers, and the freckled page produced some vellum with a quill to write. Philippe dashed off a few lines and tried to hand the permission to Thomas. Llewellyn smoothly intercepted it and read it over before rolling the document up.

"Thank you again for your help, Prince Philippe." *Such as it was.*

Philippe returned Thomas a bare nod, not even civil, and Thomas left the prince's presence without another word.

"That went well," Llewellyn muttered darkly.

"Do we have enough horses for our men?"

"We are short one horse, Sire."

"Mine, yes? Well, I'll ride pillion behind you if I must to get out of this damned camp."

Llewellyn brandished the prince's note. "I'll see if this stretches far enough to cover a horse."

They walked in silence through the camp for a moment more before Llewellyn asked with deceptive mildness, "Will you take formal leave of the Princess Aliénor?"

"No. I'll not create further problems with her troublesome wretch of a husband. Besides, I hardly know the woman." He would never know her better now. *I'll probably never even see her again.* Bitterness burned in his gut at the thought. How cruel the Fates were to throw such a fascinating, lovely woman into his path when she belonged to someone else.

"I think you *must* take formal leave of her."

Thomas flicked an annoyed glance at his second. "Why is that?"

"Because she's sitting just up there, watching us."

Like a compass needle seeking true north, Thomas's head whipped around almost against his will, and his hungry gaze sought sight of her. *There.* She sat on one of the grassy hills well above the river, her legs stretched out before her.

Thomas broke off from Llewellyn and cut through a line of tents, his path an arrow shot straight for Aliénor. *Princess* Aliénor. He sighed to himself. *Old fool.* It had been twenty years since he'd felt so silly-headed around a woman, and that had been his late wife. He frowned, disconcerted by the thought.

Aliénor smiled at him as he approached, her clear brown eyes shining, her cheeks flushed in the gloomy light of this miserable morning. She wore another plain, almost dun-colored gown today with a short leather riding jacket over it dyed a soft blue. Both garments were weather-beaten but clean, like something a merchant's wife might wear. He felt a strangely wistful urge to see her in all her royal finery. How beautiful she would look with that red-gold curtain of hair loose about her shoulders, jewels at her creamy throat. *Best to get this over with.* "Princess Aliénor, I come to take formal leave of you. My men and I are going."

Her pale brows drew down. "But you cannot. You have no supplies. Do you even have enough horses?"

Thomas felt his mouth twist. "Your husband has most generously gifted us with whatever supplies we need to be on our way."

"Most of your men are injured. *You* are still injured, no matter how you go charging about the camp. Forgive me, but this does not seem wise."

His chest ached with bittersweet warmth, as if a bird were unfolding its wings over his ribcage. "You speak true, my lady." Truer than she knew. "Yet for all that, we must go."

"But—" Her eyes widened, and her gaze flicked back to the way he had come, toward Prince Philippe's tent. She caught her breath on a scandalized gasp. "I think I understand now."

Thomas made a small gesture of negation. "'Tis well enough."

Her already ivory face had paled now almost to the color of snow. "Philippe is a jealous fool." She spat the words out, yet tears glittered in her eyes, and her lip trembled.

"Princess Aliénor, what is wrong?" Thomas knelt beside her and took her hand before he could think better of it.

Her graceful fingers gripped his for one brief moment before she jerked her hand back and looked about as if someone might be watching.

They probably are. He shifted further away from her.

She sent him a quick, despairing glance, and pulled her knees up to her chest like a castle lifting its drawbridge. Truly, she seemed besieged in that moment. Caught, trapped, utterly alone.

"Princess, is there any assistance I can render you? Anything I can do?"

One small tear broke free to slide down the fullness of her cheek. She turned her face away, and wiped the betraying wetness against her skirt over her knee. "No one can help me while I abide in Philippe's camp."

Come away with me. Thomas bit the words back, just barely. His hands were curled into tight fists as he fought every urge within himself that cried to draw his sword and pledge it to this sweet lady's defense.

Come away with me. He could still taste the words, heavy and tempting on his tongue as some rich wine. And just as foolishly intoxicating. For surely the quickest way to start the next war between Jerdun and Lyond would be to steal away the Jerdic princess.

As if sensing his inner battle, Aliénor looked at him, her face sad. "I think you are right and you must go. Kind Fate walk with you and keep your steps safe from harm." She rose as she said it and offered him her hand in parting.

Thomas stood with her and caught her fingers. He bowed low and pressed a small, tender kiss against the skin of her hand. When he would have released her, her palm turned against his, and he felt the feather touch of her fingertips against his cheek. It was the barest touch—he might have imagined it. Yet the princess's face was wistful, her eyes brimming with tears again when he glanced at her.

His chest ached, as if a split were starting, a crack like a jagged fissure in the heart of a glass window. "Good-bye, Princess Aliénor."

"Good-bye, King Thomas." She wheeled away from him, folding her arms over her chest.

He forced himself to turn, to take one step and another away from her until he could not even see her anymore when he looked behind.

Chapter Eight

The army moved out the next morning later than usual, shuffling and slow after the disaster by the riverside. Aliénor watched the ragged line straggle up the road behind her, men limping, dirty, empty-eyed. She couldn't help but think they looked more like a mob than an army.

Philippe seemed to notice nothing. He was still as neat as ever in a parti-colored surcoat of now-faded purple and white with his chain mail beneath. He wore the uniform of a common soldier, but it was cleaner and well-mended. His cheekbones had no hollows beneath them from lack of food or sleep—although his eyes were pinched today, and his mouth set in an unhappy line.

The clop of their horses' feet and the men's on the road was dull, but the jangle of all their harnesses, the creak of leather and chain mail seemed impossibly loud in the still morning air. She and Philippe did not lead the column, and ahead of her were the backs of men and horses. She could not see the road at all, except for the craggy red stone of the mountains looming in the distance.

Her horse stumbled badly on the path, rattling her. When she looked down, a body lay in the road.

Her stomach clenched, and sourness burned her throat as she stared at the dead man. Her horse had recovered his footing, but Aliénor's stomach felt less sure. Covering her mouth with one hand, she cast her gaze wildly about and was shocked to see more evidence of slaughter: blood staining the rocks and clumps of carrion birds still feasting to the side of the road.

She could hardly believe her eyes, but yes, they had left the river valley and climbed steadily toward the higher ground offered by the road into the mountain passes. The rocky foothills loomed before them, and the higher peak of the imposing Mt. Calismos towered over her like an enemy's blade about to fall.

The blood jumped in her veins. "Husband, we're heading into the mountain passes?"

A muscle flexed beneath Philippe's beard. "Yes."

Aliénor lowered her voice, but she could not stop a small tremolo of fear from leaking in. "The same mountain where King Thomas's army was attacked? Philippe, are you *mad*?"

His head snapped her way, and his eyes were tight with the same fear souring her gut. "What choice do we have? My advisors went over and over this yesterday. The weather along the river path is disastrous. If we stick to the river we shall all be drowned, and we lack the supplies to go the long way around the mountains. Instead, we must cut straight for Anutitum, straight as the crow flies, and then we shall be there within the week." A brave speech, and yet her husband's voice wobbled on the end.

"We will all be killed by the Tiochene first."

"I have no *choice*, Aliénor." He scraped a shaking hand through his dark hair. "Anyway, I'm sure the Tiochene have moved on with their spoils by now. Why should they attack a well-armed force like ours when their victory over King Thomas is so fresh?"

"Why indeed?" Aliénor pressed a hand to her face, rubbing at the sudden ache behind her eyes.

"You question my methods, wife?"

I question your sanity. Aliénor bit those words back, chewing on her cheek, her stomach feeling as storm-tossed as the dark river from the other night.

The blood witch rode somewhere just behind them, and Aliénor felt the witch's presence like a rolling boulder at her back. Between the looming mountain pass and the threat of the blood witch's control, Aliénor wasn't sure which Fate she feared more.

"Monstrous. *Monstrous* that the Jerdic boy would kick us out of camp." Godric fingered the scab on his face from his interrogation, his expression surly.

Thomas simply kept his eye on the uneven trail along the riverbank. They were taking that shorter path to civilization, hugging tight to the riverbed. This trail would be more dangerous with the winter rains and flooding, but the chances of supplying themselves were better. After what happened to his army in the mountain passes, Thomas would take the dangers of the riverbed over the dangers of the Tiochene raiders any day.

"It's for the best, really, that the Jerdic lad kicked us out," Llewellyn murmured.

Thomas shot his friend a quick, accusing look. "What do you mean by that?"

Llewellyn's mouth quirked, but instead of making some comment about the Jerdic princess, his second merely raised his mail-clad arm. He pointed behind them toward where they had left the Jerdic camp.

Thomas craned around in his saddle, but it took him a long moment to understand what he was seeing. A column of dust rising high on the road. A column such as a moving army might produce with their many trampling feet. When he recognized the direction of the dust, he felt his temper spike. "That foolish, arrogant little *ass*."

"Yes."

"He's leading them through the mountain passes."

Llewellyn dropped his gaze, and his shoulders hunched over. His voice was quiet, almost soundless as he said, "Yes."

"We warned him. He saw our wounded, our dead. Why would he do that?"

"Perhaps to prove he is the better man, the better general. Perhaps he feels he cannot support his army through a long trek around the mountain passes.

Perhaps he simply has a horrible sense of direction." Llewellyn lifted one shoulder in a shrug, but his face was pinched and unhappy as his gaze wandered toward the trailing column of dust.

Thomas had a violent urge to wheel his horse about and ride straight back into the Jerdic column. Gallop through until he found Aliénor, toss her over his saddle, and ride off with her to safety. Foolishness, of course. Even if he were to attempt such a ridiculous rescue, the odds that he could find one fair lady among a rabble of thousands of soldiers on the march were slim.

Still, he stared at that column of dust steadily marching toward doom, and he wished he'd had the audacity to ask her to run with him when he'd had the chance.

With a firm hand, he turned his horse back onto the river path. "Come on. We don't have enough supplies to dawdle."

Llewellyn urged his horse alongside Thomas's and kept his voice low. "Perhaps they will fare better than we did in the mountains. Perhaps the Tiochene won't attack. Perhaps Philippe is a better leader than we give him credit for, and he will fight them off."

"Yes." Thomas stopped himself from looking back again. Instead he turned his eye toward the roaring of the river. The waters were still dark and heavy with storm runoff, bracken, and tree limbs swirling in the wild torrents. He could almost imagine he saw that brave, small figure dressed in pale blue fighting her way through the wild rush of the river again. *Fight hard, Princess Aliénor. I cannot help you this time.*

Chapter Nine

The army passed more bodies with practically every step they took up the treacherous road into the mountains, but Aliénor knew better than to look. The soldiers, though, marching on foot as they were, could not help but notice—notice and fear. A ripple of alarm and dismay passed through the column, starting at the front and passing backward in a low, muttering wave. Men were tense now, watchful.

Aliénor kept an iron grip on her own reins, and the leather straps were slick in her sweaty palms. Her shoulders were stiff and aching from tension, and she seemed to have passed her jitters on to her horse as the damned nervy beast kept twitching and sidling sideways under her hands.

Philippe seemed no better. He'd caught his lower lip with his teeth and worried at it absently. She wasn't sure he realized he was doing it. His eyes scanned the tops of the hills above them, and Aliénor found her own gaze following his even though she wasn't sure what he feared.

Constant alertness, constant worry. These made the army cautious, slow, scared to take every step forward. A strong leader might have been able to hurry them forward, to reassure. Philippe just sat atop his horse and grew paler and paler as the day passed, deep lines etching themselves into his face. Some turn in the path appeared ahead and Philippe, atop his horse, wheeled toward Aliénor. "Wife, take yourself to the women's wagon. You look overtired."

She opened her mouth to protest, but Philippe's gaze warned her that his mood was dark. Feeling an itch behind her shoulder blades that might have been the blood witch's stare, Aliénor dropped her head. She nodded, hating herself and him. "Of course, husband." Her obedience tasted heavy and bitter on her tongue.

"My princess." Philippe lifted her hand to his lips for a careless kiss and dropped it just as quickly, his gaze returning to the cliffs above.

Aliénor motioned for her personal guards and Noémi to follow as she turned her horse about. The small group of them worked their way back from the vanguard to the middle of the column along a narrow band of a wash beside the old mountain road.

"My lady," Noémi murmured.

"What?"

Her handmaiden nodded to Aliénor's hands on her reins. A long moment passed before Aliénor realized she was scrubbing the back of her left hand with the heel of her right. *Stop.* Still her skin prickled. Strange that the memory of one small kiss should leave her so warm while the feel of her husband's lips only made her skin crawl.

She urged her horse forward faster, just short of a trot along the narrow basin path. Her mount huffed in annoyance but obliged her. She felt suddenly as if she were back in that dark river, watching the waves rise over her head, seeing her doom approach. *All I can do is take a deep breath before the wave washes over me. All I can do is hope for the best.*

The ladies' wagon appeared before her: a squat wooden box set on six wheels and drawn by four horses. The driver, Michel, rode atop the right horse in the front line, controlling it and the other beasts with a long whip. When he saw her approach, he tugged on the reins, then reached behind to pull the harness on the rear horses until each animal had stopped. Aliénor dismounted, then nodded hello as she climbed inside the coach.

Violette was bundled up on one of the benches, still tired after her adventures in the river. The girl looked up from a sewing project as they entered, her hazel eyes wide in her dark face. "My lady?"

"Get out your armor and put it on at once." Aliénor worked her way past the two women and told the driver to start moving again.

"Princess?"

"My lady?"

She flung her hands up amid the chatter of their voices, and silence fell as the wagon rolled into motion, rocking gently like a boat. Violette rose from her seat, pressing one hand against the wall to keep her balance. Her usually rich brown skin looked sallow, the skin around her mouth and knuckles a pale yellow. "Why, my lady?"

Because at least then you'll have some protection against arrows and blades. Aliénor did not say that. Best not to scare them. Instead, she gave them each a gentle smile. "Because your princess asks it of you, and you are both my Amazons. Is that enough for now?"

Violette swallowed, perhaps in belated realization that this was not an idle whim. "Of course, Princess."

"Let's put yours on first, my lady." Noémi sat stiffly in one corner, arms folded.

Aliénor opened her mouth to argue, but before she could speak, Noémi popped up and set about digging in the storage space under the wagon benches. Philippe had not allowed her to keep swords or bows in the lady's wagon, but each set of armor had a knife in a scabbard to belt at their waists.

For a good while, the wagon rocked with a bustle of activity as the ladies pulled their brave red leather breastplates from the storage under the benches and fastened the armor over each woman's gown. Each Amazon had a red gown to match her armor, but Aliénor ordered them not to change into those.

As she surveyed her women, she restrained a sigh of deepest frustration. Red. *Scarlet* red. What an idiotic choice for armor. They would all stand out like a beacon in the countryside. There were no good choices here. She had rather they have the protection their armor could afford if it did come to fighting. She would just make them all stay in the wagon so they could not provide tempting targets to any eagle-eyed archers on the hill.

Their breastplates were old-fashioned leather ones, dyed that ghastly red, more like sturdy vests, really. Philippe had forbidden them real chain mail, and Aliénor rather thought he was right about that. They weren't strong enough to wear that heavy stuff—she'd rather they be able to move. *To run.* Beneath their brave red breastplates they all wore plain-colored split-skirts for riding and their sturdiest boots.

Violette toyed with the dagger at her side, drawing it in and out.

Aliénor reached over and gently squeezed her handmaiden's hands to get her to stop her fidgets. "It'll be all right."

The girl pursed her lips but nodded. She didn't look like an Amazon. She looked like a child playing dress-up, frightened and queasy. Aliénor felt the same. Noémi was the only one among them who wore her armor as easily as she had worn her gowns. Once they were all dressed, the stout handmaiden had settled back into sewing with never a pause, looking completed unruffled. Aliénor deeply envied Noémi her poise in this moment.

The wagon rolled over a large rock, making Aliénor sway and throw a hand out to steady herself. They all tilted a little as the wagon rolled its way up a steep hill, ever further into the mountains. Aliénor fisted her hand against her knee but then forced herself to uncurl her fingers, trying to calm the ragged hammering of her heart.

But even as she did, a piercing cry filled the air. Not of fear, but of fury. A loud wail.

The three women in the wagon jumped. Violette uttered a small shriek and buried her face against Noémi's shoulder. The men outside cried out, their voices dulled by the heavy wooden walls of the wagon.

Aliénor crawled forward, tossing aside the decorative pillows as she moved. She called out to her driver, a stout sailor from her island. "Michel, what's happening?" She could only just see the red hillside looming ahead through the gauzy curtains that divided her women from the outside world.

Beads of sweat poured down Michel's temples, and he half-turned, his face screwed up in fear. "Some shrieking barbarian on a horse came tearing down out of the hillside, swinging that curved sword of hers like a madwoman. She tore right into our line of men."

"A woman?"

"Ay, these Tiochene even make their women fight, my lady."

Aliénor swallowed. "Just the one warrior?"

"Yes, my lady."

No arrows yet, and no spell-casting, either. "Is she dead?"

Michel shook his head, his face pale. "No, that's the worst of it. She rode straight up and lopped off one of our own lads' heads, then went tearing off back up the hillside. Gone out of sight, and none of us dare follow."

"No." That would surely lead to an ambush. Aliénor pressed a clammy palm to her throat, her pulse pounding.

"*Aieeeeeeeee.*" The hills around them erupted with sound. This time it was many voices, all screaming as one. The whole hillside seemed to vibrate around Aliénor, as if the very rocks and sand were screaming for the blood of the Jerdic army.

Something dull thumped against the wagon's side, and then another *thump* and another until it sounded almost like raindrops falling.

"Michel, what is—?"

Michel let out a low, pained grunt and toppled sideways off his horse.

Thomas and his men had stopped to water and rest their mounts. The first sounds of battle reached them even as he rechecked the straps of his horse's bridle. He and his men were still close enough to the mountains that the cries of the soldiers could faintly reach their ears, but the terrible sounds were faint, far away. They could have been bad memories or half-remembered nightmares.

Except they aren't. Thomas stood braced, staring at the hard line of the mountains behind them as if he could send himself there through sheer will.

"What are we going to do, Your Highness?" Godric asked.

Thomas tensed all over, as if his body were straining to go without permission from his mind. *How can I ask it of them?* After he'd led his men into disaster once, how could he ask this of them again?

"They wouldn't have helped *us*," Ned murmured, but loudly enough so all could hear.

Godric wheeled toward the boy, his nostrils flaring with indignation. "Which is why we should lend Jerdun our aid and teach them better manners."

Thomas drew close to Llewellyn. "What do you think of all this, my friend?"

"I think it is a fine bit of foolishness, and we might all be killed." Llewellyn's lips gave a wry twist, and his eyes were sad. "But I don't see that there is anything else you can do. This is who you are."

"An incompetent leader? A vainglorious fool?"

"A good man." Llewellyn turned at the words and swung into the saddle of his own horse, taking it for granted what order his king would give. "Better to die in battle than starve in the desert anyway, eh?" His eyes twinkled with the light of adventure.

Thomas puffed out a pained laugh. "Mount up, men."

As the wagon driver's dead body rolled off the lead horse, Aliénor gritted her teeth to keep a scream back. She took a breath to steal herself then crept forward and peered out.

A rain of lethal arrows battered her husband's army. Each arrow found its mark with deadly accuracy, which made her believe they were guided by supernatural means. She watched men fall all around through the gauzy curtain that divided her from the world. It felt unreal, almost dreamlike, watching the arrows punch their way into the men, watching the men fold up like forgotten dolls.

The wagon horses sidled in their traces, their eyes rolling over white with fear. The fact that the arrows kept missing her horses also seemed to argue for magical intervention. She was sure these desert raiders could use good mounts.

Another shriek of fury washed down from the mountains as hundreds of their enemies bellowed at them from the hilltops. The wagon trembled. *An earthquake?*

But no. The Tiochene emerged from the hills at last, pouring down to rush the line of Philippe's army. The raiders rode furry, stocky little ponies that moved like the wind, and they carried thick, short bows that they fired from their horses' backs. Their arrows sang through the air with a precision that made Aliénor shiver. Most of the warriors wore heavy wool tunics in various bright colors. Some had strange scale-like armor all over their bodies. Others wore northern chain mail likely looted from King Thomas's poor dead soldiers.

Several riders lifted their arms high, their hands glowing, full of spell-fire. As the first of the Tiochene spell-casters hurled their deadly curses, she closed her eyes. But she could not shut her ears to the screams of the soldiers, the crackle of flame as men were burned alive. *Just like Thomas said.*

The wagon lurched forward, and one of the horses whinnied.

Aliénor swallowed and forced herself to move.

"My lady, come back inside!" Noémi cried.

Holding her breath, Aliénor slithered out of the safety of the wagon's back compartment to huddle atop the empty driver's seat. It was like swimming up from the quiet of underwater to the surface to find the world in chaos above her. For a moment she could only sit stunned, bombarded by the screams and cries as the men around her grappled with one another. The arrows had stopped and most of the spell-fire. The Tiochene hacked their way through the line of surviving Jerdic soldiers now, the foreign warriors faster and fiercer than anything she'd ever seen.

Small spells still sounded occasionally with flashes and booms around her. Screams rose from a clump of Jerdic soldiers as a fiery cloud engulfed them, setting fire to their surcoats and hair. Heat blasted Aliénor's face, and one of the horses on her wagon half reared in its traces.

The path ahead was a tangle of fresh bodies, horses and men jostling and swiping at each other, blood splashing on the path and against the men. Her wagon horses shrieked again, and the wagon rocked as one of them kicked out at a jostling pair of soldiers who came too near. Her personal complement of guards was either dead or locked into the melee ahead of them on the road.

Tears stung her eyes. *Papa's songs never spoke of this.* Even from a distance she could tell Michel was quite dead, one arrow through his eye and another in his neck. She hovered on the edge of the wagon seat. Either she needed to go out and get the reins from Michel's body, or she and her ladies needed to leave this wagon. Neither option appealed. Still, nerves jangling, she eased her way forward, ready to hop down.

A Tiochene warrior came roaring up. He slashed at one of the horse's sides, and the animal screamed and pitched forward to run. The other horses, alarmed, stampeded forward too. She tipped backward and might have fallen straight off the wagon had not her two ladies reached out to grip her arms.

The wagon rocked and lolled, wallowing over the bodies in the road, and then it burst forward at a breakneck speed. The panicked horses kicked their way through the chaos to a small strip of clear land just off the road, and then they *flew.* Aliénor jolted upward in her seat as the horses fought their panicked way over rocks and small hillocks of sand, trying to escape the chaos of the battle. Without a driver, there was no way to regain control of them. Aliénor didn't quite have the courage to attempt a leap onto one of their backs in this wild, tumbling run.

She held on, her muscles screaming protest as she fought to keep her seat amidst the pitching, bumping path the horses led them on. They rolled over another large rock and her teeth jarred together. Beneath her a crack sounded, and the wagon suddenly listed to one side.

"The axle!" Noémi cried from the back of the wagon.

Another large rock loomed ahead, and their wildly bumping, tilted wagon was about to sideswipe it. The horses could dodge around, but the wounded carriage was going to hit it almost head-on.

"Hold on!" Aliénor threw herself into the safety of the back compartment. She rolled herself into a tight ball and prayed her other ladies did likewise. With a terrible crash, the wagon collided with the boulder.

———— ◆ ————

Thomas and his men made good time riding back toward doom and disaster. The mountain pass and the river road paralleled each other a good bit of the way. Soon enough, Thomas could hear the chaos of the battle, although he had yet to see any Tiochene or Jerdic soldiers. Not even dead bodies.

He called a halt and rode with several of his men a little ways off the road to huddle in the bushes while they held counsel on what was best to be done. His nerves twitched and his body ached, wanting to be moving, wanting to be doing. But it was no good riding headlong into the battle. They needed some sort of plan. Thomas crouched in a small circle among his men. "All right, Llewellyn, do you think you're strong enough to create the distraction alone?"

"Since that is our only option, I will do what I must."

Thomas pressed his friend's shoulder. "Without injuring yourself?" Llewellyn was known to try his strength too far, even to the point of illness and collapse.

Llewellyn snorted. "Do not worry about me, my king. It will be a strain, and I don't know how I can create something big enough alone, but perhaps I can—"

A low, animal grunt sounded from the brush to their right, and a shaggy-furred brown bear reared onto his hind quarters. He was a massive, heavily muscled brute with large, powerful paws as big as Thomas's head and claws half again as long.

Llewellyn slammed his hand onto Thomas's shoulder. He and Godric yanked Thomas back, dragging him through the dirt, away from the bear.

The beast's head swung round and surveyed them, but he did not charge. The animal only sat there staring at them, tilting his head to the side to scrutinize them in a very un-bear-like way. Llewellyn frowned and eased closer to the bear, his own head cocked in a fascination that almost mirrored the beast's.

"Llewellyn..." Thomas reached for his friend's arm to haul the damn idiot back.

Llewellyn sat back on his heels with a short, somehow bitter laugh. "Mistress Helen, is this your work?" he called out softly.

The bear slammed down onto all fours, then lowered himself to lie on the ground, like nothing so much as a tame dog. Brush crackled away to their left, and Thomas whirled around to watch Mistress Helen pick her way through the heavy bushes toward them.

Dirt and streaks of blood smudged her pale skin, and her hair was a dark cloud of tangles. She grinned as she approached them. "Oh, thank goodness. I thought you were farther along the road, and I should never catch up to you."

"Impressive work with the bear," Llewellyn murmured.

Mistress Helen waved that away. "With all the soldiers occupied, I needed some way to defend myself." She clasped her hands together then and gazed beseechingly at Thomas. "Please, please, gentle king, give me one of your horses and get me out of here."

Thomas recoiled, and eyed the witch up and down in surprise. "You would abandon your army? Your prince?"

Her face contorted, her lip curling in a sneer. "King Thomas, you've already watched the slaughter of one army. What makes you want to watch another?"

Thomas reared back, as startled as if she had slapped him. Where was her loyalty? Her compassion? "We are going back to save what men we can, or die trying."

"They're all dead already, and you will be too if you keep riding." The blood witch had been walking toward them. Now she stopped and braced her weight on her heels, poised as if to run. Thomas felt Llewellyn tense beside him, watching the woman.

Thomas kept speaking, hoping to keep her attention on him. "Nevertheless, we mean to continue. I hope you will help us."

"What? A poor, feeble woman like me? Oh no, my king. I cannot. I've no strength left." A scimitar-sharp smile crossed her face, and her gaze flicked toward the bear. Behind them, the bear rolled onto his hind legs and voiced a low, rumbling growl. The blood witch wheeled around as if to run.

Llewellyn flung his hands up, magic coiled around his hands, pooling against his palms like liquid fire. "No, you don't." He flung the spell like a snowball and it thwacked gently into the bear's chest. The witch let out a shriek of outrage even as Godric caught her by the shoulders and banded his beefy arms around her body.

The bear sat there blinking a long moment, the spell soaking into his fur like water. The animal swung his head around, unsteady as a drunkard, and looked at Llewellyn. Llewellyn made a small flicking gesture with his hand. "*Go.*"

The bear slammed onto all fours again and took off running. The brush crashed and swayed at his retreat. As Thomas approached, Mistress Helen squirmed and thrashed in Godric's arms, but the large knight had her securely pinned. Her face was parchment-white with outrage and fear. Though Thomas was closer, her burning gaze fixed itself firmly on Llewellyn. "You're a spell-caster."

"Mistress Helen," Thomas murmured, "meet my royal magician, Master Llewellyn."

Llewellyn made a small bow as he eyed the blood witch in assessment. For her part, Mistress Helen let out a high keen of rage and redoubled her efforts to break Godric's hold on her. "*Fools.* You're all fools riding back to that slaughter. Leave *me* out of it."

Thomas drew close, and—though he did not like touching her—he turned her chin gently toward him so she could look at his face. "Come along now, Mistress Helen, let us see what can be done for your army, eh?"

The blood witch spat on him.

Chapter Ten

Aliénor's head buzzed and she slowly woke up, groggy, her body aching. She stared around, wondering how the wagon's pillows had come to be so scattered about. *Why is there blood on the walls?*

"Aliénor." Philippe's voice. He tucked his hands under her arms and tugged. She wished he wouldn't. Everything in her ached, and her head felt woozy.

"*Damn you.* Help me get her out," Philippe snarled. More hands, more pulling, and a sort of weightless sensation as she was lifted up. Screams and cries still filled the air, but they sounded farther away, distant. *The battle.* The sun stung her eyes as the men carried her from the wagon. Philippe had about two dozen of his soldiers surrounding them. The wagon was a broken wreck. The horses were gone. "Noémi? Violette?"

"Can you walk?"

Aliénor touched her aching head and gasped when her fingers came away bloody.

"Dammit." Philippe hefted her awkwardly in his arms and took off at a trot over the sand. She blinked and stared into her husband's face as he shot her a harried look, fear lurking in his eyes. He stumbled once and nearly dropped her. "Aliénor, I need you to walk."

"I...think I can."

He set her down at once, and she wobbled on her feet to be so abruptly standing, but she didn't fall. The battle did lie behind them, but not far. Any moment some of the Tiochene warriors might break free to pursue them up the road.

"You'll ride with me, Aliénor. We must *go*."

Even as he said the words, some half dozen Tiochene plowed into the line of his men, cutting them down, breaking the protective line. "*Go!*" Philippe grabbed her arm and jerked her along after him toward his horses. A group of Tiochene rushed forward, cutting off Aliénor and Philippe's route to their mounts. Philippe slid to a stop, breathing hard, eyes frantic.

Aliénor yanked on his arm. "The river."

"What?"

She tugged on him, trying to get him to move with her. "Their spells won't work over water. Maybe we can swim downstream. Get away."

He wheeled about, towing her along behind him. The two of them cut over the long mountain road and stumbled down a rough patch of hillside. Slipping and sliding in the loose dirt, rocks cutting into her feet, Aliénor could hear more Tiochene yelling behind them. Following them, it sounded like. Sweat beaded at her temples. Her Amazon armor cut into her thighs and armpits as she ran. Philippe held her hand painfully tight as they made their frantic stumble down the hill, but she gripped him back just as hard.

Water gurgled ahead, the sound like music, and her heart clenched. *Please, oh please.*

More shouting behind. A skitter of pebbles banged into her ankles, and she dared to turn around. A half dozen Tiochene had chased them this far. They too were jumping and sliding their way down the treacherous hillside. Philippe shoved her ahead of him as the silver glimmer of the river came in sight.

Aliénor rushed into the stream, the water sloshing over her ankles, then her knees. It was still so cold, like a slap that shocked her to breathlessness. Dizzy, off-balance, she teetered on her feet and reached back for Philippe's arm. He wasn't there. "Philippe, come on—" When she looked back, Philippe had not followed her. He stood a few feet behind, guarding her back, and drew his sword as the Tiochene came on toward them. Aliénor's heart throbbed inside her like someone had squeezed it in their fist.

Philippe squared his shoulders. "I surrender and demand ransom. I am the Prince of—"

One of the Tiochene lifted his short bow before Philippe could finish and put an arrow neatly through her husband's neck.

Aliénor screamed. Philippe's hands pawed futilely at his neck, trying to stop the bleeding or wrench out the arrow. He folded up facedown on the ground, his blood soaking into the damp earth of the riverside.

The archer drew his bow again, aiming for Aliénor. She flung herself backward into the river, letting the water rush over her face and body. The arrow sliced into the waves, nicking her arm. Too befuddled to swim well, Aliénor stayed under but clung to the roots of one of the trees snuggled up to the water and worked her careful way downstream. This area of the river was heavy with bushes and trees that had been swamped by the river's rising levels the night before. Carefully, hidden by the screen of a half-submerged bush, she lifted her head to survey the shore.

Several Tiochene stood by the riverside, arguing amongst themselves. The archer pointed angrily down the river in Aliénor's direction, though they couldn't seem to tell that she was still close. A female Tiochene wearing ornate robes stepped forward and held her cupped hands in front of her. Spell-light gathered in her palms. The woman rolled her hands as if she were making a dough ball, then flung the accumulated magic toward the river. Aliénor flinched as the spell drifted in her direction. But as the magic sailed over the water, the spell seemed to unravel. The light dissipated, and the spell-caster turned to her fellow Tiochene with a shrug. The archer stamped his feet angrily, then motioned for everyone to follow him back up the hillside toward the battle. They left Philippe where he lay, facedown in the dirt.

Aliénor waited, heart hammering, for them to walk out of sight up the hill. She worked her way back down the riverside, pulling herself from one submerged tree to another. At last, she dragged her sodden, shaking body out of the water toward her husband. *"Philippe."*

He was still alive when she turned him over. His skin was clammy. He fastened his gaze on her, eyes wide with fear, his face ghastly pale. His mouth moved, but only blood leaked out.

She caught his hands and clasped them tight, her vision blurring with shocked tears. "I'm here, Philippe. I'm here." Her voice sounded thick, cracking. She shook her head, pushing the wild tangle of emotions back. She smoothed her husband's dark hair and held his gaze as his limbs stopped flailing, as the light in his eyes died away. She wrapped her arms around him. Philippe closed his eyes and rattled his last breath out against her heart.

She held him for another moment, feeling dizzy, storm-tossed, as if the whole world were spinning around her, whooshing, roaring. Faintly, she heard a trumpet sound somewhere in the distance, but she couldn't think what it meant.

As the heavy metallic smell of blood dug its way into her senses, her gut roiled. She eased back, laying Philippe against the ground. Her armor was almost entirely stained now with his blood. Her skirts clung wetly to her skin, the blood and river water mingling to turn the fabric pink. Her hands were bright red, sticky with his drying blood.

Her mouth burned, and she crawled sideways a few feet to vomit away from his...body. *Oh Fate spare me. Oh please.* The ground was sharp with rocks and over-hot, but she wanted nothing more than to curl into a ball and lie there until the world slowed down. Until her life made sense again.

Cloth rustled beside her, and she startled away from something glimpsed out of the corner of her eye. As she tumbled backward onto her rump, Violette loomed above her. Only Violette. "My lady?" Tear tracks shimmered on the young girl's face, and she cradled her wrist against her belly. "Are you all right?"

No. Aliénor's stomach clenched as savage emotions whipped through her, shaking her head to toe. Her gut hurt holding it all back, and she gasped for breath as more hot tears burned her eyes. The walls of her mind might have been caving in. She felt wild and numb and utterly lost.

"My lady?" Violette sounded terribly young and frightened.

Aliénor shook herself. "Yes, yes. I'm fine." *All right. Enough.* The Tiochene might be back at any time. Her hands shook as she used her own damp skirts to mop what blood she could off her hands. She swallowed and set one hand on the ground, using the other to dash the last of the wetness from her eyes. Scuttling across the ground on all fours, wet, dirty, what a picture she must make. Philippe would be scandalized—

The thought slashed at her chest like a sword wound. Philippe would never be anything. Never again. She closed her eyes, but the image of his body flashed through her mind at once. His eyes emptying, the fear on his face as his life bled away. *Oh Philippe.*

"My lady?" Violette knelt beside Aliénor, and the younger girl's chin trembled, though she tried so bravely not to cry.

A loud blast of trumpet sounded again, startling Aliénor into standing. "What was that?" Her heart felt twisted and raw, like a garment wrung out after a hard wash in the river.

Violette shook her head—she'd seen Philippe's body and was now sobbing too hard to speak well. She pointed up the hill.

"Is it safe?"

Violette nodded and rubbed her cheek against the shoulder of her gown to wipe the tears away in a heartbreakingly childlike gesture.

Right. Aliénor composed her own face, and if it felt like she was holding herself together with only her bare hands—and that not very well—it didn't matter. Her legs were still uncertain as she moved. Still, she worked her way up the hillside with Violette. The sun beat hot against Aliénor's back, drying her clothes and warming her armor until sweat beaded against her chest to trickle between her breasts.

As they crested the hill, she forced herself to look back at the mountain pass, then had to swallow sickness down as she did. The Tiochene had fled, yes, but they had left seemingly all of her husband's army dead behind them. The men who hadn't been killed with arrows and swords had been burned with the horrible spell-fire. Bodies of soldiers and horses littered the ground. Now that the fighting had stopped, vultures were already landing. Aliénor looked away when the carrion birds began to feed.

Violette's good hand crept into Aliénor's. "My lady, what are we to do?"

That brave, bright trumpet sounded again, and Aliénor turned in the direction of the faraway call. Once she did, she found it very hard to look away again from such a sweet sight. Shimmering in the distance like a heat mirage, the proud line of an army approached. No Tiochene army either. These were men of the colonies, men of Anutitum perhaps. It might even be her cousin leading them. She hugged her arms around her belly and drank in the faraway vision. "Was this why the Tiochene left?"

"Yes."

Then this could be no fevered heat dream, for the Tiochene had seen the army as well and fled. Aliénor glanced sidelong at Violette and softened her voice. "How—how did you survive?"

Violette sucked in a long, ragged breath. "We were in the wagon, and we heard the fighting outside. Noémi hurt her head in the wagon, or opened the wound on her head again from the storm."

"Yes?"

"Anyway, her head was bleeding very badly, and she reached over and smeared some on my face too. Then she whispered for me to lie still and quiet. Play dead. The Tiochene were...well, it took them a long time to...to deal with Philippe's guards. After that, they only glanced inside the wagon. Everything was all tossed about, you see. *We* had a terrible time getting out without help. They would probably have had a difficult time crawling in. I think they were all too tired after the battle to try."

Aliénor reached over and squeezed Violette's good hand. "I'm so glad you're all right. And Noémi?"

"Yes, yes. She didn't feel up to the hill to check on you and Prince—to find you."

Aliénor swallowed. "I understand." She gave Violette's hand a small tug, toward the wreck of the wagon.

The colonial army still shone like a beacon on the horizon, though they seemed no closer yet. "We must ride out to meet the army. Is Noémi strong enough to ride?"

"Yes. Like me. My lady, we want to get *out* of here."

"All right." The weight of responsibility settled on Aliénor like an over-heavy cloak. "All right."

"The Tiochene have almost all cleared out now," Godric reported as he peered over the edge of the rock they sheltered behind.

"Any sign of survivors?" Thomas asked, although he had little hope of it. *Too late. Too late again to be any use to anyone.* The Tiochene were swift and thorough.

Godric peered anxiously around the vast mountain road then swallowed. "None...none yet, my lord."

"Can I drop this bloody glamour then?" Mistress Helen snapped, her fingers twitching as if she meant to do that very thing.

"You will hold that glamour until we are certain the Tiochene have gone."

Mistress Helen's lip curled at Thomas with dislike, but she continued plucking and strumming at the air above her as if playing an invisible lute. Beside her, Llewellyn sat with his eyes closed. Thomas could almost imagine his friend was sleeping except for the tense lines etched on Llewellyn's face and the sweat beading on his brow.

"How are you holding up, Llewellyn?" Thomas whispered.

His magician only grunted in reply, clearly not wanting to risk his concentration by speaking.

Thomas gave Llewellyn's shoulder a small, encouraging pat.

"Riders," Godric murmured, practically humming with excitement as he wheeled to face Thomas.

"Tiochene, or...?"

"Definitely not, my lord. I—I think it is the Jerdic princess and her women."

Thomas's pulse jumped at the words. "You three, with me. Godric, stay behind to guard Llewellyn and Mistress Helen."

Thomas did not even wait to see his order acknowledged. There was a chance Princess Aliénor was alive. His whole body prickled and chilled in cresting waves as fear dueled with the stirring hope in his chest. *Alive. Aliénor is alive.*

Aliénor did not understand how they could be riding so fast toward the approaching army and yet the line of men never seemed to be any closer. The sound of the army too seemed to cut in and out like an ill-played instrument. With a sense of sinking dread, she realized what she must be seeing. *Magic.*

Though it pained her to do it, she reined in her horse at once and motioned for her ladies to stop as well. They'd grabbed a packhorse and taken what supplies they could from the broken wagon, need warring with their desire for haste. Fortunately, the pack animal was well-trained and stopped when her horse stopped without her having to tug on the leading string.

"What's wrong, Princess?" Noémi asked. She was pale and cradling her head. Poor Violette had to ride in front of the much larger woman because she could not control a horse with her own broken wrist. They were all three a proper mess.

Aliénor pointed toward the horizon. "I do not believe that is a real army."

"An illusion?"

"Yes."

"But *why*?" Violette's voice threaded upward with strain and fear.

"Either this is a trap meant for us or it is a trick to drive the Tiochene away. But we dare not ride further until we know which."

Violette voiced a low moan, and her shoulders rolled down with defeat. "Riders approaching."

Aliénor wheeled around in her saddle, and her nerves jolted to see three men riding hard toward them from a small outcrop of rock on the road ahead. Aliénor had finally thought to grab herself a sword off one of Philippe's dead guards, but she didn't really know how to use the thing. She'd looked for a bow, but all the ones she'd found had a draw too heavy for her to manage. Besides, it had hurt too much to linger on that field of death for long.

She drew her borrowed sword and braced her feet in the stirrups. Violette kicked her horse forward, Noémi grimly clinging to the back. Violette drew her own sword. "We're with you, Princess."

"No, no, look." Noémi pointed, a smile blossoming on her face. "Those riders are not the Tiochene."

Aliénor squinted, and it suddenly felt as if her heart had sprouted wings. "Thomas!"

Chapter Eleven

P rincess Aliénor might have been a vision from myth or legend as she rode
toward him, her long hair streaming like a banner behind. He smiled to
himself and admired the way her summer-red hair glinted in the sun.

She reined her horse in beside his, the packhorse tied behind sliding to a stop a
moment later with a puffing grumble. Aliénor flung out a hand to greet him. He
caught her fingers and dropped a quick kiss against her palm.

"You found us—"

"Thank Kind Fate you're alive. We feared—"

They talked over each other but stopped after a moment and laughed. Thomas
looked down and realized her slim white fingers were still tangled with his own.
Embarrassed, he gently released her hand. Blushing, she settled it in her lap and
covered the hand with her other.

It was foolishness on his part—still Thomas let his eyes drink their fill of her.
That hair. A bright, coppery red that flashed in the light like a live flame. It looked
almost warm to the touch and temptingly soft. Yet his stomach quailed as he took
in the rest of her and realized she did not wear a red gown as he originally thought.
The poor woman was soaked all over in blood. "You're hurt."

She frowned in confusion then looked down at herself. Her face tightened, her
lips going white. She shook her head. "It's Philippe's. He…" She broke off, a puff

of air escaping her lips, a dark laugh entirely without mirth. "Everyone. *Everyone* back there is dead. All our men."

A band of grief tightened around his chest. *So much loss, so much waste.* "Come. Let us collect the rest of my people, and we will be on our way."

Aliénor's hands fluttered in confusion toward the illusion of the army. "Is that you then?"

Thomas quirked his mouth, already turning his own horse toward the rocks. "Yes, come and—"

His men erupted out from behind the sheltering rocks, Godric in the lead with Llewellyn riding half-conscious in front of him. Thomas surveyed his men in confusion. One knight's clothing was actually smoking as if it were recently on fire. "What happened?"

Godric swallowed, his jaw tight and angry beneath his dark beard. "That blood witch, sir. As soon as you were gone, she let off some kind of spell."

"Tried to set me on *fire*," one of the knights muttered.

"And then, while we were running around all distracted, she took off with two of the horses." Ned's gray eyes were wide in his ruddy face.

"Two? Why would she take two?"

Godric shrugged. "Maybe she plans to eat the other one."

Aliénor, whose mount was still close to Thomas's, shook her head. "I think she did it just to be spiteful. She saw you were short of mounts, and she doesn't like you, so she took two."

Thomas raised an eyebrow. "How do you know she doesn't like me?"

"She doesn't like anybody. She didn't even like Philippe, I think. Just what he could do for her position."

"I hope the Tiochene murder her in the wilderness," Godric muttered.

Llewellyn stirred in the knight's arms, and the illusory army began to fade, like bits of fabric tearing at the seams. The music and other sounds had already stopped when Mistress Helen fled. The magician's gaze fastened on Thomas, his face grave and pinched with worry. "It does one other thing besides inconvenience us—it slows us down." Llewellyn looked to Princess Aliénor. "Can you think why she wants us slowed down, Your Highness?"

Aliénor shook her head. "I'm scared to think why she would. King Thomas, one of your men is welcome to my packhorse."

"Thank you, Princess Aliénor." He gestured behind, and his page, Ned, hustled forward to wrestle the women's meager belongings off the horse. Thomas noticed it had a saddle, which meant it wasn't originally a pack animal. Llewellyn slid off the other horse out of the supporting knight's arms and, with a loud groan, heaved himself atop the packhorse. Ned darted a look at Thomas, his lips twisted with uncertainty. Thomas gave a short nod, and the lad scrambled atop the horse behind Llewellyn, taking the reins away from the exhausted magician. It was an alarming testament to Llewellyn's exhaustion that he didn't protest any of this.

But there was no time to worry about Llewellyn just now. Thomas drew in a deep breath and hissed it out through his teeth. He pitched his voice to carry toward all his assembled knights and the ladies as well. "We must ride hard today. We need to get as far away from here as we can." He was turning to apologize to Aliénor. "This will be difficult for you and your women—"

"Never mind that. Let us be off at once." Suiting words to action, she spurred her horse forward.

Grinning, Thomas urged his own mount forward to catch up to her. *Oh, I like this princess very much.*

Too much, probably, but that was a concern for a different hour.

One good thing about riding to the point of total exhaustion was that Aliénor had no energy left to think about Philippe or to worry over the fact that she was not heartbroken. King Thomas and his men set a brutal pace. It was all she could do to keep her seat on a horse that was meant to be ridden by someone much stronger and larger than her. Her eyes were gritty and burning with lack of sleep, her muscles stiff and aching. Yet she felt almost as if the king gave her that discomfort as a gift, gave it to all of her ladies, really. They could lose themselves in the very real struggle of staying on their damned horses for just one more minute despite an aching back and chafed thighs and weary minds—and they didn't have to remember that battlefield, didn't have to remember their lost men for this small respite of time.

When the sun at last sank toward darkness, and King Thomas finally, *finally* called a halt for the night, Aliénor practically had to fall off her horse into his arms. Her muscles had locked up, her legs like runny pudding. King Thomas even went so far as to carry her himself to one of the bedrolls set up by the fire.

Once he set her down, she snuggled into the rough blankets on the chill ground, her mind fuzzy and already running toward the welcoming arms of sleep.

"Shouldn't you eat, Princess? And wash?"

"Hmm..."

"Are you already asleep?" His voice was tender, warmly amused. She could actually hear the smile in it.

As her mind floated away to blessed blankness, she smiled into the folds of her blankets, carrying his warmth and gentleness with her into her dreams.

When she awoke, much later, it was early morning. Her body was almost unbearably stiff, and Aliénor's muscles burned and protested when she sat up. Her rump especially was afire with pain. Still, the sleep had done her good, refilling some well of energy inside her.

The camp seemed mostly empty except for Violette sitting on her bedroll a few feet away, propped against a rock and dozing. Some healer in the king's party had set her broken wrist. Of Noémi there was no sign, and few of King Thomas's men were around except for one or two drowsing in their bedrolls, including the king's young page. The horses were all still in camp, though, tied up together next to a small stand of trees.

A low baritone voice rang out nearby from behind the clump of horses. He was humming under his breath as he worked. She caught the tune, an old song about spring flowers and a maiden's hair. Aliénor sang a few of the verses low and half under her breath as she rolled her blankets up to be packed.

Unfortunately, her singing had opposite to the desired effect, because the deep baritone humming stopped at the sound of her voice. Still, her singing did produce some good results, as King Thomas appeared from behind the horses he'd been tending and approached her. "You slept as if bespelled, my lady."

"It was a good spell if so." She stretched and it hurt—of course it did—but it brought warmth and a tingling into her muscles, a healing kind of hurt. "I feel much better."

"Good. Your other lady is stealing a chance to wash while my men hunt and gather for some food. We want to save the packed supplies for any bare stretches."

"Food." Her stomach emitted a most unladylike grumble, and she clapped a hand over her gut, hoping to muffle the sound.

The king's eyes crinkled with amusement, but he made no comment. "Godric caught two rabbits, and Llewellyn coaxed some fish out of the river."

"Llewellyn's your magician, isn't he? Did he use his magic to catch the fish?" She had been trying to sound light, unconcerned, but she was rather afraid her voice came out stiff or stilted. She dropped her gaze from his and nervously pleated the fabric of her filthy skirts.

The king cleared his throat, gruff but clearly embarrassed too. "You are Jerdic. You were all Jerdic in that damned camp. How was I to risk telling you, even you, that I had a Lyondi magician with me?"

She worried at her lip and stared at a cluster of pebbles on the ground before her. "You were right not to tell anyone in that camp. I don't blame you. If I'd found myself lost in a camp of Lyondi strangers, I would have kept every advantage I might have as a secret too."

"You're very understanding, Princess."

"No, just practical." Still, there was a sick sort of aching in her gut. Thomas was not just a man of Lyond—he was the *king* of Lyond, a nation that had been fighting her own for her entire life and more. Even with Philippe gone, she was still the Jerdic princess. Thomas—*King* Thomas—was still her enemy, and the enemy of her whole people.

She allowed herself to sneak one small glance at him, at the rugged handsomeness of his face, the line of his leonine nose, the softness of his lips, those clear, piercing gray-blue eyes of his. *He does not feel like my enemy.* He felt like warmth and safety and solace. He felt like home.

You're just overwrought. Latching onto the nearest strength and comfort. These wild, foolish feelings didn't mean anything.

Aliénor shoved herself to her feet. She teetered unsteadily, and King Thomas caught her elbow to keep her from falling down again. They stood close enough that his breath stirred against the skin of her face.

"Your Lady Noémi will be missing you by the river, and there isn't much time left before we depart. You should go. 'Tis that way, over the hill. I have a guard posted, but he will not disturb you."

"Thank you." She walked away, stopping to rouse Violette enough to tell her handmaiden where she was going.

Violette looked thoroughly ashamed to have fallen asleep. "I am supposed to be guarding your honor while we travel among these rough Lyondi men. I failed you, Princess. I'm sorry."

Aliénor only motioned Violette to follow her up the hill. The king had returned to the horses, stroking his hand down the silky neck of one of the geldings. She looked back at King Thomas once on her way to the river and saw he had not returned to his work yet. He was watching her walk away.

She tore her gaze from his. *Oh, what fools we are.*

———————◄O►———————

Godric probably should have been content with the two rabbits he'd already brought back to camp to stretch their supplies, but they had those three lovely ladies to feed now too. His luck had already been good that day. He hoped Kind Fate would extend her care to two or three more rabbits.

The land along the river was craggy with rocks, but further from the shore was the forest with tall pines and scrubby brush. It felt almost like home, although winter here was warmer and dryer than in Lyond. His lips and knuckles were already cracking. Still, he could hardly hope for another rainstorm after the last one.

Godric bent to set a new snare.

"Sir Godric, how lovely to see you. I've been looking for you."

He froze and had his knife half-out as he whirled at the sound of her voice. *Her.* The blood witch. Even as he tensed his muscles to face her, he felt his body lock up, stopping his motion. As pain stabbed all up and down his arms and legs, he swallowed a scream. His muscles flexed and strained, dueling impulses coursing through his blood, her magic burning him from the inside out.

The blood witch stepped out from the line of trees. She twirled her dagger between her two hands and smiled at him. "I have need of a guide and a guard. You shall take me."

He flexed his jaw, trying to form words, trying to deny her. He managed only to let out a half-swallowed moan. Nausea roiled in his gut as she took a firmer hold on her blade and crossed toward him. With a soft, warm smile she drew her knife across the meaty part of his forearm, a line of blood oozing up. She smeared the blood away with her thumb and popped her finger into her mouth with a long sucking noise.

Her eyes glowed like a candle flame as she wiped her blade clean and resheathed it. All the tension of his body left him as she stripped away even his ability to resist. She made a small *come along* gesture with her hands, and he hopped to his feet as if tugged by an invisible rope, leaving his snares behind.

"We'll ride hard, Sir Godric. I have surprises I want to leave for your king along the road."

"Yes, my lady." Godric followed behind the witch like a trained dog at heel. His face was calm, still, almost lifeless. Inside was different. Inside he was screaming.

Chapter Twelve

In the grim aftermath of the battle, Violette and Aliénor might have walked off in only the clothes they stood in, but Noémi had insisted they linger on that field of horrors long enough to scavenge supplies for themselves: food, weapons, even some extra clothes. They didn't have much, but it was still some salve to Aliénor's pride that she and her ladies were not wholly dependent on Lyondi generosity. Although their Jerdic food rations looked just as unappetizing as the ones the Lyondi were eating. Difficult to embellish upon hard bread and dried meat, after all.

Once she and her ladies had forced themselves to choke down a small meal, they took themselves off to wash. Aliénor had never been more grateful to be clean than when she was finally able to drag off her soiled gown, which had gone stiff with drying blood. She scrubbed her skin raw in the chilly river, liking the clean bite of its water. Trading pain for pain felt right. It *should* hurt as she scrubbed her husband's blood off her skin.

Violette helped Aliénor into a fresh chemise after her wash. Noémi had pinned Aliénor's hair around her head like a silken crown. Violette usually did everyone's hair, but her injured wrist had created difficulties. Aliénor returned the favor next for Violette, carefully finger-combing out the tangle of Violette's tight, tiny black curls once Noémi had shown her how.

Aliénor knew that they could not stand on ceremony in this place. Not anymore. She was a princess, but that did not mean she was too fancy to help her friends. After some fumbling, she managed to put Violette's hair into two serviceable braids. Violette gave her head a small shake to test if they would fall out, then grinned at Aliénor. "Well done, my lady."

Aliénor smiled, probably more proud of herself than the simple task warranted. Still, she'd finally been *useful* to someone. Noémi had moved away to start cleaning all their brave red breastplates—a task neither Violette nor Aliénor had had the stomach or the heart to face themselves.

Their armor was too uncomfortable to wear for riding—another irony with symbolic bite to Aliénor—but the ladies all agreed they would keep the breastplates for now. Aliénor privately vowed that, if she were ever in a position to again, she would get real armor for her ladies. Not the pantomime version they were stuck with now.

In her shift and shivering, Aliénor rifled through the one bag of clothing they had managed to pack. Her ladies' dresses had weathered the battle all right, but Aliénor's was ruined—torn and stained with Philippe's blood.

She pulled out her one remaining garment and winced. She had a plain brown skirt left, but the only top she still had was a daring dark purple jerkin with a low-cut bodice and slashed sleeves to tug her linen chemise through.

Aliénor shivered but still felt foolishly reluctant to don these clothes, even though they were the only ones she had.

"Princess?" Violette murmured. Noémi, perhaps hearing something in the other handmaid's voice, left the riverside to stand beside Aliénor too.

Aliénor shook her head. Tears stung her eyes as she looked down at the bodice, and she wasn't entirely sure why. "Philippe hated this jerkin. He forbade me to wear it."

Noémi sighed and looked away.

"And now I must wear it in mourning for him."

Violette pressed Aliénor's shoulder, her eyes shining with wetness. She had lost her husband John in the battle too. "Your husband would want you to be warm. Cared for. We can cover the jerkin with a cloak or something. It'll be all right."

Aliénor shook her head, a bramble bush of emotions tumbling through her, pricking at her heart.

"Violette, you look tired. Why don't you sit a moment over there?" Noémi jerked her chin. "I'll tend the princess."

Violette narrowed her eyes, looking suspiciously back and forth, but then she tromped off to the shady trees, pouting only a little and cradling her wrist.

Noémi watched her go, then turned back to Aliénor with raised eyebrows. "Well?"

Aliénor shook her head and shivered, hugging the fabric of her chemise closer to her bare skin. "I don't want to cover the jerkin. I love it. I've always loved it. But…"

"Philippe is dead."

Aliénor winced, her chest hurting. "He's barely been dead a day. Shouldn't I honor his wishes? Now?" Emotion clogged her throat. "I was such a horrible wife to him. I couldn't be obedient while he was alive. Shouldn't I—"

"*Shh, shh.*" Noémi flung an arm around Aliénor's shoulders and drew her close for a tight, comforting hug. "This isn't about a jerkin, my lady."

Aliénor pressed her eyes closed and turned away. A tear slipped free to slide down her cheek in a chill drip onto her chest. "What sort of woman am I?"

"A lonely one. A frightened one. You cared for your husband, didn't you? You were sorry to see him killed?"

"*Of course.*"

"But you were never in love with him."

Aliénor swallowed, the brambles tugging at her heart, making her insides sting with shame. "No."

Noémi eased her back to sit on a boulder with her, her arm still a comforting weight around Aliénor. "My second husband died barely a month before I signed up for this journey."

"Oh?"

"He would have hated this. Would have forbidden my going. And never mind it was my own money we were living off all the time we were married." Noémi snorted.

"What are you saying?"

"I'm saying you can't lock yourself up for Philippe's memory. You didn't let him have that power over you while he lived. Don't do it now he's dead. Not out of pity. Or guilt." Noémi met Aliénor's gaze with a directness that made Aliénor squirm. "You have the power to do what makes you happy, what feels right to you. So do it."

The brambles shifted in Aliénor's heart, scratching, but maybe breaking apart too. She let out a small laugh. "What I want is not so very wise, Noémi."

"Well." Noémi shifted off the rock and stood. She plucked the purple jerkin out of Aliénor's hands and shook it out, holding it up for Aliénor to slide her arms through. "Come on, my lady. We shouldn't linger."

"No." Aliénor wet her lips as the soft leather of the jerkin slid her over her shoulders. "No lingering." And no hesitation. Not now.

———◦———

As the three ladies walked over the hill, it was to find a camp in chaos. King Thomas's men were furiously packing their supplies and distributing them among their too-few horses. Thomas glanced up at her arrival and walked briskly toward her. "Good, I was about to send for you. We must ride at once. One of my men has gone missing. Sir Godric."

"Missing?"

"There was no sign of a struggle. We found only his snares in the forest. No sign of him."

"The blood witch."

"That was my thought as well. But we can't take the risk that it might be the Tiochene catching up to us, either."

Aliénor wrapped her arms round her middle. "Set a guard on your magician and yourself. Let none of your men go out alone again."

"You think she is that dangerous?"

"Yes." Aliénor took a deep breath, then let it out, trying to calm her racing heart. "She tried to convince my husband to let her use her powers on you. To control you and take the kingdom of Lyond under Jerdic control."

His jerked back in surprise, and his brows lowered in rage. "After killing all my men, no doubt."

"Philippe did not agree to the plan." King Thomas sent her an assessing look from under his lowered brows, and Aliénor felt her cheeks warm in a blush. "She is a powerful witch and ambitious. I do not like to think what she might do if she were to get yourself or your magician under her control."

"All right." King Thomas called out instructions to all his men to pair up. As soon as he'd spoken, Llewellyn jogged over to stand beside King Thomas. The magician gave Aliénor a friendly nod in greeting, but she walked away without speaking to him. She found it hard to trust magicians at just that moment.

———◆———

The next several days passed in a blur of riding and exhaustion. Their path was circuitous but well-kept, and the river seemed content to behave itself for the moment. No winter storms had troubled them yet. They did lose half a day when one of their scouts spotted a Tiochene raiding party farther downriver.

King Thomas's troops split into two and hid in the nearby forest, keeping quiet and still as the Tiochene warriors moved past. The Tiochene remained oblivious, laughing and joking with each other as they rode along on their furry little ponies.

Aliénor huddled in the shadows of the forest, and her gut roiled as she spotted several of the Tiochene in Jerdic surcoats and others with stolen chain mail. Spoils. Brow knit, she cast a glance over at her two ladies. Noémi stared on stone-faced, lips pursed into a thin white line. Young Ned had his arms round

Violette, helping to smother the sound as she sobbed into her hand. Maybe with fear or rage. Or simple grief.

Soon enough, the raiders had passed them by, but King Thomas waited another half hour before he let any of them move, his face calm, his steady gaze assessing their situation. Aliénor's admiration for the Lyondi king grew with every moment. He seemed to her like a rock along the seaside—solid, immovable. Centered in himself and sure. How desperately she envied his certainty, his calmness.

Everything inside her felt like a luggage trunk with the contents tossed all about. She was sad for Philippe's death, relieved to be out from under his thumb, guilty to *be* relieved, grateful to be alive, drawn to King Thomas but hesitant, scared, exhilarated, exhausted, worried, fascinated, giddy. Most of the time, she felt like the wreck of her wagon—something once elegant and ordered that'd been smashed all to pieces. And she wasn't sure if she could put herself back together or not. Certainly, even if she did, she would never be quite the same Aliénor again.

The magician Llewellyn brushed her sleeve and nodded for her to get moving. With a sigh, she shook away the troubling spin of her thoughts to remount her horse and fall into the line of riders.

———◆———

They rode for several hours that night until the ground became too rocky and uneven to risk traveling by moonlight. They ate only the supplies they had in their packs: dry bread and smoked meat. Aliénor longed for one taste of a bright orange fresh from her garden at home. Or a strawberry. Even some of that violently yellow, sweetly tangy fruit they'd had at Ordinobl. The pineapple. She forced herself to keep chewing anyway and washed the dry, tasteless food down with an ice-cold mouthful of river water that she could feel inside as it trickled through her chest.

When they all bedded down for the night, she shivered and wrapped her blanket more tightly around herself. The days were chilly but manageable—the nights she often worried she might freeze to death before sunup. Noémi and

Violette sandwiched her in between themselves, and they all huddled close for warmth. Her two ladies dropped off to sleep almost at once, Violette snoring softly, Noémi muttering through her dreams.

Aliénor's rest eluded her. *No hesitation. No regrets.* She had regrets about so many things in her life. Was it selfish to want one less? Not that there was anything to be done tonight, but still...

Well, the least I can do is let my ladies sleep. She, at least, seemed incapable of sleep at the moment. She pushed onto her elbows and gently kicked the blankets away from her legs as she stood.

The men had made no fire when they bedded down, not wanting to risk anyone spotting the light. The moon was up, and bright enough for her to pick her way through camp. Aliénor tugged a blanket free and threw it around herself. One of the Lyondi knights sat posted as guard. She could just make out his silhouette where he sat propped against a boulder with his sword to one side and his legs stretched out ahead of him.

As she drew closer, she frowned and paused. *Surely not*—and yet something in her was vibrating, thrilling with recognition. She dropped down beside him with a small murmured "hello" and felt him jump. "I didn't mean to startle you." She kept her voice low.

"I heard you coming, but I thought you were one of my men." King Thomas leaned against his rock, but there was a tension in his body, a stiffness to his shoulders.

"Should *you* be on watch?"

"Why not?"

She tried to imagine Philippe acting in this way. If he'd ever spent a single night on watch like a common soldier, she would be shocked. Yet she could almost picture her father doing such a thing. He had valued his soldiers, and he had fought in real wars, not played at it like—

Aliénor gusted her breath out through her teeth. *I must not think ill of the dead.* Philippe had been spoiled, coddled, catered to—but then, so had she. How could she judge him so harshly and not examine herself with the same attitude?

What a mess it all was, a tangled knot of darkness and dissatisfaction that seemed ready to poison her whole life with its contagion. She drew the folds of her blanket tighter around herself, hunching into them.

She and the king sat together quietly, although the night itself was not silent. To her right, the river rushed and gurgled, busy as ever, and the brush rustled in the forest as night creatures went about their business.

"How do you know which noises are dangerous, and which are not?" she asked, breathing the words out in a whisper.

The king shrugged, and she felt the movement all along her side. "The sound of steel being drawn is fairly distinctive, but any soldiers would be at just as much of a disadvantage as us if they tried to attack. The real danger will come when the sky brightens toward dawn, and there's light enough to shoot straight."

"What about their magicians?"

He made a small grunt. "If they set their magicians on us, there's nothing for us to do anyway."

"So why worry?"

"Exactly."

She shivered in her blankets. His fingers brushed her arm, making her jump, but he only reached for the edge of her blanket and tugged it more snugly around her shoulders.

"You should go back to bed, Princess."

"I cannot sleep, and I do not wish to think. Or remember." She curled her hands into fists inside her blanket and tucked her arms up around herself. Her stomach churned. Whether it revolted at her dry, unappetizing dinner or the wet, sticky memory of Philippe's blood on her hands, she did not know. It had been days, and she had washed her hands many times since. Still, the coppery smell of blood seemed to linger in her nose. The memory of it pressed on her heart.

"I am sorry for your loss, Princess. I'm not sure I said so before. Your husband...he seemed a good man. Dutiful. Pious."

Aliénor stifled a snort, something in her chest twisting to hear this gentle, straightforward man lie through his teeth like that. "Philippe was a sweet child when we first married. His family expected much of him. I think he would have been happier in some monastery studying omens and reading signs. He could have served Fate well, been a good oracle if his father had let him take vows."

"I suppose I can understand why his father forbade him that path. With only two sons and a war on at the time, King Bernard probably worried he might need Philippe to ascend the throne someday."

"He did, yes."

"Was this campaign Philippe's idea?"

"No. It might have been his brother's, or mine. I hardly remember. I helped with the organizing, once we'd decided. I coaxed and cajoled the noblemen loyal to me to go, may their ghosts forgive me. I had no idea what real war would be like, and I wanted so badly to get away from Jerdun." King Thomas made some noise of surprise. Aliénor could not see his face, but still her insides writhed. "I was raised on my father's brave tales of the south, you see. The exotic palaces of the colonies. The wild weather and soaring cliff tops. Wind in my hair and a sword in my hand. Valiant deeds and treasure. All the stuff they sing in those jaunty war ballads. My father even composed a few of those songs himself."

"I never knew maids hungered after such accomplishments." His voice was warm. Quietly amused, perhaps? Not disgusted, though. Not bitter or angry.

She blew out the breath she'd been holding. "My father buried all his sons and had me when he was too old and stubborn to care about what was proper. I learned to ride and swim, hunt, shoot a bow."

"And fight?"

"No." She vented a wistful sigh. "Never that. His eccentricities only went so far."

"He named you his heir, though. There was a male cousin he could have named instead, wasn't there?"

She let out a low hum of pleasure. "Yes. Papa named me heir and said he was proud to do it. He knew I would take care of our island." A chill breeze danced over her face, blowing bits of her hair to tickle across her cheekbone. She scraped her hair back, but the teasing wind only plucked it loose again. Irritated, she tugged the blanket up over her head and tucked her hair underneath it. "Philippe didn't want a crusade at all originally. He certainly didn't want to lead the thing or come along himself."

"What changed?"

She drew her legs up, pillowing her cheek against her blanket-covered knee. "He wanted redemption for his sins."

"His sins?"

She shook her head, which was foolishness since King Thomas probably couldn't see her in the dark. She should not speak, should not tell the Lyondi king these things. Yet the memories boiled in her mind like dark, sticky oil. Her gut roiled. Philippe was dead, and she lived. It felt as if these memories, these regrets would burn her from the inside out if she kept them quiet and unvoiced. "Last year one of my husband's vassals revolted, refusing to supply funds or men-at-arms. My husband led his soldiers in to take the town and castle. Philippe was angry, wrathful, and ordered his men to set fire to the castle.

"In the heat of battle, they started torching the town as well. The townspeople took sanctuary in their local temple. And then the—the temple caught fire." She let out a ragged breath, and dashed away a tear with her thumb. "Philippe has—he *did* dream of it every night after that. He'd wake up screaming, weeping. After that, all his thoughts were about atonement. About living his life with decorum and honor." About making sure she lived her life by the same code. "The guilt was a terrible burden for him."

Yet that tragedy had spawned this one as her husband moved from rash revenge to rash redemption. "When word came that the Tiochene were taking over our territories down here, Philippe decided the way to redeem himself was to reclaim our colonies single-handedly. Yet he never gave a real thought as to the how. The practicalities of the thing."

"You cannot blame yourself for what happened."

Aliénor swiped away more tears with chilled fingertips. "But if only I'd put my foot down, told him to wait, forced him to give this action the proper planning it needed." But she hadn't. For, truth be told, she'd been as anxious to escape their life, their problems, as her husband had been to escape his guilt. "This was supposed to be our grand adventure, a new start. But you cannot run from yourself, can you? Philippe and I might have traveled a thousand miles together, could have walked the whole world from end to end, and still the two of us could not have outpaced our failings. Our unhappiness."

The king had been quiet so long while she vomited out her secrets to him. What must he be thinking of her? *Curse this wretched dark.* Her blood flamed hot underneath her icy skin. "Forgive me, my lord, for burdening you with my secrets. I'll go back to bed now and cease to trouble yo—"

His hand brushed her shoulder and followed the line of her arm until he found her fingers and squeezed them. His hand was cold, but his grip was firm, and warmth began to uncurl inside her wherever his skin touched hers. "You do not trouble me, Princess. And nothing you could ever say would be a burden too heavy for me."

Her heart hammered now, punching away at her chest until she felt almost sick with it. "Th-thank you." Alarmed and excited all at once, she tried to calm her racing heart, to quiet her panting breath. Never, *never* had she felt like this before. *No hesitation—*

"My king?"

Thomas jumped beside her, his shoulder knocking into hers, but his voice was calm. "Yes, Llewellyn?"

"Shift change, Your Highness."

"Right."

Thomas pressed Aliénor's hand and nudged her gently with his arm. She pushed to her feet, gathering her blanket around herself as she scurried away in the dark, back to her ladies. Her cheeks burned with excitement, with shame. She had been very foolish tonight, speaking with King Thomas so long. And alone.

True, they'd been surrounded by his soldiers, and her own ladies had been within hailing distance. Still, the easy intimacy of the dark could be intoxicating.

Foolish girl. To risk your reputation. The voice in her head sounded very like Philippe.

Aliénor bit her lip, trying to rein in the smile that wanted to blossom. She *had* been foolish, but she had no regrets.

Chapter Thirteen

Thomas wasn't surprised Llewellyn wanted to lecture him about his talk with Princess Aliénor—he was only surprised the magician waited as long as he did. Llewellyn had let Thomas retire to his own bedroll and sleep the night through. Indeed, the magician did not broach the subject until they were up and riding beside the river the next morning. "What were you and the Jerdic princess talking about last night, my king?"

Thomas gathered his reins and idly glanced about to see how close the others were. Aliénor—*Princess* Aliénor—rode toward the back, surrounded by Thomas's men and her ladies. Thomas and Llewellyn were a little ahead of the others, within calling distance, but not so close that anyone could hear their conversation. Thomas sighed as he reconciled himself to his lecture.

"Well?" Llewellyn said, raising one pale eyebrow.

"Well what?"

"What did the two of you talk about?"

"Nothing that I will tell you."

"You trust her?"

Thomas gritted his back teeth. Llewellyn's paranoia had kept them alive many a time, but it could be wearing. Especially in this instance, when the magician was not entirely in the wrong. "She is the Jerdic princess. Of course I don't trust her."

Yet that was a lie, wasn't it? He'd trusted her with his life several times. Even last night. She could have easily slid a knife between his ribs and slipped away into the dark. Still, he'd let her sit close enough to him that he could hear each breath she took, feel her shoulders brush against his arm. Smell her hair, her skin.

Llewellyn studied Thomas's face. "She's rather young for court intrigue, I grant you."

"Rather young for *me*, you mean."

Llewellyn's pursed his lips in a look that almost certainly meant, *You said it, not I*. He was a wise man as well as a magician, and he knew when to keep his mouth shut. Llewellyn tilted his head side to side in a so-so gesture. "Certain sure, the princess seems very kind, very generous. But she *is* young, and perhaps she doesn't understand as well as you do the consequences."

Anger spiked in Thomas's belly, sharp and hot, but he kept his voice even. "Consequences?"

"It's clear to everyone here the girl is half in love with you. Even her idiot husband saw that."

"*Llewellyn.*"

Llewellyn must have heard the warning in his king's voice, but the magician only shook his head and leaned closer, made his voice even more urgent. "If her dear brother-in-law, the Jerdic king, thinks you have trifled with the girl's honor, it will mean war with Jerdun. *Again.* You know the man wants another chance at seizing our lands. Don't offer him so convenient an excuse. Not over something like this."

"I'm not *trifling* with her."

"But you can't marry her, can you? The Jerdic king will want to keep her lands in his family. Moreover, after so many years without a queen, I don't think our people will take kindly to a Jerdic princess. 'A Jerdic princess to replace our dear departed Queen Rosamund? What is ol' Thomas *thinking*?' They'll be suspicious of her, angry. They'll think you're an old fool taken in by a pretty face."

"Flattery, flattery. Please, feel free to speak your mind, oh wise Magician."

Llewellyn sighed. "I don't mean to be cruel, my king. I'm just worried. You haven't looked at a woman like that since—well, since your poor wife died. And that was fifteen years ago. I like Princess Aliénor. I truly do. I just don't see how this can end happily."

Thomas ground his teeth together as he stared straight ahead. The mountains soared high away to the west, snow-capped peaks stabbing into the gray morning sky. The air blew heavy and scorching today, muggy with the coming storm. His skin was clammy and burning despite the chill in the air. Even though he had his armor stowed across his saddle, everything in him felt over-hot and tired. *I wish I were a simple farm lad.* Although, even if he were a farmer, he'd still be too old for Aliénor.

Anyway, he wasn't thinking of marrying her. That was absurd. She'd just been widowed. She was Jerdic. And since he wasn't going to marry the girl, he should stay far, far away from her as Llewellyn advised. To do anything else was to court scandal and dishonor. Thomas straightened on his mount. "I thank you for your wise counsel, Llewellyn."

"Which means, 'I'll do what I damn well please and keep your bloody nose out of it.'"

Thomas bit back a grin. "No, you're right, old friend. I'll stay away from her. Better that way." Easier on his old heart, certainly. He allowed himself one small look behind, watching as the sunlight caught on a stray lock of red hair that slipped free of her braid. "Bah." *Foolish old man.* He had half a mountain range still to cross and a dozen people to see to safety. What cared he for red hair at such a time?

———◆———

"*He's* watching you again," Violette whispered as she passed Aliénor the canteen. They'd stopped by the river to water the horses and eat quickly before continuing.

Aliénor took a long swallow out of the canteen, then wiped some of the sticky paste of sweat mixed with dirt off her face with a handkerchief. As she passed the canteen on to Noémi, she frowned at Violette. "What?"

"That...their king." Violette's lip twitched with dislike. "He watches you, Princess. I think he means to attempt some impropriety. And here we are, stuck in the wilderness with only his men to protect us." The younger girl pressed a trembling hand to her throat and looked wildly toward the line of trees just up the ridge. "Perhaps we should try to get away from them."

Aliénor stifled a groan.

Noémi was not so sensitive and laughed outright. "Child, we'd be dead in a day without these knights around us and their supplies. If they meant to demand such favors for their aid, they would have asked by now."

Violette drew herself up. "He wants her. I know the look of a man with that on his mind. Why, my husband always—" She broke off as sudden tears shone in her eyes.

Aliénor's own chest ached with sympathy, and she reached out to squeeze Violette's small hand. "It's all right, Violette. Really it is."

The girl gave one quick, fierce shake of her head. "He ought not to look at you like that, my lady. Our prince dead not even a week and him looking at you like *that*." She hurried away to the river to splash water on her face.

"Go with her, Noémi."

Noémi passed Aliénor her canteen and followed the younger maiden down to the river. Violette was without a protector now that her much older husband was dead.

Although she was sorry for Violette's grief and fear, Aliénor couldn't help thinking the girl would be better off with a husband nearer her own age this time. *Or none at all*. Perhaps Aliénor could arrange things so Violette could keep her freedom. Fifteen years old had always seemed far too young to be married anyway. *I was certainly too young*. Of course, that hadn't stopped King Bernard from giving Aliénor to Philippe.

Yes, Aliénor would have to arrange something for poor Violette, and those plans would *not* include marriage. Not yet. *Of course, in the meantime we might all be killed.* Aliénor pinched her eyes closed, her shoulders bowing with the weight of fear and uncertainty. What good was there in saying, 'I shall do such and such a thing if we ever make it back to civilization'?

If, if, if. Aliénor slapped the cork into her canteen with more force than necessary and tied the jug back on her horse's pack. What use planning anything with such a large *if* looming over her head?

"Are you all right, Princess?"

The rich baritone voice made her chest flutter with emotion. She didn't trust herself right now with him, with this wild tearing frustration bursting inside her.

She heard his foot scrape against the turf and pebbles beside her, as if he'd made a move closer to her. Aliénor jerked her shoulder up so she would not have to see his face. "I'm all right, King Thomas. Are we setting out again?"

"Yes." His voice was tight, uncertain. "Do—do you need assistance to mount up?"

It's not you. She wanted to tell him. *You've done nothing.* She went to her horse as the unspoken words burned on her tongue. As she swung into the saddle and settled her weight down, she voiced a small groan. Her chafed skin and bruised bottom protested, and every muscle in her body ached.

The king came to her horse's side and looked up at her. His skin was red from the sun and peeling a little on his forehead and cheeks. The laugh lines around his eyes were deep, and a dark brown beard with gray patches shadowed his cheeks. His dark hair looked temptingly soft.

"I'm all right, King Thomas. Truly."

He ran his gaze all over her face, as if he meant to memorize each line of bone, each freckle. He opened his mouth to say something, and she caught her breath.

"My king, all is ready," Llewellyn called out from the front.

Thomas puffed out a small laugh and lowered his face. "All right." When he looked up at her again, a wicked gleam of humor had animated his face. All at once, he transformed from a dirty vagabond to a man who took her breath away.

"What an old fool I am." He breathed the words out softly, wryly. No one farther away than Aliénor would have heard him.

She ran her tongue over her lips to try to bring some moisture back. "I am barely twenty-two, my king. What's my excuse?" Their gazes met, the feelings between them like kindling, like a spark catching on dry brush. An aching, an urgent need. "Are you on guard duty tonight, King Thomas?"

His lips flattened, and he lowered his eyelids, veiling his thoughts from her. "Do not seek me out, Princess. It is folly."

"I asked only if you take a watch again tonight." She tilted her chin in the most regal manner she could manage, staring down her nose at him.

"I will. And shall do every night until I have seen us all safe out of this mess."

"My king?" Llewellyn called again from the front, clearly worried something was wrong. All eyes were on Aliénor and Thomas now.

"Do not come, Princess Aliénor," Thomas gritted out from between his teeth, and he stomped to the front of the column to get them all moving again.

Aliénor watched the broad line of his shoulders as he retreated from her. *I did not listen to my late husband, and I do not heed the advice of my own ladies. What makes you think I will let a foreign king order me about, Thomas of Lyond?*

Even if Aliénor or Thomas had managed to work themselves up to try some more daring indiscretion, they each found their movements impeded. Aliénor, despite her best intentions, was asleep that night almost as soon as her body hit her bedroll. Still, Thomas found when he was awoken for his watch that he would not have to face the long night alone, after all.

Llewellyn grinned at his king's approach, the magician's teeth a white gleam in the moonlight. "With that blood witch about, Your Highness, I thought it better if no man stood his watch alone."

Such worries had not troubled Llewellyn last night. Still, Thomas held his tongue and settled in beside the magician. He drew his cloak more tightly about his own shoulders. "An excellent precaution."

"I promised long ago that I would guard your life, my king."

"I know, old friend. I know." Thomas hugged his cloak tighter.

Llewellyn shifted, and a small pebble went tumbling to the ground, overloud in the darkness. "I've been thinking. Perhaps we should—"

A branch cracked in the quiet night, and the both of them tensed. Thomas flung back his cloak and reached for his sword. Llewellyn shifted his weight to balance on the balls of his feet. Neither of them spoke. They hardly breathed as they waited together in tense anticipation.

———— ◈ ————

Godric's head throbbed and pounded as the blood witch's voice reverberated inside his skull, like an echo chamber that would never be silenced: *Bring me the princess.*

He jogged through the dark. She'd kissed her finger, then touched each of his eyelids, and now he saw in the dark as easily as if it were high noon. His muscles shook with quivering tension as he moved, and tears leaked out of his eyes that he did not—could not—stop to brush away. *Bring me the princess.*

The blood witch had given him one of the princess's sun veils, a light, gauzy thing. She'd wrapped the fabric around his bicep in mockery of a lady's tournament favor. The witch had woven her magic in with the warp and weft of the cloth, and the tracking spell pulsed now like a living thing, tugging him along like a dog on a leash. Leading him toward their camp, toward the girl. *Bring me the princess.*

Quiet voices sounded up ahead and he hurried onward, wanting this errand over with. The witch had promised he could sleep once he brought her back the Jerdic girl. He was not used to a spell-caster who spent her magic so freely. Perhaps Mistress Helen was more powerful than even Master Llewellyn, or perhaps she was simply more desperate. The witch certainly looked as exhausted as Godric felt, with great dark circles under her eyes and lines around her mouth. Perhaps he could use her fatigue later to get away from the woman.

Bring me the princess. Bring me the princess. Bring me the princess.

He didn't even care anymore whether the witch meant to kill him or not. He only wanted a release from the terrible grip of her control, the endless cry of her voice in his mind. *Bring me the princess.*

He took an incautious step and a branch cracked beneath his foot. The voices in camp quieted, and he waited a long while, his hands fisted against his knees as he squatted and examined the lay of the camp.

The king and Llewellyn stood guard, but the princess and her ladies were on the opposite end of the small circle from them. Risky, risky...

BRING ME THE PRINCESS.

Godric lifted a small stone and drew back his arm, hurling it far away. The rock crashed into the brush on the other side of the camp. The king and Llewellyn whirled, trying to see what had made the noise. King Thomas rose to his feet, sword drawn and ready.

Bring me the princess.

Godric scurried forward to where the Jerdic princess slumbered among her blankets. She remained peacefully oblivious, snoring softly as he loomed over her.

Forgive me, my king. Godric grabbed for the woman.

Chapter Fourteen

Aliénor startled awake as a cold, clammy hand settled over her mouth. She instinctively shrieked and thrashed, clawing for her attacker's face. Her fingernails raked deep into his flesh, but he seemed oblivious as he grasped her wrist in a bruising grip and hauled her to her feet.

Violette stirred beside her. "My lady—"

The man jerked violently, lashing out in some way, and Violette fell back with a cry, landing atop Noémi, knocking the older woman backward.

Aliénor pawed at the hand over her mouth and twisted and wrenched her torso, trying to break free. The man banded an arm like iron around her ribs and dragged her against his chest. Her breath left her on a small, pained gasp into his hand. The world swooped around her as he dragged her away from her tumble of blankets.

"Help..." Violette coughed the word out, her voice little better than a croak. "*Help.*"

"*Princess?*" The king's voice.

Light flared behind them. A fire? No, it was blue. A bright ball of light shot into the sky like a falling star in reverse. *Llewellyn.*

Her attacker moved at a run toward the tree line, fast, unhesitating. As she watched the light fall, the spell illuminated the ground all around the camp. From a distance, she watched as the knights hurried to awaken and strap on their gear.

Aliénor realized with a sinking heart she was already too far away. Her kidnapper had carried her into the shelter of the trees, where Llewellyn's blue light did not touch them.

Aliénor rocked her shoulders, fighting, but she felt light-headed now, her air coming in small fits and starts, while her attacker covered her mouth and crushed her lungs in his cruel hold. The rest of the camp was stirring, but their forms were indistinct in the faint moonlight.

"Split up!" King Thomas called, his voice distant. "Find the princess."

She and her kidnapper crashed deeper into the trees, but at the first small-ish clearing, he set her down at last. She sucked in a deep breath through her nose, ready to scream the forest down once he removed his hand. Unfortunately, he lifted his hand only to shove a foul and metallic-tasting rag between her lips. He held her head in place and poked hard until the fabric was so far down her mouth she nearly gagged.

Aliénor's eyes watered, and she worked her tongue, trying to spit the fabric out. He gripped both her wrists in one of his, and twisted something tight round both her hands so the bones mashed together. A rope or cord. Rough. Aliénor thrashed, trying at least to make it hard for him to tie her.

With a small, impatient grunt, he sat back from her. The wind whistled, and the next thing Aliénor knew, her cheek was stinging from the force of a brutal slap. Her face throbbed so badly it took her breath away.

"I'm sorry, my lady."

Aliénor flinched, her body locking up with a chill terror. *Godric.* Her head still rang from the blow he'd dealt her, but she found some reserve within herself and lurched away from him, furiously kicking out with her feet. *No, no, no*—where Godric was, his new mistress the blood witch was surely nearby. *Nonono*—

He hauled her back, half dragging her across the ground. He slapped her again, and her head went fuzzy as he flung her weight about, then tossed her over his shoulder like a sack of flour.

Aliénor's stomach swooped, her throat burning, but she took deep breaths in through her nose and pinched her watering eyes tightly closed. She could not be sick with the gag in her mouth. *Will not. Don't.*

Godric moved with swift, unfaltering steps through the night, though she could barely see a foot in front of her own face. Still, her weight slowed him down, and she did not make an easy burden for him. She wriggled and squirmed, and knocked at his belly with her knees, trying to impede him any way she could.

Finally, when that didn't seem enough, she clawed with her bound hands at the gag he'd shoved into her mouth. She spat as the fabric came free and drew a long, deep breath. "*Help!*"

"*Aliénor*? Princess?" The king's voice. Close by.

Her heart soared with hope. "Here," she squawked out. Using her bound fists, she pushed up against Godric's back to make her voice louder. "Here. *Thomas!*"

Godric swore and firmed up his hold on her body by wrapping his arms around her legs. He broke into a run, heedless of noise as the brush crunched and broke around him.

An impact. A grunt. Something slammed into them from the side, toppling Godric over. *Thomas.*

They all three tumbled together in a tangle of limbs. Godric's elbow banged into her ribs and she keened at the jolt of fire in her side. The king clawed for her arms, and she kicked out, trying to twist toward him, her nerves vibrating, charged with fear and anger.

She scrambled to her feet, but Godric caught her ankle and tugged. She lost her balance and went face-first into the dirt and bracken on the forest floor. Spitting leaves, she kicked behind and felt his head snap back. Thomas shoved Godric away from her, and the two men locked arms, jostling above her.

Aliénor elbow-crawled to a safe distance and worked at the knots on her wrists. The rope burned and cut at her skin, refusing to loosen.

"Fight the magic, Godric. Damn you," Thomas gasped out. "You are stronger than some evil witch."

"I'm sorry, my king. *I'm sorry.*"

As she heard the sound of Godric drawing his sword, her heart froze. Steel glinted briefly in the moonlight as Godric slashed at his king's belly. Thomas blocked the blow with his own blade, and the swords clanged loudly in the night.

Nerves jangling like discordant bells, Aliénor pawed at the ground with her still-tied hands and came up with a heavy rock. She lurched to her feet and ran at the bespelled knight before he could swing again. She brought the rock down hard against the back of his head. He crashed to the ground, still slightly awake but groaning.

Thomas was by her side at once, clawing at the knots of rope on her wrists. The scratchy loops fell away, and Thomas whirled with the rope toward Godric. He lashed the burly knight's hands together while the other man was still stunned. With a savage sort of satisfaction, Aliénor crawled forward and shoved the gag Godric had used on her deep into the knight's mouth.

Thomas caught at her hand, and she swallowed a gasp as his fingers brushed over the raw, bleeding skin of her wrists. She curled her fingers around his hand and gripped him brutally tight. "Where are the others?"

"Looking for you."

"What do we do with Sir Godric?"

"He's still bespelled." Thomas combed his fingers through his hair, tension radiating off him.

Aliénor chafed at her chill arms, her stomach roiling. She didn't want Sir Godric anywhere near her, and yet... "If we leave him, the witch will find him again. If we take him with us, her spell will wear off, won't it?"

"If we take him, he might attack you again. Overpower me." Thomas snorted. "He is quite a bit younger than I, and one of my best knights." He shifted from foot to foot, still with that same frantic jitter about him. At last he shook his head. "I can't do it." Thomas's voice cracked on the end. "I won't risk him hurting you again. I'll see you to safety. That is my first duty. After that I'll return for Godric."

What about your *safety?* Aliénor bit her lip. Men never worried over such things, she found. *They leave that burden of worry for us.*

Thomas was still watching Godric as his knight moaned half-conscious on the ground. "Hopefully, he'll still be here when I return."

"It will be all right." She tugged on his hand, and with reluctance Thomas let himself be pulled away from Sir Godric's prone form.

"Another man lost." He shook his head.

"You must not blame yourself. You will get him help when you can."

Thomas tossed her a wan smile and, still gripping her hand, moved in front of her to clear their path through the woods. They hurried through the trees, but not with the headlong rush of Godric's flight. Clouds had blown across the moon, and it was bitterly dark now. Cold. They had to be careful to feel and pick their way through the trees lest one of them take a bad fall.

Aliénor had slept in her clothes, but Godric had not thought to grab her good heavy cloak when he'd snatched her. Distracted, tired, bruised, she stumbled over a rock and went down hard on her hands and knees.

"We'll stop and wait for better light." Thomas settled onto the ground beside her, and the two of them pressed their backs up against the nearest tree. He reached over and hauled a screen of broken branches around them. She hoped that would be enough if Godric managed to slip his bonds and come looking for them or, worse, if the witch were prowling these woods too.

Thomas untied his cloak and draped it around the both of them like a blanket. Aliénor slid close to him, pressing her side tight against his, pillowing her head on his heart. "To stay warm," she murmured. "We shall both freeze without the other, surely."

"Surely." His voice was a trifle dry, but warm with amusement. His arm settled around her shoulders to draw her even closer. "The others will find us soon."

Aliénor nodded against his shoulder, then covered a yawn with her hand. He was so warm, and she was so tired and sore, frightened. She burrowed under Thomas's cloak, the smell of him wrapped around her comfortingly close as his arm. Aliénor slept.

Thomas was proven wrong. For though he watched and waited the whole night through, none of the others found them. When dawn broke, he nudged Aliénor awake. "It is light enough now that I think we must look for them."

She rubbed sleep from her eyes and pushed disheveled red-gold hair back from her face. An ugly bruise darkened the skin of one cheek, and deep red lines of blood and bruises circled her wrists where the rope had dug in. Something clenched in his gut, a tight burst of anger and fear that he immediately locked down. He drew the cloak off himself and wrapped it around her shoulders. His knuckles brushed the bottom of her chin as he fastened the clasp. She caught his wrists with her small, soft hands, and his gaze darted up to hers in surprise.

Her brown eyes were warm, and still soft with sleep. "Thank you, King Thomas."

He swallowed, and his fingers twitched before he jerked his hands away. They had each been foolish before on this road. He could not afford to be foolish now, when they were alone together. He pushed to his feet, creaking and moaning at the stiffness in his limbs. He offered his hand down to help Princess Aliénor stand, but then he dropped her fingers almost at once. Every moment with her was temptation. Best not to magnify it with touch.

They were deep in a small forest, but he could hear the river somewhere away to the east. Anutitum was to the south. It was enough to be going on with. "That way." There were no paths cut through this forest, and it was slow going, having to clamber over bushes and under hanging limbs.

"*Bahhh.*" The high-pitched sound made them both jump with its sudden-ness. And then, "*Bahhh, Bahhh,*" sounded again.

Aliénor laughed. "Sheep?"

Thomas craned around, but he couldn't see the animals. He heard more muted *bahhh*s now that he was listening for them. "There must be pasturage up ahead." He kept an ear cocked, listening to the sheep. Perhaps, if they *ever* found the others, they could then find this shepherd and buy a few of his flock for dinner. Thomas was getting ever so sick of hard biscuits and dried meat.

After a little while longer of trudging and grunting effort, Princess Aliénor asked, "May we speak or do you think we ought to keep quiet?"

"It is all right to speak, I think. It might help the others find us faster."

"What about the Tiochene? Or...or Godric and the blood witch?"

"This forest is quiet enough that we'll hear anyone's approach. Don't worry. I'll see Godric and the blood witch coming if they find us. The Tiochene—well, if they're near enough to hear us, we have larger problems anyway." He smiled at her, trying to be reassuring.

She grimaced a smile back at him and huddled deeper into his cloak. She had the hood up, shadowing her face, but her posture was slumped with defeat.

He slowed his pace a little so they could walk side by side, and so he could see her profile. "What troubles you, Princess Aliénor?"

She gave a bleak little laugh. "Oh, many things, King Thomas." Her fine brown eyes darted up to meet his gaze. "I was just thinking about...well... You were married once, weren't you?"

"Yes, a long time ago. Before I was even crowned king. She and I were childhood sweethearts. She was a good woman and a wonderful queen." Was he trying to remind himself? To use the memory of Rosamund to shield him from Aliénor?

"Your father let you marry for love?"

"My elder brother was alive then. My father didn't know he would need me for a strategic marriage. He didn't know my bride would become queen, so he let me have my way. Did your father not ask what you wished before arranging your marriage?"

"My father might have let me pick, but he died too soon and left me a ward of the old Jerdic king. King Bernard." Aliénor sighed. "And King Bernard rather fancied my lands and treasury for Philippe, who is—*was*—the second son. Poor Philippe Lackland, the nobles at court used to call him before our marriage. One of the last things King Bernard did before he died was marry me off to Philippe."

"That was a monstrous abuse of the king's power. You were his sacred charge. He should have at least tried to arrange a respectable match for you outside his family." He grunted. "I never did like Old Bernard."

Her lips pinched with anger, perhaps, or remembered despair. "I was scared and alone after my father died, vulnerable. If I'd kicked a little, the king might have called it off. I think he believed Philippe and I could do well together. But then, King Bernard didn't know me very well when he arranged the marriage. Otherwise he might have hesitated to chain his son to such a harpy. No matter how rich I am." She hugged her arms around her stomach. "Silly girl that I was, I liked the idea of being Princess of Jerdun. It seems such a foolish reason to take a husband now."

"You'd just lost your father. It's understandable that you'd want protection. Security."

"Family." She bit her lower lip.

Cursing himself for a fool, still he reached out and caught her hand. He'd missed this. Missed the kindling heat of feelings like this. Aliénor was clever like his first wife. Kind. Beautiful. Brave. But there were rougher edges to Aliénor, brittle places that his sweet, soft Rosamund had not had.

Perhaps it was the hurt in him attracted to the hurt in Aliénor. She knew loss and bitter disappointment as he did. That gave them a common ground that he'd lacked with all the other sunny-souled ladies his courtiers had thrown his way over the years. No, he didn't need another sweet-voiced Rosamund in his life. He'd had her and lost her. This...*thing*, this awareness between himself and Aliénor, was entirely different. And wonderful. And terrifying.

Having lost something so precious once, how could he willfully turn away from his feelings now? He knew how rare this connection was, how precious. He'd never thought to have this again. How could he throw this unexpected gift back at Fate like an ungrateful child?

She faced him, tilting her chin so the soft morning sun caressed the contours of her features. Her skin was still pale from the chilly morning air, and her freckles stood out like constellations on her skin. He wanted to trace them, learn their patterns. He wanted to trail the pad of his thumb across her mouth and see if her lips were as pillowy soft as they looked.

She caught her breath and leaned, ever so slightly, toward him. "Thomas..." There was a question in her voice, perhaps an invitation too.

Before he could do anything, before he could decide, a drop of water splashed against her face, making her flinch. Another dropped onto his head, cold and hard. He turned his face up, and more rain broke through the screen of branches above to splatter like ice against his face. The rain plopped against the leaves all around them and wet the ground at their feet.

"We shall be soaked."

"*Bahhh.*"

Thomas took a tight grip on her hand. "Maybe not." He towed her in the direction of the calling sheep.

Chapter Fifteen

In the end, Thomas led her unerringly toward the grassy hill where a flock of sheep were grazing, as well as two miserable-looking guard dogs. Just in time too, for her boots had begun to slide in the new mud. Her skirts were an inch deep in the muck, heavy and dragging against her legs when she walked. The king's cloak, at least, kept her nice and warm, which gave her a pang of guilt. Without his cloak he was wet through, hair plastered to his head and little runnels of water coursing down his nose.

As they drew close, Aliénor flinched at the sight of two muscular brown dogs amongst the sheep. The hounds wore fearsome spiked collars round their necks. Both beasts' heads lifted to attention when Aliénor and Thomas broke from the tree line. A small shepherd's hut lay up ahead, more of a lean-to, really, with no door, only a small opening. Nevertheless, it had a roof, and it looked dry inside.

Aliénor wiped the streaming water off her face. "Are you sure we should go closer, King Thomas? The dogs don't look quite friendly."

"As long as we make no move toward the sheep, I think it will be fine. They are here to guard against wolves. See the spiked collars?"

"Yes."

"Those are to keep a wolf from getting a good grip on their necks. Come on." He gave her hand a friendly tug. Strange that her hand seemed linked to her heart now, for when he tugged on her arm like that, she felt a similar pull in her chest, a quick jolt of excitement.

Thomas approached the dogs warily, and fumbled for the pouch at his waist. He drew out two strips of the dried meat they'd all been eating for weeks and held them out in his palm.

One of the dogs hesitated with a small whine in the back of his throat, but then he popped to his feet and padded over to the king. Thomas stayed crouched down and watched the dog out of the corner of his eye, slowly easing forward a step at a time. Eventually, he was close enough that the dog sniffed his hand, then took one of the strips of meat. The animal walked away to chew on it happily, its skinny tail wagging in spite of the rain.

The other dog was more standoffish, and though it stood and came closer, it would not come near enough for Thomas to touch. Thomas set the meat on the ground and backed away. The dog darted forward and snatched it up, then scuttled away again with its tail down. Still, it chewed on the treat happily enough. Neither dog made a move to stop them as Aliénor and the king ducked inside the small hut.

As soon as she swung inside the little wooden structure, Aliénor let out a groan of relief. She was wet, aching, and miserable, but there was no more rain pounding against her shoulders. The shack was warmer, with a pile of straw and blankets on the floor. Aliénor threw herself down with a thump.

Thomas did not duck inside but hesitated, staring at her. Her cheeks warmed, and she looked away. There was space enough for two in the small room, maybe even three, but somehow being alone together inside felt more intimate than being alone together out in the woods.

"Oh, do come inside, King Thomas," she said at last, without looking at him. "My reputation is in tatters already, and I don't wish to start another war with Lyond by letting you drown out there."

He leaned against the hut's narrow doorway and looked out.

"You're not going back to look for Godric, are you? Or the others?" She did not want him to. She wanted his solid, comforting presence beside her.

"No, I don't like to leave you alone. Besides, I'm an old fool, but I'm not stupid." He sighed. "Much as it shames me, I truly don't think I can take on a bespelled Godric by myself."

"You did before."

"No. I had you." His voice was soft, grateful.

Heat pooled in her belly, and she looked away.

"We'll linger here—see if we can wait out the rain."

"All right." Aliénor took off his heavy cloak and laid it out on the straw to dry. She lifted one of the musty—but delightfully dry—blankets off the floor of the hut and wrapped it around her shoulders instead. Her skirt was still soaked and heavy with mud, but her shoulders and chest were instantly warmer. She cast a glance over at the king, watching as his muscles quivered and twitched with the cold. "What if I were to close my eyes, King Thomas? Then you could take that drenched tunic off at least, and wrap up in one of these dry blankets."

He cast a mischievous glance her way from under his lashes. "No peeking."

"I would never." She grinned at him and held her hands up before her eyes like a child.

He laughed, and she heard the sounds of wet cloth slapping against the ground. Something tugged under her hip, upsetting her balance, and she accidentally opened her eyes and looked up at him.

The blanket he'd chosen had had a corner resting under her hip that he hadn't noticed. "Beg pardon." He dropped the cloth at once. For a moment his arms bobbed up in the air as if he were unsure whether to cover his chest or brazen out this moment.

Aliénor could be no help to him—she could only stare. He had a marvelous body, a soldier's body, tall and strong, with broad shoulders and tightly corded muscles in his arms. Something uncurled in her gut, a small feeling almost like the vibration of a cat's purr. *Mmmmm.* She bit her lower lip to keep a laugh back and finally tore her gaze away from him. Shifting uncomfortably, wobbling her hips back and forth, she tugged the edge of the blanket out from under her bottom and blindly tossed it toward him.

"Thank you." He wrapped the blanket around his shoulders and collapsed into the straw beside her.

He sat as far away as he could in the little hut, and yet Aliénor felt his presence with an almost throbbing intensity, as if every beat of her heart came from his body. She felt over-hot and all tingly along her arms and chest with a heady kind of anticipation.

Perhaps if the threat of her normal world had seemed more real, Aliénor could have controlled herself better—kept her distance, kept to what was proper and expected. But she had stared death straight in the eye so many times, and that black terror seemed to stalk her now each night in the darkness.

Hard to care what tomorrow might bring. Hard to tell herself *no* when every moment felt like the edge of a precipice. Each second felt precious now, finite. She didn't want to waste them in gray mourning for her bitter past with Philippe or this dark fear of the unknown. She wanted to coax high that kindling warmth she felt whenever she was with Thomas. If her life was to gutter out like a flickering flame, then she wanted to burn now like a lightning strike, like a falling star.

She tucked herself deeper into her blanket, hunching into its warmth. "Will you think me presumptuous if I ask something, King Thomas?"

"No."

"Were—were you happy in your marriage?"

"Very." His voice was rough. "For the little time we had."

"Was she?"

"I think so. I hope so."

"With one successful marriage to your credit, why did you never marry again?"

He shifted, and the edge of his blanket fell across Aliénor's lap. He didn't notice. "I never...there's never been anyone who made me feel the way Rosamund did." His gaze flicked toward her, and their eyes caught. *Until you.*

Aliénor hissed in a startled breath, her pulse thundering. He had not said the words, and yet the tender warmth in his eyes said everything for him anyway, whether he meant it to or not. He looked away again, but she had seen, indeed she had *felt* those unspoken words deep inside. She studied the line of his cheekbone, the soft curve of his mouth. *I've never felt this way about anyone.* Her tongue felt heavy with the words, but she swallowed them back.

When he spoke again, his voice had a hearty cheerfulness she could tell was forced. "Anyway, I was quite spoiled by my love match, you see, and anything less than that, anything based on practical or political considerations, just doesn't tempt me."

"*Hmm.* You seem to be an anomaly." She kept her voice friendly as she said this so he would know she was teasing. "Most men I know of, who have had one happy marriage, are eager to try their luck again. 'If I had it once, I can do it again.' Whereas women, widows, they are usually the ones reluctant to try their luck again, to let go of the past to try for present happiness."

"Or perhaps I'm too old now and set in my ways."

Aliénor snorted. "Oh yes. That's probably it. You being so wizened and decrepit with age and all."

"Anyway, there are women exceptions to your rule. Like your Lady Noémi. Didn't you say she'd been married twice?"

"Well, yes, but Noémi says she hasn't yet managed a really good marriage, so she must keep trying her luck until she does."

"And you?" His gaze flicked all over her face, studying her, a notch between his brows. "What about you?"

She swallowed, her heart hammering. Just the thought of another marriage made sweat pop out along her hairline. To belong to a man again, to be under his rule. No, to try that again would be to break herself utterly. "No. Never again. I am the Duchess of Catarlia once more, and well-contented with what I have. I have no need to marry again."

King Thomas was quiet for a good long while. She even began to wonder if she should stay silent and leave him in peace, if she had offended him. A black despair loomed at the thought, but then he spoke, and his voice was quiet, sad. She realized he'd only been silent so long because he hadn't known what to say. "I think your husband did love you, my lady. In his way."

She winced. "Yes. I think that was our greatest problem. If he'd loved me less, he might have been able to see how miserable we made each other. If he'd loved me less, he might have been able to let me go."

"Let you go?"

The rain pounded with renewed fury against the roof, and the world seemed dark outside, even though it was midmorning. The two of them were in almost total darkness together in this stormy world. In this quiet, intimate darkness, divorced from real life, it was easy to say these things. Aliénor blew out a slow breath. "I was going to leave Philippe when we reached Anutitum. I was ready to admit my failure as a wife even if he could not. So you see, King Thomas, how unfit and unwomanly I am. No proper wife for any man."

He shifted in the straw beside her with a small sound of denial. "I do not find you unwomanly. Not in the least."

His voice felt like a caress against her skin, and she shivered, imagining his touch—his fingertips tracing her skin, his hand against her jaw, his breath stirring on her cheek. The gentle pressure of his mouth against hers. Aliénor exhaled a ragged sigh. "I wish I were a dairy maid."

"What?"

"And you a simple page or a man-at-arms. A groom in the stable."

"I don't understand—"

She let herself lean against him, resting her head against his shoulder, and her skin seemed to catch fire at the contact. A sweet fire, though. Cozy. Caressing. Warming instead of burning. She lowered her voice too, until she was barely breathing the words out. "I wish we were anyone but who we are. I wish I was not the Princess of Jerdun. I wish you were not the King of Lyond."

He tensed, but he did not push her away. "This is foolishness, Aliénor. We cannot stop being who we are."

"I know. And yet..." She followed the strong cord of his neck with her fingertips up to his jaw and ran the back of her hand against his cheek, listening to the rasp of his stubble.

"Aliénor."

"You don't wish we could be other people? Just for a minute? An hour?"

The silence between them lengthened, pulsing in the air as if it were a living thing with a heartbeat she could count. When Thomas finally spoke, his voice was low and rough. "An hour wouldn't be enough. I'm not sure even a year would be." He turned toward her. "But yes, you make me wish I were the lowliest cowherd, and you a simple milkmaid." His dragged her closer to him, and she lamented the great tangle of blankets between them.

His hands carded through her hair, and his fingertips tickled against her skull. He cupped her face in his large hands, his thumb tracing the line of her cheekbone. She made some needy noise and fought her other arm free of the blanket so she could touch him better. Her skin felt alive under his touch. A strange fluttering started in her gut, and her lips ached, burned. *Touch me, hold me.* She curled her hand around his neck and tugged him closer. "*Please,*" she breathed against his mouth.

"Aliénor." It came out a low groan, a prayer, a breath of wonderment. His lips brushed hers, soft and warm, his kiss better than she'd dreamed. She groaned, rising toward him, reaching, wanting, and he slanted his mouth against hers, swallowing her needy noises.

As he teased her lips apart with his own, she fought back another noise of aching delight. *Yes. Oh yes.* She twisted and tugged and pushed to press every bit of her against every bit of him that she could reach. He knotted his fingers into her hair and kissed her harder, his tongue massaging hers with delicious friction.

Philippe had never kissed her thus. No one ever had. She liked it *oh so very much.* This tense tangle of limbs, the wet press of lips and tongue. The fierce, hot urgency of this embrace. This was how lovemaking was supposed to be. How she'd imagined it. The few times she and Philippe had tried, the act had been cold and painful. Short.

Thomas kissed her like he could go on forever, like she was appetite and nourishment for him smashed altogether, and he could never get enough. Great harlot that she was, she wanted to climb on his lap and fill the ache within her.

Fill herself up with this tender, fiery need between them and let the scandalized world think what it would.

⸻⬦⸻

Thomas knew he should stop. Had to stop. This kiss was a disaster, a calamity...and the single most satisfying thing he'd done in fifteen years.

She twined her arms around his neck, digging her fingers into his hair. He wanted to savor every moment, experience each discrete touch and stroke of their bodies together, but it was all going so fast, and all he wanted was *more. All. Everything.*

A loud cough just outside the shack caused him to jolt in surprise. A chilly fear followed soon after. He broke away, putting Aliénor behind him so he stood between her and whoever might come through that doorway. "Who's there?"

A strange voice called out something, the words indistinct over the rain.

"It's probably the shepherd." Aliénor cleared her throat, then yelled something back to the shepherd with lots of hard consonant sounds.

A grunt came from outside, and their intruder swung through the doorway into view. He was indeed the shepherd. A young lad, short and stocky, and soaked through from the rain as they were. The boy had dark skin, and black hair braided away from his face. The shepherd's eyes widened as his gaze flicked back and forth between the two of them. A slow smile spread on the boy's face. He laughed and said something in Tiochene.

Aliénor gasped and made what sounded like a very sharp retort to the boy.

"What?" Thomas fumbled for his damp tunic and shrugged the garment over his head, shivering as the chilled fabric touched his bare skin. "What is he saying?"

"Oh." Aliénor huffed, glaring at the shepherd while the boy just grinned back. "Nothing. The lad is insolent."

"How do you know the language?"

"My handmaiden Violette has been teaching us all these past few months on the road. Her—her mother was Tiochene."

"Ah. So this is the lad's hut?"

"Yes. But he says we can shelter with him until the rain lets up."

The shepherd's gaze lingered on Thomas's sword, and the boy kept his hands up and visible as he walked farther into the shelter. He settled against the wall across from them. The boy carried a small sack, and he held it out to them with a polite smile.

"He has food in there," Aliénor explained.

As if in response, Thomas's stomach let out a loud wail easily heard by all three of them.

Aliénor puffed out a laugh and bumped Thomas's shoulder with her own. "I'm hungry too."

Thomas continued to study the shepherd. The lad wore a coarse brown wool tunic, longer than the fashion of Jerdun or Lyond, with intricate red embroidery around the collar. Thomas's head felt fuzzy of a sudden, clouded. A strange tremor started in his hands and arms. *Perhaps I am hungrier than I know. And yet...something about the shepherd...* "The boy is just offering us his food?"

"Oh no. He's offering to sell it to us." Aliénor and the shepherd exchanged a few quick words before she continued, "He says he has some apples, I think, and then a word I don't know. Some kind of cheese? Goat cheese, maybe?"

As if to demonstrate, or perhaps just to twist the knife, the boy drew a large green apple out of his bag and bit into it. Thomas could hear the juicy crunch of the apple's flesh even over the still-pouring rain outside.

"Buy the lot of it," Thomas muttered.

She snorted. "I would if I had a single coin with which to cross his palm."

Thomas smiled and plucked his own small money pouch off his belt.

"Such a wise ki—man." She darted a nervous glance at the boy. "Philippe never carried his own money. He did not wish to taint his hands with such worldly considerations."

"As a young man, I was stranded once after a battle on the wrong side of a river, in enemy territory. I didn't have any money on me at all. Nothing to trade. I nearly starved to death before my father's men found me." Thomas thumbed through his pouch and came up with the smallest possible coin. It wasn't that he minded paying more for the food, but he didn't mean to let the shepherd know how deep his purse was.

The shepherd held his hand out for the coin. Thomas pressed it into the lad's small hand. The lad flexed his fingers a little and grinned, clearly waiting for more. Thomas's stomach chose that particular moment to betray him again by emitting another high-pitched growl. The shepherd gave him a toothy smile and wiggled his fingers again.

Thomas dug out two more of the small coins and dropped them into the lad's palm. The boy at last pulled his hand back and dug in his bag. The first thing he came up with was another apple, and such an apple: perfectly round with a delicate red blush to the green.

As Thomas weighed the ripe fruit in his palm, it took all of his willpower to turn and offer the food to Aliénor first.

She gave Thomas a startled glance and tried to push the apple back to him. "No, no, you first."

The shepherd made a sound of protest, frowning mightily, and let lose another long stream of angry words.

Aliénor frowned. "He says I must eat first. Bad luck otherwise. A local custom, I guess."

"It's fine." Thomas clapped a hand over his gut in an attempt to muffle its unmannerly noises.

Aliénor smiled at him. "I'll just take a small bite, then hand it to you." Suiting action to words, she sank her teeth into the apple with a loud crunch. Juice from the apple dribbled down her chin, and Thomas laughed a little.

She froze and stared at the apple in her hand.

Thomas stilled too, watching her face contort. "What—"

She choked once, gagging, her frightened gaze darting to his face.

"*Aliénor.*" His heart clutched with fear.

She toppled backward, away from him, and the apple rolled out of her nerveless fingers.

Chapter Sixteen

T homas reached for Aliénor as she collapsed, his pulse thundering with
fear. "No—"

Movement at the corner of his eye made him instinctively flinch back.
The shepherd lunged toward him. Thomas caught the boy's wrist, anger and
alarm flaring in the king's gut. "What did you *do* to her?"

The shepherd let out a husky laugh, feminine and low.

Thomas gaped.

"Hello, King Thomas." The shepherd's skin cracked. The shepherd's dark
face shredded away to reveal Mistress Helen's lighter cheek like a snake
shedding its old skin. The last traces of illusion peeled away from the blood
witch, and she combed her fingers through her hair, smiling at Thomas.

He jerked away, but she flicked out her sharp little knife, slashing at him.
He dodged, trying not to topple over Aliénor in the small hut.

The blood witch bit her lip in concentration and threw herself at him
again. Her shoulder slammed into his chest. He caught her hands, holding
that accursed blade of hers away from his body. A nasty fighter, she managed
to sink her teeth hard into the bare skin of his wrist.

He yelped as her teeth opened his skin and shoved her violently away from him, hard enough that she banged into the wall and made the whole hut rattle with the impact. Thomas whirled and fumbled on the ground for his sword.

"No, no. Stop that," she snapped.

Thomas froze, but his hands shook as he tried to make his body obey his own will and not her damned spell. *Move. Go.* His muscles remained stiff and unyielding, under his command no more. His body might as well have been stone for all he could do with it.

"Turn around, King Thomas."

Breathing heavily, stomach roiling with acid, Thomas wheeled around—and it felt as if an invisible hand were moving him the whole time, twisting his torso, shifting his legs.

Mistress Helen raked her gaze slowly over him. His blood still stained one side of her mouth, and she absently flicked her tongue out to lick at it. Her slow perusal of him complete, she met his stare at last, and her lips widened in a smile. "Well, this is lovely. A king to call my very own. A handsome one too. You and I shall be quite good friends, I think. Do sit down, Thomas."

His legs crumpled beneath him, and he hit the dirt hard. His mind seemed to throb with the effort to think, to resist the creeping numbness and confusion of her spell. *What can I do? How can I fight this?*

Mistress Helen sat gracefully across from him, arranging her legs *just so*, then smoothing down the line of her masculine hose over her knee. "Dear Thomas, tell me: how large is your country?"

Over the next half hour, she asked many such questions of him. How large was his treasury? How many men could he muster at need to fight? How much land belonged to him alone?

"And the succession? Who is your heir?"

Thomas swallowed, the words bitter on his tongue as they forced themselves past his unwilling lips. "Gabriel. My nephew. But he's gone missing."

"Well, good." Her lips pinched. "Although dead would be better. Well, I'll take care of him eventually if I must." She tapped her little dagger against her knee as she thought. Then she looked again at Thomas, and her face broke into a large smile. "Now, tell me true, dear Thomas: do you think it better if we marry here or wait until we reach Lyond?"

Marriage. Married to this harpy and his whole country under her thumb? Thomas had to lick his dry lips. His voice was thready, strained and throbbing with his own fury. He still answered her truthfully, though his tongue felt thick, his stomach nauseated as he did so. "I think, however you drag me back to my kingdom, the people will be suspicious. If we are unwed, they will more easily see you for the scheming, manipulative adventuress that you are."

She narrowed her eyes, scowling, and let out a gusty sigh. "I suppose it shall have to be married and pregnant, then, with a lovely long tour through your country first to tell your people the good news."

Married. Pregnant. And Aliénor's motionless body on the floor behind him. What sort of hellish, devastating land of nightmare had he walked into? And how could he free himself from it?

The blood witch peered out the hut's small opening. "The rain's letting up. We should be going. Get your cloak, dear Thomas." She had a malicious glint in her eye as she said it.

Hands shaking, Thomas turned toward Aliénor where she lay unmoving on the floor atop his cloak. Her skin was blanched a ghastly white, but her red hair lay spread about her like a spill of rosy gold. His late wife, his dear Rosamund, had looked that pale, that still as he'd held her and watched the life leave her body. His eyes stung. *Aliénor.*

He had to lift Aliénor into his arms in a mockery of an embrace in order to yank his cloak free. Her limp body sagged in his grip, and he felt dizzy, off-balance, as if the world were tilting beneath him. Suddenly he knew the witch had given him this order to be cruel, to make him feel how futile all his half-imagined hopes and dreams were now.

Aliénor's skin was corpse-cold, and no breath seemed to stir in her breast. "I'm sorry, Aliénor. I'm so sorry."

The spell would not even let him hold her or touch her face, though he tried to make his hands obey. He could touch her only as much as he needed to in order to carry out the witch's order, and no more. Once he had tugged the folds of his cloak free, he had to lay Aliénor gently back on the floor and step away. *Aliénor.* He gritted his teeth, a scream of fury and loss and fear building behind his locked teeth. But the spell choked his cry back as firmly as a hand round his throat would.

"Come along, dear Thomas."

His whole body trembled as he turned away and left Aliénor's poor cold body behind him on the floor.

To lose a princess was bad enough. To lose a princess and a king all in one day made Llewellyn feel an utter fool. And the princess's ladies did not soothe his pride or his temper any either.

"Your king probably stole our princess in the night." This was the younger one, Lady Violette. She'd been muttering such things the whole night through. The other one, the stout Lady Noémi, held her tongue. Still, she kept a wary eye on Llewellyn and all the king's knights, and she made sure to keep little Violette close to her side like a mother hen with only one chick. Lady Noémi hadn't liked any of them, but she'd trusted the Lyondi knights yesterday. Now she stayed with them only out of necessity.

Llewellyn understood the women's suspicions, but he could do little to assuage their fears when he could not keep track of his own bloody king. *Oh, my king, what have you gotten yourself into this time?* He did not want to believe King Thomas had absconded with the girl, but everything had been so dark and chaotic the night before. They'd seen no sign of King Thomas or Princess Aliénor all the long night they had been searching. Now their whole group was wet through, tired, sore, hungry.

If we do not find them soon... Llewellyn winced and pushed aside the branch just ahead of him. The rain, at least, had petered out. Perhaps they might even have time to dry off before the next winter storm swept through to pummel them.

The sound of sheep caught at Llewellyn's senses, and he cast his eyes around in the gray light until he saw what must be a shepherd's hut. Perhaps he could leave the two ladies there with one of his men and take the rest of his knights to—

Lady Noémi gasped and pointed. "*Look.*"

Two dark figures had ducked out of the hut and were making their careful way down the muddy hill.

Llewellyn's breath caught as he recognized the king's form up ahead. The other wore hose and a tunic, but had the silhouette of a woman.

"Hallo there!" Llewellyn hollered and hurried forward.

Both figures froze. The smaller of the two yanked hard on King Thomas's arm. Instead of this speeding him along, they lost their balance together and fell with a wet splat into the mud.

"Are you all right? My king?" Heart fluttering with an alarm he didn't quite understand, Llewellyn jogged forward up the hill toward the two figures. He was certain now that one was King Thomas. But the other—

"Burn. *Burn.*" The blood witch's voice boomed over the hillside, and a ball of red heat rolled off her palm like a flung stone, hurtling down the hill toward him.

Llewellyn threw himself into the mud, pressing flat. The heat rolled over him and hit against the trees. The princess's women cried out behind him, and he heard the crackle of flame as the damp trees caught fire. A powerful spell, then, to make even the wet wood burn.

Llewellyn wasted no time and pushed to his feet, racing after the blood witch.

"Stop him, Thomas!" she hollered over her shoulder and took off down the other side of the hill.

Llewellyn raced past his king, then suddenly went flying, landing hard enough to knock the breath out of him. The king had yanked Llewellyn's legs out from under him, and he leapt onto the magician's back. Llewellyn thrashed as King Thomas ground his face into the cold mud.

Llewellyn gagged and bucked, clawing at the ground. Mud went up his nose, down his throat. He could feel desperate magic building in his chest, wild, dangerous spells. *I do not want to hurt you, Thomas.* Llewellyn's eyes burned as the king's fingers dug into the back of his skull, crushing Llewellyn's face into the wet muck.

"No, my king. *Stop.*" The voices of the other knights. They yanked the king's weight off Llewellyn's back. He rolled over and coughed up the chilly black mud. Stumbling forward, Llewellyn touched the king's hand as his friend thrashed and fought at the knights pinning his arms.

Llewellyn rubbed his fingers together, drawing up the purging spell, rolling the stinging filaments of magic between his palms like a glowing snowball. *"Out."* He slapped the hasty spell-ball against the king's chest, and it shattered with crystalline brightness. The witch's spell coursed like poison through his king's blood, but as his own magic worked, Llewellyn could smell a faint coppery tang. At last, his spell had burned the contagion out of King Thomas.

The king groaned, and his muscles seized up. With a gasp, the king collapsed in the other knights' holds. Llewellyn himself doubled over in the mud, breathing hard, his heart racing. *Too much magic.* He blinked his eyes open, and the world spun. Rolling over on his back despite the icy mud, he gulped in several deep breaths, trying to regain his balance.

"The princess?" Lady Noémi rushed up, her hair in disarray. She threw herself right in the king's face. "Where is the princess?"

The king's face crumpled, still white with shock and pain. His eyes shone wetly. "The hut. The witch gave her an apple. I—Llewellyn?"

With a groan, Llewellyn rolled onto all fours. "I'm coming, I'm coming." He did not move. His muscles were too tired, his head too dizzy. *If only I had a spell to compel my own body to move.* After a moment, young Ned yanked on Llewellyn's arm, pulling him to his feet. The page would have stepped away, but Llewellyn clung to his arm and pointed to the hut. "There."

With a sigh, Ned walked forward, Llewellyn leaning heavily on the page the whole time.

Lady Noémi raced in ahead of them, and her shrill cry when she hurried inside made the rest of them redouble their pace. Llewellyn ducked through the doorway and stopped short at the sight of the princess's body splayed out on the ground. An apple with one bite taken out of it lay near her hand.

"She's *dead*." Lady Noémi's voice shook, and tears spilled freely down her round cheeks.

"Please, let me see her." Llewellyn tried to move past the woman.

She shoved him away. "Don't you touch her, you bloody Lyondi spell-caster."

Llewellyn took a deep breath to calm his temper. "I am a healer. I set your friend's arm, didn't I? Bandaged your head. Maybe I can do something for your princess. You must let me try."

Lady Noémi's chin crinkled with emotion. At last, she curled into herself, crying softly, and turned away.

Llewellyn brushed past her and knelt beside the princess's still form. "My king?"

"Here." King Thomas hunched down next to Llewellyn.

Black spots swam at the edge of Llewellyn's vision and he blinked, trying to banish them. *Too many spells*. He needed a rest, but there was no time. "What happened?"

"The blood witch in disguise gave her the apple." King Thomas chafed his hands together, nervous, in pain. "Aliénor—the princess took one bite of the apple, choked, and collapsed."

Lady Noémi's lip curled. "And you didn't help her?"

King Thomas's nostrils flared, but his voice was calm, controlled. "I tried, but the blood witch attacked me. She bit me to get a taste of my blood, and after that I was powerless." He swallowed, his gray-blue eyes shadowed.

Llewellyn touched his friend's arm and moved closer to the princess. As he leaned over her face, her breath stirred ever so softly against his cheek. "She lives."

Chapter Seventeen

L ady Noémi sobbed as they knelt beside Princess Aliénor's still form. "The princess is still alive?"

"*What?*" The king moved Lady Noémi out of his way to get closer to the Princess Aliénor's body.

Llewellyn ignored them both and hauled the princess into his own arms. She was light and so limp as to be practically boneless, cold as marble. "A bite of apple, you said?" As gently as he could, he tugged her mouth open with two fingers and felt inside, his knuckles brushing her teeth. The bite of apple was still there, resting against the back of her throat like the cork in a bottle. He tugged the bite free of her mouth and tossed it away. The princess gulped in a deeper breath, but her eyes didn't open.

"Damn." A flash of anger blazed through Llewellyn. *Of course it couldn't be that easy.* "I'll have to draw the spell out."

Lady Noémi wrinkled her nose. "Draw it out? Like a splinter?"

"I need something small, sharp. Something to prick her with."

The king moved to draw his dagger.

Llewellyn held his hand up. "Too large."

Lady Noémi frowned, then fumbled in her hair, tearing at the coiled braids. At last she jerked out a small hairpin with a circular design like braided rope on the end. "Here."

Llewellyn took the pin and tested its point against his finger. "Sharp, good. And silver. All right. Back up, you two."

"What are you going to do?" The king took Lady Noémi by the elbow and tugged her to the wall of the hut.

Llewellyn shook his head. "Something stupid." With a deep breath to steel himself, he stuck the hairpin into the tip of the princess's finger. He closed his eyes, the better to trace the dark web of the sleeping curse inside the princess's body. He couldn't really see it, per se, but he could feel it. Almost like a chill cocoon of mud slowly covering her body, ready to entomb the girl forever. And the longer the princess lay under this darkness, the harder it would be to drag her out.

Llewellyn ghosted his hands just over her skin, using his magic to push Mistress Helen's curse down and out, channeling it all toward the silver hairpin in the princess's finger. The sticky black muck of the curse was stubborn, clinging to the princess's body like a stain. Llewellyn pushed harder, his hands tingling and then burning from the magic. He gritted his teeth, fighting the pain, ignoring the spinning sensation in his head. *"Come on."*

The king traced a fingertip along her cheek. "Aliénor, please." His voice broke.

Cold. And dark. Like the long, deep dark at the ending of the world. Like the black tide of the river rolling her in its waves. Aliénor gulped in one breath after another, thrashed, pushed, twisted, but she could not make her body move, could not open her eyes. Her throat burned and throbbed.

"Arrogant girl. Weak. Foolish." Her father's voice.

"Papa?"

"I should never have left my lands to you. I should have drowned you first."

"Papa." Aliénor curled into herself, heart hurting, but ghostly hands brushed across her skin, and more ghostly voices whispered in her head, the words like knives.

"*You pride led us here!*"

A susurrus of voices rolled over her. Some she recognized. Her guard captain's. Lord Ysen's. It was like a thousand men crying out all at once, accusing her. Hating her.

"*The quest was your idea.*"

"*Fool...*"

"*Harlot...*"

"*You've killed them all. Killed me.*" Philippe's voice. "*Unnatural woman. He doesn't want you. Who could? He left you at the first opportunity.*"

Aliénor turned her face away, sobbing hard. She hurt inside. Everything hurt.

"Aliénor, please..."

"Thomas?" She twisted, looking for him, but there was only that same clinging, boiling blackness.

Or, no...the darkness was lessening, the black water receding. Aliénor felt life returning. Light. Something was pulling the consuming dark away from her.

"*Slut. Liar. You'll spread your legs for a Lyondi killer?*" Philippe's ghostly hand grabbed for her, trying to pull her back.

She flung him off and drew her shoulders back, walking toward the growing light ahead of her. "Good-bye, Philippe."

<hr/>

With a grunt, Llewellyn plucked the last clinging strand of the curse away from the princess's head and shoved it into the pin. He removed the pin slowly, cupping his palm over the end of it to plug the curse up inside. He carefully held the pin in one hand, point up and away from his body. "There." With a deep drawn breath, he looked down at the girl.

Princess Aliénor's face contorted with pain, tears leaking from the corners of her eyes. Lady Noémi bustled forward, drawing the princess up into her arms. With keen good sense, Lady Noémi immediately turned the girl onto her side as the princess retched.

"Poison?" Lady Noémi murmured.

"Magic?" the king asked.

"A bit of both." Llewellyn held the hairpin up close to his face. It had an inky black aura around it now, tinged with yellow. He sighed. "A rather complex sleep spell, and the apple was what the blood witch used to carry it into Princess Aliénor's system. You're all right now, Princess."

She gasped in a deep breath, and Lady Noémi helped her sit up, still in her arms. The princess had finished retching, but she shook like a leaf, frightened tears still leaking from her eyes. "Magician, what was that?"

"What do you mean?"

She swallowed with difficulty, shaking her head, her eyes haunted. "I heard voices. My father. All those dead soldiers. Even...Philippe. Was that real? Were they—?"

He gripped her hand and gave it a strong, bracing squeeze. "No, no. That wasn't real."

"Was the witch in my head? Controlling me?"

"No. Part of the nastiness of sleeping curses is they place their victims in a perpetual state of nightmare. All their worst imaginings forever. But it's not real. None of it. I promise you."

Her shoulders sagged with profound relief, and Lady Noémi gave the princess a tight one-armed hug. "It was like being in the river again, drowning with no way to fight it," Princess Aliénor murmured.

The king made a small, instinctual grab to take her from Lady Noémi, but stopped himself at the last moment, curling his hands into fists. Lady Noémi's eyebrows climbed in surprise.

Llewellyn managed to control his own face a little better, but still felt a flash of exasperated resignation. The Lyondi knights did *not* need further complications on this trip. He held the hairpin aloft to distract everyone. "The curse is contained in this pin. Unfortunately, it is stronger now. It's all tangled up with my magic, with the magic I had to use to draw it out of you, Princess."

"We should dispose of it," the king murmured.

Llewellyn recognized the vengeful gleam in Lady Noémi's eyes. "It's my hairpin," she said. "I'll give it to the princess. She can use it on that damned witch if the evil woman ever comes back."

Llewellyn hesitated, his gut uneasy, but he finally handed the pin over to the lady-in-waiting. "Be very careful and mind that none of you ladies stick yourselves with it ever again. I'm not sure I could remove this curse from someone so easily again."

Lady Noémi nodded and hauled out her canteen. She unwrapped the string keeping the cork tied to the jug and instead stuck the hairpin into the cork. "Good enough?"

Llewellyn gusted out a weary breath and leaned back hard on his hands. "I suppose." The room spun again, blackness on the edge of his vision. He should not have done so much magic in so short a time.

"Please send in Lady Violette. We'll see to Princess Aliénor now." A cool dismissal from Lady Noémi. Never mind Llewellyn could barely keep himself upright, let alone stand, let alone walk.

"No." Princess Aliénor pulled away her handmaiden's hands. "We must move. We must get to Anutitum."

"My lady—"

"*No.*" Princess Aliénor pushed to her feet.

Llewellyn flung out a hand to help her, though he was still a little dizzy himself. The king, Llewellyn noticed, had his hands clasped tight behind his back. Perhaps to keep himself from reaching for the lovely princess?

Said lovely princess flung a hand out against the rough wall of the hut, clearly still woozy. Yet her voice was forceful as she stared around at them all. "The Tiochene still roam these hills, and Mistress Helen means us all more mischief,

I'm sure of it. The best thing we can do is get ourselves safe behind the walls of my cousin's city." Her gaze flicked to King Thomas. "Yes?"

"Yes." King Thomas sighed. Llewellyn wondered if Lady Noémi, if the princess, could hear the sadness in the king's voice.

The princess and the king looked at each other like no one else was in the room. Their gazes held, and Llewellyn looked away hurriedly in the face of such naked despair, staring anywhere but at his king, anywhere but at the princess. *They will have to do better than that.* If the two royals looked at each other like that in the city, it would set a scandal burning that could consume both their nations. *Again.*

"We should get you some food, Princess. Then we can be on our way." Lady Noémi broke the silence as she bustled out the door and called for Lady Violette to bring the other canteen and some supplies.

Llewellyn and his king left the ladies to it, stepping just outside but no farther. Llewellyn dragged a deep breath of fresh air into his lungs, still dizzy, still weary.

"Sit down, you fool." Thomas followed his own advice and folded his legs up beneath himself to lean against the side of the hut. Llewellyn gratefully followed suit, leaning hard against the rough wall of the hut and wishing he need never move again.

"Did you find Sir Godric?" King Thomas's voice had a bleak edge to it.

Llewellyn winced. "No, my king. I'm sorry. We found some bloody rope farther down the hill, but nothing else."

King Thomas punched the side of the building. "Damn. Send some of our men to look again, would you? I will not lose another man to this damned wilderness. Or to that damned witch. I will not." A muscle ticked in the king's jaw as he looked away.

"Of course, my king." Llewellyn beckoned Ned over and sent him off with orders to summon their four best knights. "I could go with them."

King Thomas glanced over with one eyebrow raised. "Certainly. If you can stand up."

"Of course I can *stand.*" Llewellyn rocked forward and got his feet underneath him. Unfortunately, when he pushed to stand, his willful limbs refused to obey.

He teetered on his heels a moment before sort of listing to the side. He was saved from another face-first landing in the mud only when the king caught his arm.

King Thomas hauled him back against the side of the building and pressed a hand over his chest to keep him there. "Stay still, you idiot. Rest, for once in your life."

Llewellyn subsided with a small grunt, closing his eyes. "What did she want with you?"

"Hmm?"

"Mistress Helen? What did she want with you?"

King Thomas cleared his throat but said nothing.

Llewellyn forced his eyes open, gazing at his king's discomfort in confusion. "What is it? What did she say?"

After hearing of the blood witch's plan to wed and bed herself forcibly to the Lyondi king in order to steal his crown, his magician insisted that Thomas keep *two* of his knights with him at all times. *At least.* That way, if the blood witch compromised one man, there would be another left to defend the king.

Thomas hated the fact that he needed constant watching like an infant, but he resigned himself to it. He hadn't liked being under the blood witch's control, after all. As king, his personal safety was more important than his personal preferences. He had let himself forget that. Aliénor was right—they had to get to the safety of the city with all possible speed. The blood witch had too many possible traps she could lay for them—for *him*—in the wilderness.

He'd dispatched four knights to find Godric, and now the rest of their party was limping down the hill to where the horses had been left. Llewellyn leaned on sturdy young Ned to get him down the hill. *Foolish magician to spend his magic again and again without worrying about the cost to his body.* Still, Thomas couldn't help but be grateful.

Aliénor walked behind, crushed between her two handmaidens as if they meant to provide a bulwark against the world for her with their own bodies. He remained uncomfortably aware of the princess. His ears seemed trained now to listen for her voice and perk up hopefully whenever she said anything to anyone. He was half-distracted, infatuated with her. Had been for days.

Llewellyn was right, though. Aliénor was too young for him, and his people would never accept a Jerdic princess as Queen. Not after living so long with the beloved memory of his late Queen Rosamund. Anyway, it wasn't fair to Aliénor to ask her to give up her home, her friends, everything to travel to a strange land just to marry him.

Was it?

Marriage. Thomas shook his head, angry at himself. Aliénor didn't even want that. Not again. And who could blame her after Philippe?

I could make her happy. I do. An arrogant thought and a foolish one. But Thomas couldn't seem to help it, couldn't stop his mind from daydreaming. Couldn't stop his heart from hoping.

They reached the small clearing where they had camped—*had it only been last night?* Two knights had been left to guard the supplies and horses. The men breathed sighs of relief as they caught sight of Thomas and the others.

"Everyone eat and rest a bit. We've all had a long night. We'll leave when the men searching for Godric return." He wiped a weary hand over his face, scrubbing hard at his chilled skin. He wanted to find Godric, to save him, but not at the expense of every other person in their party. At some point, they would have to move on.

The spell was fading. After almost a day or more out of the witch's power, Godric at last felt like himself again. Some weak, fumbling version of himself, anyway. The world seemed vague still, sort of fuzzy around the edges, and his limbs fumbled often when he walked—as if they weren't used to taking orders from him anymore. Nevertheless, each hour that passed he felt better, more sure in his movements, more certain in his mind.

King Thomas had almost found him a few hours ago, and then a few of his brother knights had come looking later. Godric had tried to call out, but the damn spell still had its grip on him—slackening, yes, but still strong enough to keep him from rescuing himself.

It was good Godric hadn't seen the princess. The compulsion was still on him to grab her and bring her back to the blood witch. He could fight it a little, but probably not if he actually saw Princess Aliénor.

Unable to reach for rescue, fighting not to return to Mistress Helen, he'd sat in the woods and waited, hour after hour, imagining he could almost feel the poison of her spell dripping out of him. At last, when the desire to find his king trumped the compulsion to chase Princess Aliénor, he'd left his hideout among the trees. *They might still be in camp. I might still reach them.* He scurried down the hill, rushing, falling occasionally, just praying all the time that he would not be too late.

Voices. Up ahead. Voices in the direction their camp had been last night. *Please, oh please.* A branch whipped at his cheek as he ran past, cutting his skin. He barely noticed—the witch had been cutting on him for days. What did one more scratch matter?

Please. He stumbled and skidded a few feet down the hill on his bum, but he thought he could pick out distinct voices ahead. The king. Master Llewellyn. Men were calling out to each other. The jingle of harness sounded. "Move out!" King Thomas yelled.

They were leaving. He stopped his downward slide and braced to push to his feet.

"Hello, Godric," her husky voice whispered behind him, syrupy and sweet.

"*No.*" He twisted to stand, to run, opened his mouth to scream for help.

"No, you don't." Her little blade whistled past his sleeve, nicking his arm. The blade landed to stick hilt up in the dirt. Godric's chest swelled with anger, boiling inside him like dark oil. He clawed the blade out of the turf and wheeled toward the blood witch. His balance was off, and he had to blink to clear his vision. "You will not take me again."

She rolled her eyes and flicked her fingers in a summoning gesture. The little blade tore itself out of his hands to fly into hers. She drew the flat side of the blade against her tongue, tasting his blood once more. She closed her eyes and moaned.

"Please, no." Godric fell to his knees, sinking his head down in despair. *I should have slit my own throat with the knife.*

"Come now, *up.*" She snapped her fingers.

All at once the languidness in his limbs disappeared. He moved with purpose again, precision. His mind was sharper, clearer. It was like being sober again after a weeklong drunk. He actually smiled at Mistress Helen as he pushed to his feet.

She smiled warmly back at him, tracing her hand over his beard. "That feels better, doesn't it? You must not try to leave my protection again. Now, let us hurry. I have the horses, and we must ride hard if we're to beat dear Thomas and that little slut to Anutitum."

Chapter Eighteen

Thomas drove his people hard after the confrontation with the witch in the shepherd's hut. They rode faster now, stopping less, sleeping less, eating less. Their group almost ran into another small patrol of Tiochene, a dozen or so, but his people hid despite their greater numbers. Llewellyn recognized the Tiochene had several spell-casters among their troop, and he did not want to set his talents against *two* unknown magicians.

Of the blood witch there was no sign. Thomas uncharitably hoped she'd run afoul of the Tiochene and had her neck slit. Of Godric there was no sign either, and Thomas regretted that more than he could say.

Several days of hard travel at last brought Thomas's party out of the high mountains and into the lowlands, where the river gentled, and more villages cropped up. Llewellyn refused to let them pass through any of the towns. He was still wary of traps set by the blood witch, and a town full of strangers seemed like too much risk. Instead, they hunted rabbits, fished out of the river when they could, and bartered with farmers on the outskirts of civilization. All Thomas's people were filthy and hungry, every one of them at the ragged end of their endurance.

"Anutitum should be just over this next ridge," Llewellyn announced after consulting their maps. The magician urged his mount forward, moving to the front of their ragged column.

Thomas grinned and tried to urge his mount faster also, but the stubborn beast just grunted. The horses too were at the end of their stamina.

A small chuckle sounded behind Thomas, and he half turned in the saddle as Aliénor approached on her own horse. "Anutitum at last."

"Yes."

"Well," she said, and her eyebrows crimped as if with pain. She opened her mouth, then closed it and looked around at their small retinue with frustration. She appeared so alone, so distressed, that his chest ached with it. She had so much brightness inside, so much life ahead of her.

She should not be so sad, so hopeless. That was for shriveled old men like him. She was a rose that should have been bursting into bloom. Dried roses and regrets should not have been her lot in life. "I am..." He broke off and wet his lips, his throat suddenly tight. "I am glad I met you, Princess Aliénor. I wish..."

"I understand."

"Good-bye. My lady."

She winced at his words—all the sign he needed that she understood this too. *This is where I lose you, my princess. This is where the world takes you from me.*

Watching him, her delicate face firmed up as if with great resolve, as if she meant to argue with him. Oh Fate spare him, but he wanted to let her, he wanted her to convince him, to cajole him to being unwise and reckless again. He wanted—

"*Halt.*" Llewellyn flung his arm up.

"What is it, Llewellyn?"

The magician sat on his horse almost at the very crest of the hill. He had a perfect view into the valley below. He grinned back at the rest of them. "Anutitum."

The city lay like a box of spilled jewels along the floor of the canyon. Hundreds of crisp marble buildings with domed tile roofs and narrow, spindly towers stretched toward the sky. The marble walls of the city glinted in the decadent golden sunlight. And straight through the heart of Anutitum, the river wound like a fine silver thread. Clean, modern, Anutitum gleamed like a beacon for them, calling them to home and safety with the failing of the light.

The road down the mountain to Anutitum lay empty and seemed somewhat ill-kept to Aliénor. A dead donkey lay off to the side of the road with flies buzzing all over. At another point, Thomas and his men had to dismount and shove an overturned farm cart out of the way.

It was near dusk as they neared the city, and yet they passed no other people. Their whole party had fallen silent without having to be told. The hairs on Aliénor's neck stood on end, and she chafed at the goose bumps on her arms.

At last, the tall white gates of the city and the long walls of Anutitum loomed above them like benevolent giants. Aliénor puffed her breath out with relief.

"Who might you lot be?" someone called down from the top of the bronze gate doors—the gates that remained resolutely shut against them.

Thomas urged his mount forward. "We are weary travelers who seek the protection of your city."

A snort sounded from the watchtower above. "Are you now? Well, it's your bad luck that we don't let folks into the city after sunset. Especially not now."

The sun was busy rolling down behind the mountains, and a chill breeze fanned across Aliénor, tickling her skin with icy fingers. She let out an impatient humph.

"Please open the gates," she called out. "I know Lord Guillaume. He will vouch for me."

The unseen guard cackled. "Oh, certain sure he will. I'm sure he's friends with all sorts of dirty guttersnipe girls. Doesn't mean I'll let you into the city."

Aliénor recoiled, anger blazing through her. Then she happened to get a glimpse of her own hands in the torchlight—dirty skin with broken nails and scrapes all over. Her face couldn't have been much better. Her clothes most certainly weren't. Anyway, for all intents and purposes, she *was* a poor guttersnipe girl begging on her cousin Guillaume's doorstep.

The only thing left to tell her that her life as Princess Aliénor hadn't all been a mad fever dream was the golden signet ring of her father's twisting on her thumb. "Look, you," she hollered, picking out each word with precision, speaking in her most cultured accent. "I've got a gold ring down here that your Lord Guillaume will want to see, and he'll want to see it tonight. If you make me wait even one minute more outside these gates, believe me that it will mean your head come morning. Now *open these gates*."

There was a brief silence from above and then some frantic mumbling. "You, go fetch Guillaume."

"No, *you*."

She didn't bother yelling again because a loud cranking had started, and the two large doors of the gate swung inward just wide enough for their horses to pass through. Aliénor urged her horse forward first, with Thomas's close behind.

"Good job," he murmured.

She lifted her chin high as she passed through the gate, into a torch-lit courtyard beyond.

Their small, bedraggled party was barely all the way through the gate before a great commotion sounded on the wall above them. "*Princess Aliénor.*"

She whirled toward the sound of the voice and watched as a tall redheaded man clattered down the gatehouse steps. "It *is* you. Cousin." The tall man cut straight past her companions to stand beside her horse.

Aliénor smiled down into his handsome face. "Hello, Guillaume." He had grown from a gangly youth into a man since she'd last seen him almost a decade ago, and yet he'd not changed much for all that. He was a little over ten years her senior, a tall, strong, handsome knight with a square chin like granite and a long scimitar of a nose slashing down his face. His eyes were the same dark brown as hers, his hair a paler shade of red, more blond than ginger.

"Bring me my horse!" Once Guillaume was properly mounted on his own horse—a fine white stallion—he wasted no time ushering their little party away from the gatehouse and up the winding road that led to his own palace on the high hills of the city. Guillaume rode at her side. Thomas rode just behind them, a lethal shadow ready to step in if Guillaume was not who or what he seemed to be. That blasted paranoia of the Lyondi must have been catching, because she was actually grateful for Thomas's care of her.

Unnecessary in this moment, though. Noémi had taken to hiding the cursed hairpin in Aliénor's coiffure each morning. 'Just in case.' The damn thing gave Aliénor the chills every time she touched it, but still it was a comforting weight in her hair.

"We heard of the slaughter of Prince Philippe's army." Guillaume's mouth pinched with unhappiness. "It is a miracle any of you survived. I'm just sorry that Anutitum cannot offer you better protection, cousin."

"What do you mean?" Was Guillaume going to turn them out into the wilderness, after all?

Her cousin let out a deep, heavy sigh. "A Tiochene army marches even now to lay siege to us. The whole countryside knows Philippe's army is lost. I have no help coming, so the Tiochene mean to try their strength against my city's walls. They should be here in a day, maybe two." He flung his hands out, and for the first time Aliénor noticed how empty the place was, how unnaturally quiet. "We sent all the families we could down the river. I'll try to get you out that way, cousin. As soon as a boat can be prepared."

She should say something, of course, but her throat was thick, her eyes stinging. It was with a very great effort that she did not look behind her at Thomas.

"Here is my palace." Guillaume dismounted first and lifted Aliénor down from her own horse. He offered his arm to her as they walked into his palace. More high walls surrounded the building, this time made of a warm brown stone, with towers springing out of the wall every hundred feet or so. The towers were round-walled and stockier than the architecture of Jerdun, with squat, rounded tops that seemed cheerful somehow to her eyes. More beautiful tile work covered the outer walls, subtle mosaics of the river with bright blue-and-green details that popped against the dull brown stone.

They passed through the main gate, and she couldn't help herself—she looked back to make sure that she hadn't lost anybody. Thomas's gaze caught with hers, his blue eyes dark, his face solemn and worried. He gave her a small nod of encouragement. One corner of his mouth twitched in an almost-smile. Taking heart, Aliénor drew her breath in and straightened up.

Guillaume paused in a large courtyard with even more intricate tiling and decoration. The space was open and airy with arched doorways leading off to the rest of the palace. Aliénor gaped. Even the finest castles back home would have looked cramped and barbaric compared to this elegant splendor. "This is beautiful, Guillaume."

He grinned. "It is, isn't it? This structure was once an old Tiochene fortress that our Jerdic forces took over when we came south in your father's day. I inherited it from the last Jerdic governor."

Aliénor swallowed and looked away from the intricate tile mosaics, the beautiful stonework her artisans back home could not possibly recreate. How much might her people have learned if they had worked with the Tiochene back then instead of trying to conquer them all?

Guillaume dismounted and clapped to summon his servants. Two young boys emerged from the shadows at once. They looked barely old enough to be servants at all, not even ten, she would guess. *All the older boys must have been called to man the city's walls.*

Guillaume scrubbed a hand over his face. "I'm afraid I cannot offer you much in the way of refreshments, though I think we do have some good meat left. Maybe some fruit?"

"That sounds fine, Guillaume."

He didn't seem to have heard her, for he still rambled on like a horse heading home for his stable that would not let his rider turn him from the path. "The bathhouses still work, so you can clean up. I'll dig up some fresh clothes for you and your ladies. The knights too. I'll speak to my steward about arranging a boat."

"Guillaume, thank you—"

"Have to give you some supplies for the trip. Can't spare much. Maybe send your horses with you, but no, we might need them. Perhaps I can—"

"Guillaume." She gripped his arm and gave it a little shake. "I'm sure whatever you arrange will be suitable, and I thank you for thinking of my comfort at all in such a desperate time as this. I am most sorry to be adding to your burdens."

He covered her hand with his own. "Here, let's get your men and the other ladies settled while you and I make our plans."

Aliénor swallowed as she looked back at Thomas. She raised her eyebrow, asking silent permission. He nodded and stepped forward. Aliénor drew a deep breath in. "By your leave, cousin, there is one more of my party that we must include in our plans."

Thomas moved to stand at Aliénor's side, and Guillaume frowned at him, raking his gaze up and down Thomas's tall form. "Who—"

Aliénor wet her lips. "Lord Guillaume of Anutitum, allow me to present to you King Thomas of Lyond."

Thomas watched Guillaume closely, but the man had a soldier's training, and upon hearing Aliénor's pronouncement, he merely blinked. "Well." The master of Anutitum turned away and motioned for the two of them to follow him. His face had gone blank, his eyes distant like windows with the shutters closed. "All right. This way."

Aliénor fell in step behind her cousin, chewing on her lower lip. Thomas wondered if she knew she was doing that. He settled his own hand carelessly on the hilt of his sword. *I hope we have not made a very grave error in trusting this Guillaume.*

Her cousin's office was large but simple, with a table and several chairs. Rows upon rows of shelves filled with parchment and sheaths of vellum were stacked behind the table with all kinds of colorful stones to weigh the loose leaflets down. Reports, inventories, correspondence. The sight made Thomas homesick for some reason. He had been gone too long from Lyond. He only hoped his regent was managing. It had been months since Thomas had received any news from home.

Guillaume settled behind his desk and steepled his fingers under his chin. "I am sorry for the loss of your men, King Thomas, and I regret to tell you that your colony cities have all been overrun by the Tiochene already."

He'd been expecting this, but still it was like having a knife shoved under his ribs and twisted. *What an old fool and a failure I am.* He hissed his breath out sharply through his teeth. "Were many of the Lyondi colonists killed?"

"Some fled here, but we were forced to send them away with our own people along the river to the last few cities controlled by Jerdic forces. A few of the colonists in your cities refused to abandon their homes. They stayed behind and surrendered to the Tiochene, even agreeing to convert. All the Lyondi cities were taken with relatively little bloodshed, so I'm told."

Thomas should have felt outrage that any of his countrymen had defected to a foreign enemy. He felt only a weary resignation. He had seen how harsh this place was, how brutal. How could he judge or condemn his people for doing what they thought best to survive?

"Now, please." Guillaume's frowning gaze flicked back and forth between Thomas and Aliénor. "Tell me how you—both of you—came to survive. And to be traveling together in this way."

Thomas glanced over at Aliénor, and she made a small *you go first* motion with her chin. Thomas snorted and settled back in his chair. "Many weeks ago now, my men and I were marching along the mountain pass..."

———◇———

As their tale continued, Aliénor watched Guillaume's expression become more and more incredulous. Though the story sounded outlandish, they even told him everything they knew of the blood witch.

"No such woman has been seen, has she?"

Guillaume spread his empty hands in a gesture of helplessness. "Thousands of people have passed through my city, cousin. I will ask my men to watch for this witch, but it's possible she's already found her way inside the walls. I wouldn't worry overmuch, though. Magic is forbidden in my city."

Aliénor tilted her head. "What? Why?"

Guillaume's jaw twitched, his eyes going distant. "Oh, the Tiochene population here were making trouble last year. The other Jerdic colony-cities too. Rumor is, the Tiochene faction in the mountains have been training anyone with a modicum of Talent in magic—even *women*. And then recruiting them for their army. So I banned magic altogether and imprisoned anyone caught practicing it."

"You don't even have a court magician?" Thomas asked.

"No," Guillaume scoffed. "More trouble than they're worth, if you ask me. Like your blood witch problem: why keep someone close to the throne who has the power to make you her puppet?"

Aliénor couldn't exactly disagree, but not all magicians were as unscrupulous as Mistress Helen. She couldn't help but think how useful and brave Master Llewellyn had shown himself to be, for instance. Having a good magician on your side could be a powerful boon. *Especially when your enemies are creating an army of magic users.* Guillaume's outlawing of magic seemed marvelously short-sighted to her, cruel even. A Talented midwife, for instance, could save more lives in her time than even a skilled court magician like Llewellyn.

"How did you break the witch's curse, cousin?" Guillaume asked, his eyebrow raised.

She dropped her gaze to the floor to keep from looking at Thomas. "Oh, 'twas the bite of apple. Once they took that out of my mouth, the spell was broken."

Guillaume frowned but did not probe further.

Thomas casually picked up the thread of the story *after* the shepherd's hut. He'd fudged the details there too, she'd noticed, so that Guillaume would not know they had ever been alone together.

Indeed, no one could ever know she and Thomas had been alone together for so long or Aliénor would be utterly ruined. So many traps in this interview with her cousin, so many details to distort and conceal.

Of course, some foolish part of her did not wish to conceal her indiscretion with Thomas. Why should that thought tempt her so? To tell Guillaume everything, to scandalize and shame her kinsman so Guillaume would force Thomas to marry her. Perhaps it was because she could feel Thomas slipping away from her. He'd already let her go on the road outside Anutitum, already switched from calling her "Aliénor" to calling her "Princess."

Each moment they spent in this city, in their real world, it felt like Thomas was being taken away piece by piece. It made her anxious, desperate, but she had enough good sense left that she did not speak. Guillaume was just as likely to kill Thomas to avenge her honor as to order them married.

No, she had to find another way to keep Thomas. They would be together on the boat up the river. Perhaps that would be enough time, enough privacy for them to figure out a way to keep each other. She smiled a little. *Jerdun and Lyond surrendering to one another.*

"I do hope you will look at my arrangements on the wall before you take ship, King Thomas." Guillaume nodded graciously. "Your strategic maneuvers at the siege of Tanab are legendary, and I would appreciate any suggestions you might have for improving the city's defenses."

"Of course." Thomas shifted in his seat and looked suddenly over at Aliénor.

She beamed at him, as warmly as she dared with Guillaume watching, but Thomas's eyes remained unaccountably sad as he gazed at her.

Thomas wet his lips. "I thank you for all your generosity, Lord Guillaume, but I must tell you that I do not plan to take ship with the princess tomorrow."

"No?"

"*What?*" Aliénor half started from her chair before she remembered herself. Heart in her throat, she clasped her hands together in her lap. "King Thomas, what do you mean?"

He turned from her. "I mean to stay in Anutitum. Lord Guillaume, I mean to help you defend your city."

Chapter Nineteen

Guillaume's face split wide in happy shock, his teeth shining as he grinned at Thomas. "This is generosity unlooked-for, King Thomas. I thank you and most humbly accept your sword to help me defend Anutitum."

Aliénor's body felt frozen and on fire all at once. She could not move, could not speak. Inside it felt like her entire body was a tumultuous mess. As if Tiochene raiders were tearing and looting through the chambers of her heart. Burning everything in their wake with spell-fire. "Thomas, no. You can't. You mustn't."

His chair creaked as he gripped the arms tight. He did not look at her. "I set out to defend my people from the Tiochene, and I miserably failed at that. I would like now to help Lord Guillaume defend his city. I am a soldier and a knight. I am an *old* soldier, but my arm is still strong, my sword sharp. I can be of use here."

Guillaume made a show of shuffling the papers on his desk. "Cousin Aliénor, perhaps you would like to eat and wash up. I will let you know what arrangements have been made to get you and your ladies safely away."

Aliénor shoved to her feet, her chair clattering behind her. Accepting her dismissal with lowered eyes and a raging heart, she walked out of the room. *Oh, Thomas, you fool. You stubborn, honorable, wonderful fool.*

Thomas and Guillaume stayed closeted together another hour or so, discussing how best to get Aliénor and her ladies safely away. After that was settled, their talk turned to how best to deploy the limited number of troops available, what precautions to take against magic, catapults, fire, disease...

Guillaume was an intelligent enough soldier, conscientious but unimaginative, and his prejudice against magic seemed to Thomas to have left Anutitum dangerously vulnerable. *Nothing to do about that now.*

Thomas was exhausted by the time their talk wrapped up. He read a similar weariness in Guillaume as the younger man pushed away from his desk and stood. Thomas clapped Guillaume on the shoulder. "You should rest, Lord Guillaume. And eat."

Guillaume waved a dismissive hand. "I will by and by. Once I've secured the boat for Princess Aliénor. I do not wish to waste a moment in getting her away to safety."

"No. Nor I." She'd looked so hurt, so betrayed when Thomas said he meant to stay behind. He'd hated to do it, but he was a knight. A solider. He could not walk away from this fight and still call himself an honorable man.

Guillaume was watching him and opened his mouth as if to speak.

Thomas raised an eyebrow in challenge.

The younger man snapped his mouth shut with a small, self-conscious laugh. "Until tomorrow, King Thomas."

"Until tomorrow."

When Thomas stepped into the hall, he was tired enough that a small growl of irritation escaped him at the sight of Llewellyn waiting for him there. "What?"

"We're staying behind, my lord?" The magician's voice was bone-dry.

"No. *I'm* staying behind with any of our other knights who wish to fight. *You* are going on ahead with Princess Aliénor to make sure that she gets to safety." Thomas started down the hallway in the direction his guest room was supposed to be in.

Llewellyn fell in step beside him. "And I don't suppose you'll see her again before she leaves."

"Perhaps in passing." Thomas clenched his fists at his side. Llewellyn must know this was a fresh wound for him, so why the devil did his magician insist on poking it? Too tired to pretend this conversation was about something else, Thomas huffed out a gusty sigh. "I'm too old for her anyway."

Llewellyn snorted. "She has the makings of a queen, sire. A great queen. You're a fool if you let her go." The magician said no more, merely stomped ahead of Thomas down the hallway, and pushed one of the doors open ahead of him. "This is your chamber. Rest well, sire."

"Llewellyn." Thomas caught his friend's arm. "You were the one who warned me away from her. Political consequences. A possible war with Jerdun. What has become of your objections now?" Thomas shouldn't have been so mad, but hot anger spiked inside his veins all the same.

Llewellyn shook his head, a muscle ticking in the magician's jaw. "You think any of that matters now with the Tiochene army about to fall on our heads?"

"What?"

"You want to stay behind and do the honorable thing. I understand that, and I would stay behind to die bravely with you if you would let me."

"No. You're to go with the princess."

"I know. I am." Llewellyn fisted his hands and shook them in front of his face with a low growl of frustration. "My king, I know what it is to lose someone. So do you. Don't double your regrets and hers."

Thomas winced. "Do you really think it would be a kindness for me to speak to Aliénor now? To tell her now?"

"You think it a kindness *never* to speak?" Llewellyn swallowed. "Go to her, Thomas."

Thomas ached inside, as if iron bands were slowly constricting around his chest. "I thank you for your wise counsel." Llewellyn's mouth snapped open to retort, but Thomas held a hand up to forestall him. "No. Really. Thank you. I will consider what you've said. Good night, my friend."

Llewellyn bowed. "Good night, my king."

Thomas stood for a long time staring at the open door to his chamber, thinking. At last, with a sigh, he went inside and firmly shut the door.

———————◆◇◆———————

Aliénor bathed and ate and changed into clean, dry clothes—three things that she'd been dreaming about for months, and she barely noticed, barely cared. Thomas was staying behind. Thomas was abandoning her. Still she felt only a melancholy resignation. *This is who he is. This is what he does.* She would not care so much for him if he were not so admirable and good. It was wrong of her to wish him to betray his honor just to be with her.

That didn't stop her from wishing he would, though.

She slept but little that night and woke early to an urgent summons from Guillaume. Her river boat was ready, and she had to leave at once for the docks. She and her ladies all helped each other dress in the near dark, Noémi braiding her hair and Violette's since the girl's wrist was still too injured to use. Aliénor doing up Noémi's gown and Violette's. Aliénor was getting quite deft at all the chores her ladies used to do for her.

The ladies had nothing of their own, so there was nothing left to pack. They made impressive speed out of the palace and down to the docks. Indeed, they moved with such haste and bustle that she hardly had time to think about the fact that Thomas had not come to see her, had not even said good-bye.

"Are you all right, my lady?" Violette asked.

"Just tired." True enough, if incomplete.

"Aren't we all," Noémi drawled.

The smell of the river reached them first, a surprisingly clean scent. Rich and earthy. The gurgle of the water sloshing against the dock made Aliénor wistful somehow.

"I wonder if your cousin will be at the docks to say good-bye. He's quite handsome." Violette dimpled at the thought, and Aliénor couldn't quite tell if the girl was thinking of Guillaume for herself or as a match for Aliénor. *It hardly matters. If the Tiochene take the city*—but Aliénor shook her head, unwilling even to finish that thought.

Guillaume was indeed waiting for them, and Llewellyn and—her breath caught—Thomas. He must have taken the time to clean up and borrow clothes from someone, for he looked magnificent. His beard was neatly trimmed, and his long, muscular body showed to advantage in the chain mail and crisp green surcoat he wore. Someone had given him a sweeping white cloak with a tasseled hood. A very dashing style. He looked like a king out of one of the old story collections her father used to read to the household at night. She wanted to fling herself toward Thomas so badly that she had to curl her fingers into balls, crushing the fabric of her skirts to stop from reaching for him.

"Cousin." Guillaume led her forward by the hand. The river churned ahead of them, looking like molten gold in the gentle pink dawn. Her ship was of simple design with a flat bottom almost like a skiff's, one lone sail, and a small, squat box, which was to be her cabin on the trip. "Forgive the simplicity, cousin. You understand I have no grander crafts to offer you."

"It's fine, Guillaume."

"Princess Aliénor."

She actually flinched at the sound of Thomas's voice, and it took all her self-control to turn and look him in the eye. "Yes, King Thomas?"

"I will pray for your safety every moment." He lowered his voice, and his gaze fluttered away from hers. "I am sorrier than I can ever say to part from you."

Of a sudden, anger flared inside her, a burning resentment that he should send her away, that he would deny what was between them at such a time as this.

Thomas must have seen some of this in her face, for his forehead crinkled, and he actually reached over to cup her elbow. "My lady—"

"*Fire,*" Violette screamed, pointing. "The ship is on *fire.*"

Aliénor whirled around, gaping in shock and dismay as the little ship went up with a whoosh of flame.

Guillaume was yelling for a bucket line when an arrow slammed into his shoulder, spinning him to the ground. Screams and cries erupted on the dock, and

Aliénor's blood went cold as she heard the high, familiar war cry of the Tiochene. Two dozen of them came running out of one of the side streets, swords drawn and already bloody. A few of their archers stayed behind a sheltering wall and fired their deadly bows at the crowd on the dock. No spell-casters yet, though.

"Rally to me!" Guillaume roared as he pushed to his feet, one hand clasped around the arrow in his shoulder.

Someone hauled on her arm, yanking her away. "Run, Aliénor." Thomas shoved her in front of him, his face a mask of panic. "*Run.*" An arrow stuck out of one of his arms, and even as she watched, he snapped the end off and tossed it away. "Go. Please." His voice was hoarse, frantic.

Aliénor tried to go toward him, wanting to help, to keep him close. She dragged her fingers through her hair, looking for the damn cursed hairpin, ready to stick all the Tiochene with it if she had to—

"My lady, let's *go*." Llewellyn caught her around the waist, bodily lifting her up, and dragged her away from Thomas.

She screamed and kicked, her heart in her throat, the hairpin forgotten. "*Thomas.*"

"Peace," Llewellyn snapped out and tapped her temple. A little spark stung against her skin. Black clouded her vision as her body went limp in the magician's arms. The last thing she saw before the darkness claimed her was Thomas cradling his injured arm as his sword clanged against that of a Tiochene warrior. Thomas grunted and lifted his arm for another swing. The Tiochene slashed with her own blade—

Aliénor fought to stay awake, to see, but at last the blackness snatched her away, and she knew no more.

Chapter Twenty

"I'm sorry, Princess."

Aliénor blinked and stirred. Her head felt foggy, her limbs sluggish. She stretched, trying to warm her body up, to make her mind kindle with something besides fatigue. "What happened?"

"A small force of the Tiochene were let in by a traitor on the walls." Llewellyn's voice. "We fought them off at the docks, but the assault on Anutitum has begun in earnest. I'm sorry, Princess, it is probably too late for you to get out of the city."

As memory returned, she sat bolt upright in bed and gripped the magician's arm tight. "Thomas?"

"The king lives. He went with Lord Guillaume to check the wall, but he'll be back later to see you."

"Good." That done, she cuffed Llewellyn hard across the face. *Crack.* "You bastard."

He sat there a moment with his pale cheek flaming red, not moving. Then he sighed and worked his jaw, wincing. "Fair enough."

"Do not ever, *ever* use your magic on me again, do you understand?"

"I had to get you to safety."

"And carrying my lifeless carcass is, of course, much easier than simply directing me where to go."

He gave her a deeply sardonic look. "You would have left the king to fight then? If I had asked you nicely?"

Aliénor primly clasped her hands in her lap. "How's this: I will endeavor not to panic in the future if you will promise to treat me as a rational, useful adult and not an idiot child who needs protecting even from herself. Deal?"

Llewellyn winced and looked away. "Yes, my lady."

"Good." She glanced around at her surroundings. The room was an opulent bedchamber with silken curtains and a heavy jacquard blanket over the feather mattress. "Where are we?"

"A nobleman's house near the dock. Guillaume is still hoping to get you out on a boat, I think. Anyway, the palace isn't safe anymore. If the city is overrun, that is the last place any of us want to be."

Panic flared inside Aliénor like lit tinder. "Noémi? Violette? Are they—"

"Safe below, tending the wounded. After I carried you here, it became a sort of field hospital for those injured at the dock."

Aliénor sagged with relief that her ladies were all right. If ever she made it safely home to her own castle, she would kiss the stones beneath her feet with gratitude.

"Master Llewellyn?" Violette's voice called up from downstairs.

"Yes, Lady Violette?" Llewellyn yelled back.

"King Thomas has returned. Did you take your nasty curse off my lady yet?" Violette's voice was unmistakably surly.

Aliénor bit back a laugh. "I'm all right, Violette. I'm coming down now."

Llewellyn took her by the elbow to help her onto her feet, but she hurried past him, practically skipping down the stairs. She shot straight past Violette to stand in the large makeshift sickroom and gaze avidly around, trying to find him. The rest of the house was as lavishly decorated as the bedroom with fine tapestries hung on the clay walls, but the place was filled now with the cries of the wounded. Injured men were stretched out on trestle tables, on the floor. The smell assaulted her nostrils, blood and death. She reeled back, her heart hammering.

"Aliénor." The low timbre of Thomas's voice filled the crowded space.

Tears stung her eyes as she wheeled around to face him. His white cape was torn, his chain mail bloodied. A smudge of dirt stained his nose. A cut bled down his cheek.

She flung herself at him and gripped him tight around his waist. He embraced her just as hard with one arm. He nuzzled his nose into her hair and took a deep breath, whispering, "*Aliénor, Aliénor*," over and over like a benediction.

"Come upstairs and let Llewellyn see to your wounds."

Thomas leaned heavily on her as they staggered up the stairs together with Llewellyn following behind.

The arrow of that morning was still stuck in Thomas's arm, the barbed head caught with the links of his chain mail and half sticking out of the meat of his bicep. Llewellyn growled and swore when he saw the wound. "Lord Guillaume came earlier to have the arrow taken out of his shoulder. Why did you wait so long for yours?"

As the magician prodded his wound, Thomas grunted. "I took command so that Guillaume would have *time* to have his wound seen to. He was hurt much worse than I."

Llewellyn made another impatient *tsk*. He'd brought his kit with him and began stripping away the links of broken chain mail with a small tool.

Thomas hissed and flinched. Aliénor squeezed his hand and smoothed back his sweat-soaked hair with a cool cloth. Thomas closed his eyes and hummed with pleasure. "Thank you, my lady."

Aliénor's heart hurt, pounding so hard with fear for him that she thought she might be sick. Still, she sponged his brow, singing a little under her breath. She smiled when she realized it was that song he'd been singing in camp all those weeks ago. That song about the maiden of spring with flowers wound in her hair.

On the other side of the king, Llewellyn swore again, and Thomas flinched with pain, his hand convulsing painfully around hers, mashing the bones. "I was thinking of you, you know. When I sang," Thomas murmured, his voice tight. "Your summer-red hair, the shifting color of your eyes."

"I know, I know..." she crooned.

He did not speak again after that, only gritted his teeth and gripped her hand hard enough to hurt. Drawing the arrow was fiddly, delicate work, but eventually Llewellyn sat back, hissing his breath out. "There." He tossed the broken bit of arrow away and wiped his brow.

"Master Llewellyn?" someone called from downstairs, voice frantic.

"What is it?"

"A badly injured woman. Lady Noémi needs your help."

Llewellyn nodded, surveying his injured king helplessly.

Aliénor jerked her chin toward the hallway. "Go. I can bandage him."

Llewellyn nodded, pushing away from the bed. "All right. Best wash his other cuts too, and dab on some of this salve." He tapped his finger on one of the little pots arranged by the bed. He left her bandages and a bowl of clean, hot water, then took the rest of his kit as he hurried downstairs.

Once he was gone, Aliénor busied herself with tending the king. They'd already stripped off his damaged chain mail and surcoat, and he lay on the feather bed, shirtless. His torso was a mess of bruises and small cuts.

She felt guilty for it, but she couldn't help but admire the chiseled muscles of his arms and chest, the broad, coiled strength under his skin. Nevertheless, she stayed brisk and efficient as she cleaned his cuts and dabbed them with salve. Inside, her body tingled, every part of her aflame. *Really, I must be the most wanton woman alive to ogle a poor injured man in this shameless fashion.*

She smirked, and after she'd dealt with his injuries, she washed his neck and face too. She traced her fingertips over his collarbone and shoulders. His eyes fluttered open as she gently sponged the dirt off his nose. She jumped in surprise but smiled. "I thought you'd fallen asleep."

"No." His gaze flicked all over her face, his blue eyes looking almost black in the weak candlelight. He touched one fingertip to her cheek and traced the bone there with a light, tickling touch.

"Does your wound hurt very much?"

His hand slid down to cup the back of her neck, drawing her closer. "No."

She narrowed her eyes and tensed above him. "Are you lying?"

"Maybe." He smiled, and she wanted to kiss his laugh lines, kiss every part of him.

Feeling very daring, she pressed her palm over his heart, sensing the vital beat of it beneath the skin. His body was lightly dusted with dark brown hair, and she danced her fingers over the hard breadth of his chest.

"What are you thinking?" he asked.

Perhaps Jerdun and Lyond can surrender to each other, after all. Her cheeks heated at the thought.

He gave a low chuckle. "Now you must tell me."

Aliénor lifted her chin, faking a confidence she was far from feeling. "I was thinking I'd like to kiss every part of you, and perhaps bite your shoulder."

His gaze warmed, the lids lowering sleepily over his eyes. He pushed himself onto one elbow so they sat pressed together on the bed. She was breathing hard now, and each rise of her chest made the front of her gown brush against the hard strength of him. Her skin felt afire, her mouth aching for his kiss. "What are *you* thinking, Thomas?"

He cradled her chin with his hand, and traced a thumb over the fullness of her lip. She tasted the salt off his skin. "I'm a fool not to send you out of this room right now."

"Thomas, the Tiochene could pour over the walls of this city and kill us all at any moment. I do not think it is wrong if we take what pleasure we can from each other while we may."

"Aliénor—"

Wetness prickled in her eyes, and she turned her face away from him so he would not see. "Please, Thomas, put aside your honor for one night. Forget we are Jerdic and Lyondi. Surrender your scruples." She faced him again, tangling her arms around his neck, breathing the smell of his skin, his hair. *Thomas.* "I do not wish to die without having ever made love to you."

He locked his arms around her, squeezing her waist.

"Wait," she murmured.

He froze and expelled a long breath against her skin. He eased back, his head hanging. "Of course. You're right. Forgive me—"

Aliénor clucked her tongue and laughed a little, tilting his chin up so he would look at her. "*Wait*," she murmured. She dug her fingers into her now untidy coronet of braids, untwisting the coil of hair tangled around the cursed hairpin. With a small oath—and a few sacrificed hairs—she at last freed the pin from her hair and set it with a small *click* next to the bed. "There." She smiled at Thomas. "Where were we?"

He puffed out a small laugh, then dropped his head, brushing his lips over the curve of her neck where it joined with her shoulder. She shivered as his breath tickled her skin. "Where were we? Let's see. You just asked me to make love to you, I believe."

Her cheeks burned, but she wasn't going to turn back now. "Yes."

"Nothing would make me happier, Aliénor."

"*Thomas*." She blinked, tears streaking down her cheeks.

Before she could say anything else, he dropped a kiss onto her neck, and then another. Slowly his mouth worked its way in a hot trail up to her jaw, her cheek, until at last his breath stirred against her lips. They were both shaking now. "I surrender, my lady," he murmured against her lips. "I surrender to you if you'll surrender to me."

"Yes." Her heart soared with a joy that made her light headed as they tumbled backward together onto the feather bed. He kissed her at last, his eyes happily crinkled, and she could taste the smile on his lips. She wondered if he could feel the love in her heart.

———◆———

Thomas woke many hours later, careful not to move too much and wake Aliénor. Her hair was a coppery, silken spill across the tumbled blankets. They'd both dressed after their lovemaking, but the neck of her gown had slipped a little, showing the delicate line of her collarbone. Her skin looked like clear, perfect marble in the gray light from the window.

His chest constricted, actually ached, as he eased his way out of that tumbled bed, walking away from her. He fancied he'd have the red-and-gold pattern of the jacquard blanket embedded in his heart forever now.

I will come back, he promised himself. As soon as he'd checked in, found out if there had been any movement on the walls. He traced his hand lightly over the silk of her hair. She stirred and smiled in her sleep but did not awaken.

"I will marry you, Aliénor." A promise not just to her and the fancy curtains, but also to himself. He would get them free of this cursed city somehow, and he would marry her. Politics and practicalities be damned. He knew what her mouth tasted like, the smell of her hair, the soft sighs and hums of happiness she made when he kissed her. To walk away from her, from the potential of the two of them together, would be a kind of curse. A flouting of Fate's gentle mercy that would be almost offensive.

With a half-swallowed groan, he left her sleeping and padded lightly down the stairs. Most of the others lay sleeping, even Llewellyn. The magician's long form was sprawled on a pallet by the fireplace, mouth open and snoring. He'd probably exhausted himself the night before, tending to patients. Thomas left his magician sleeping and nodded hello to Lady Violette and a few of the wounded soldiers who were awake.

"Lord Guillaume sent a note for you, Your Highness." Lady Violette scurried over to hand him the note, her eyes lowered. He wondered if she knew what he and her lady had been doing the night before.

Her gaze flicked up to meet his, and she gave him a small, shy smile. "I am glad you and the princess..." She broke off and shook her head, embarrassed.

Thomas grinned and patted her hand. "Worked out our disagreement?"

"Yes. That." She spoiled her recovery by giggling.

"Forgive me, Lady Violette. I didn't think you liked me much."

She lowered her dark eyes. "I saw you get my lady to safety yesterday and...and she smiles with you. That never used to happen before. With the prince."

"I see." And he softly smiled at her.

Looking flustered, Violette waved her hands in confusion and scurried back to the less confusing company of Ned.

Thomas unfolded his note from Lord Guillaume and read it over. There had been no serious incursions during the night, but Thomas's presence was most urgently requested on the wall this morning. If his wounds would permit.

Thomas hesitated. He wanted to wake Aliénor up, to say good-bye and tell her that he would be back as soon as possible. But they had been up so late—

He grinned in memory and caught at his lower lip with his teeth, trying to hide the expression. She made him so happy and light. "A scrap of vellum, if you please? Lady Violette, I'm leaving a note for the princess. Will you see that she gets it straightaway when she wakes up?"

"Of course, Your Highness."

Thomas dashed off a quick note, grinning all the while, and left it in care of Lady Violette as he walked out of the nobleman's house. He passed one group of soldiers just coming off shift and heading to their beds, but otherwise the streets were startlingly empty, every doorway closed, every window shuttered.

"Thomas."

He froze at the sound, his body jolting with alarm. "Aliénor?"

"Thomas."

Impossible. He'd left her sleeping. Safe.

The cry came again, laced with fear. "Thomas, oh *please*."

He took off running, following the sound of her cries back toward a narrow alley near the nobleman's house. "*Aliénor?*"

"Here."

He rounded the alley corner but something stopped him, a prickling on his scalp, an uneasiness that he could not name. He was reaching for his sword as someone slammed into him from behind, pinning his arms. He whipped around and caught a glimpse of his attacker. "Godric?"

Thomas's heart was pounding even before a little chuckle sounded from the shadows in the alleyway. As Godric dragged Thomas forward, Mistress Helen was still smiling. Godric pushed the king to his knees in front of the blood witch.

Thomas thrashed, but the younger man's hold was too strong. Thomas's sleeves felt wet, and he glanced over in dismay to realize he'd reopened the wound on his arm. "How did you get into the city, witch?"

She shrugged. "I've been here a few days. Just a poor widow woman and her brother. Refugees from another Jerdic colony. I suspected you were headed this way."

"How did you know where I was in the city?"

"Your blood, dear Thomas. Once I've tasted a man's blood I can always follow the scent and find him again. Anywhere."

The blood witch cooed in delight and peeled his sleeve and bandage both back to see the raw wound beneath. She stuck her thumb into the arrow wound, pressing cruelly hard. Thomas let out a roar of pain, not caring for his dignity. Maybe someone would hear and come to his aid.

The witch popped her bloody thumb into her mouth and sucked hard, eyeing him. She winked.

He spat at her and thrashed again, trying to throw off Godric.

"Ah." The blood witch sighed happily, her pupils dilating for a moment before they contracted back to their regular size.

That horrid, familiar stiffening of his limbs settled over him as the witch stripped away his will. He thrashed weakly once. The last twitch of a doomed man. It did no good at all.

The blood witch clucked her tongue. "Now, now, straighten up. We need to pay a visit to little Aliénor, and I want you looking your best."

"*No.*" Thomas gritted the words out from between his teeth. The effort made his jaw hurt, his head ache. "Why?"

The witch shook her head, raising an impatient eyebrow at him. "So you can kill her, of course."

Chapter Twenty-One

Aliénor knew she should get up. There were probably things to do, people to help, ways to be useful. But every muscle in her body was warm and liquid. The bedroom door creaked open and she didn't even have the strength to roll over. "Thomas?"

His heavy boots stomped across the floor, and then his heat settled against her body, his front to her spine. She hummed with pleasure and pushed her bottom against him. He touched her shoulder, turning her onto her back. She kept her eyes closed but smiled and toppled over willingly to lie beneath him. *What a shameless wretch I am.* She laughed happily.

His hands traced over her face and jaw, down to her neck. She arched into his touch and lifted her hand to touch his face, at last opening her eyes. Instead of the sleepy, happy expression she expected, his face twisted into a mask of anguish.

She touched his lips. "Thomas? What's wrong?"

"*Run.*" He gasped the word out, as if it were literally torn from his lips. A vein throbbed in his forehead.

"Thomas—"

His hands fastened around her throat, squeezing tight, crushing the air out of her. Her throat burned. She gagged and clawed at his hands in pure, animal instinct. He pressed harder.

Something wet plopped against her face. Tears. He was crying, tears dripping off his face and onto hers.

"Wh-*why?*" She had to mouth the words. She had no breath.

He blinked, and his grip slackened ever so slightly. "Blood witch."

"No." Her body clenched with horror and fear. Aliénor let out a hoarse sob and tugged at his fingers, dragging a shallow breath in. "*No.*"

Thomas's breath was ragged too, almost as hoarse as hers. His hands shook where they gripped her throat. "Not strong enough." His hands spasmed around her throat. She flinched. "Forgive me." His voice broke.

Aliénor's nose burned. Wetness trailed out of her eyes. Blackness edged her vision. *No.* She kicked out in a blind tearing panic. Bucking beneath him, she managed to throw him off.

"Help." She half fell off the bed, scurrying away on all fours. "*Help!*"

Thomas rounded the bed, his brow furrowed, his mouth stern as he pursued her. Tear tracks slicked his cheeks.

Someone pounded against the door. "Princess?"

"Break the door down!" Aliénor levered herself to her feet, weak and dizzy, frantically glancing around the room for a weapon. Thomas lunged for her and she ducked away, rolling sideways under the bed.

The pounding on the door increased, the wood rattling in its frame.

"*Hurry.*" She scuttled out from under the bed, making a mad dash for the door. Thomas leapt over the bed and caught her skirt, yanking her back. She cried out and slammed hard to the ground, her breath punching out of her on impact.

"Thomas, *please.*" She clawed at the floor and kicked as he gathered great handfuls of her skirt and jerked her toward him. He caught her by the arms and tossed her backward onto the bed. He pressed his body atop hers, crushing her into the mattress in a horrible parody of intimacy. His hands clawed for her throat. He froze, blinking, and shook himself. Fighting the spell. But then she could almost see the witch's leash settling around his neck as he bore in on her again.

She slapped his face hard enough to make her hand sting. As he recoiled from the blow, she twisted underneath him. Rolling to the side, she pawed at the side table, reaching for a hairbrush, a comb, *anything* to defend herself with. As he yanked hard on her leg, dragging her underneath him, her fingers fumbled over the hairpin.

She held it aloft, letting him see it clenched in her hand. "Please, don't make me."

His face convulsed, his body shivering against hers. His muscles were braced and taut as if with great effort. "I surrender. Please, Aliénor. Do it fast."

"Thomas," she sobbed.

"*I can't—*" His hands twitched, tightening around her throat.

Lungs aching, heart hurting, she stabbed the cursed hairpin into his chest. Just over his heart. He gasped in sudden pain. The breath left her in a sympathetic hurt. His hands loosened, and his eyes rolled back as he slid sideways off the bed to land on the floor. He did not move.

"*No.* Oh spare me. *Please no!*" Aliénor lay on the mattress a long moment, gasping and coughing, sobbing, wiping snot away with her sleeve. Her body hurt, and she thought she might shake apart. At last, she rolled off the bed, falling onto all fours as she crawled over to Thomas.

Thomas lay still as death, the hairpin sticking out of his chest. It hadn't gone in deep, and she ripped the silver bauble out of him and flung it angrily across the room. "*Thomas.*" She set his head in her lap, shaking his shoulder, gently slapping his face. "Thomas."

Nothing she did roused him. He didn't stir, didn't open his eyes. She pressed her cheek against his mouth and felt his breath puff against her skin, but it was so faint. His eyes wouldn't open. "Thomas, *please.*"

The pressure built behind her eyes until her mouth trembled with it. A great ache filled her as if her insides were caving in. She buried her fingers in the fabric of his tunic and shook him in anger, in desperation. "Do not leave me. *Do not leave me like this, Thomas.* Damn you." Her voice was a hoarse croak, and it hurt her to speak. At that moment, it hurt to live.

She pressed her cheek to his heart, listening to the faint beat inside him, and she wanted to die. "Thomas, no. Please no."

The door splintered behind her, and she instinctively stooped to shield Thomas's body from flying debris.

"What the *hell* is happening?" Llewellyn clattered into the room. "Sire, what is—" The magician was across the room in three bounds and all but threw Aliénor away from Thomas's body as he bent to examine it.

Aliénor swabbed at her face with her sleeve again. "I awoke—" She stopped and coughed, but her next attempt was no better. She could make her voice work, but it was still a hoarse croak, and it hurt to speak. "Thomas tried to strangle me, Llewellyn. Blood witch made him. I was so sc-scared."

Llewellyn sat back on his heels and gaped at her, his face quivering with some strong emotion.

She took a deep breath, forcing herself to continue. "Thomas couldn't stop himself. I couldn't... I used that cursed hairpin. I had to—"

"You used the sleeping curse on him?"

She pressed her hands to her face, scrubbing hard as a bout of gasping hiccups spasmed through her. *Oh, everything hurts.* At last, she simply had to nod.

"My lady, I..." Llewellyn trailed off. She looked up at him and noticed for the first time that his own eyes were shining, his voice almost as ragged as her own. "Princess, everyone downstairs is asleep too."

"*What?*"

"The sleeping curse has claimed everyone else in the house. We have to go." He reached for her.

She yanked her arm away, crawling backward from him. "You want me to leave him?"

"If the blood witch sent him then she must be nearby. And everyone who can help us is *asleep*." He dragged her to her feet, and she forced herself to let go of Thomas's hand, to leave him behind. The best way to help him now was to keep herself and Llewellyn safe.

As they passed through the downstairs room, Aliénor couldn't help but gape. Every soldier, every servant, Violette and Noémi...all of them were asleep, sprawled across tables, fallen to the floor. Every last person in the house was unconscious.

She shook her head. "How? How can they all be sleeping? The spell wasn't that strong before. It was only me last time."

Llewellyn's mouth pinched with unhappiness. "My fault, I suspect. The blood witch's small, simple spell got all tangled up with my magic when I drew it out of you. And my power seems to have magnified the effect."

After peeking through the door to make sure the street was clear, they scurried out together, stalking carefully from one street to another. Aliénor had fastened her small dagger on and borrowed a short sword from one of the guards at the house. After what happened with Thomas, she just felt better armed.

They didn't see many people, but those they did see were all as deeply asleep as Thomas and the others. A miserable light drizzle had settled over the city, dusting them with tiny water droplets, dampening the air.

"Why aren't I asleep?" Aliénor swabbed rainwater out of her eyes. "Why aren't you?"

Llewellyn gave a small shrug. "My guess is that there are only three people awake in the city right now: the two of us and the blood witch." He held up three fingers and ticked them off as he made his points. "The blood witch is immune because she cast the original spell herself. You are immune because I pulled the spell out of you in the first place. And I am immune to the spell because I'm the damn fool idiot who mixed his magic in and made this curse so powerful. Here, come on. Let's see how bad this is."

They had reached the city walls, and he climbed up one of the ladders to a lookout stand. Aliénor followed behind him just so she wouldn't be alone.

The two lookouts lay passed out and draped over each other like sleeping children. Llewellyn swore softly, standing by the window, and Aliénor came to look out beside him. "Oh my..."

All the men of Anutitum manning the city's walls were asleep. Even the horses and beasts of burden were unconscious. Across the battlefield, the Tiochene camp too lay utterly still, every man, woman, and beast sprawled on the ground in fitful slumber.

Aliénor flinched and looked away, hugging herself for comfort. "How do we lift the curse?"

Llewellyn rubbed his temples hard. "This is bad. I'm...I've never..."

"We probably don't have to go one by one curing everybody. If we can just lift the curse off Thomas, the rest should follow, yes?" That seemed logical to her, and never mind if that really was the answer her heart selfishly wanted to it to be.

"Yes, that's generally the way an enchantment like this works. Cure the king and the city will follow."

"We must get back to him then."

———◇———

The longer they went without seeing a sign of the blood witch, the more uneasy Aliénor grew. "We shouldn't have left Thomas alone. She'll guess that we'll come back for him."

"We had to see if there was anyone else in the city awake to help us, Princess."

"You don't think you're strong enough to beat her?"

"If it were only her strength against mine, I would not be worried, but I fear—" He halted in the street and gripped Aliénor's arm hard, stopping her momentum. She could actually see the muscles in his throat move as he swallowed. "—that."

Aliénor gazed at the cozy nobleman's house just ahead of them. The earlier drizzle had increased to a full-out rainstorm, and it was difficult to see through the downpour. For a moment, her heart lifted to see people moving about all around the house. She opened her mouth to cry a glad greeting to Violette.

But her handmaiden's eyes were shut tight, and the graceful Violette moved with a jerky, unnatural gait like a puppet with a particularly clumsy puppeteer.

"What is—"

"I suppose I should thank you," Mistress Helen called out. She stood on the roof of the building, her hands dancing in front of her like a musician plucking her strings or...like a puppeteer making her marionettes dance.

Aliénor drew her borrowed sword, a sudden bitterness in her throat. "Oh no."

Mistress Helen's mouth tipped up in a tight smile. "People are so much easier to control when they're unconscious. I don't have to fight their own wills for their bodies, you see. You've gifted me a city full of helpers. As I said, I should thank you." Her eyes narrowed. "But I think I'll just kill you instead." She flicked her fingers outward as if shaking water droplets off them.

Llewellyn grabbed Aliénor's free arm, yanking her backward as the people round the nobleman's house charged them. Everyone had a weapon of some kind: swords, knives, even cudgels. Violette had a wickedly sharp fishhook. Aliénor too had weapons, of course, but she wasn't willing to use them on any of these innocent people.

Llewellyn stopped in the street and made a slash through the air with his arm. Aliénor's hair stood on end, and the people chasing them bounced off some sort of invisible wall. Sweat popped on Llewellyn's forehead, and he groaned through gritted teeth. "I don't want to hurt them."

Aliénor shook her head, staring in anguish as sweet Violette hacked mindlessly at the wall holding her back from them. Her beautiful face was utterly blank, her eyes still closed. One of the men toward the front slipped, and the others, oblivious, stepped on top of him to keep pushing against Llewellyn's invisible wall.

"Llewellyn."

"I see him." With another strangled oath, Llewellyn let the shield fall. Aliénor and Llewellyn took off running.

"The river, Llewellyn. Her magic won't work over running water."

"Neither will mine."

"We'll risk it." Aliénor hauled him after her toward the gurgle of the river.

The street cobbles were slick beneath their feet. The rain beat harder now, pummeling them like an angry spirit. Aliénor's foot turned beneath her, and she went down. The breath was knocked out of her. Her sword skittered out of her hands, and one of the sleeping people snatched it up. Other hands immediately pawed at her legs, dragging her backward.

"*No.*" She kicked out, but as she looked back, she gasped in dismay to see Violette reeling away from her, holding a bloody nose. The other sleeping victims clawed at her, but their hands slid off, finding no easy purchase in the pouring rain and wetness.

"Back off." Llewellyn pushed the air with his hands, and a great wind kicked up, blowing their attackers momentarily away from her as if they were dandelion fluff.

Llewellyn yanked her to her feet and dragged her along after him. The river roared just ahead, swelling with the storm water. The river's level had risen at least two high-water marks since last night. The burned-out remains of Aliénor's boat rocked just ahead of them, still tied to the dock as it swayed back and forth on its tethering line.

Fifty feet shy of the ship, a new crowd of curse victims burst out of the small house just next to the dock. Aliénor danced free from their clutching hands, twisting and ducking. Someone grabbed her skirt, and a swath of fabric ripped away with a loud tearing noise as she jerked herself free.

They caught Llewellyn, and he howled and thrashed as they bent his arms back. "*Run.*" He shot Aliénor an anguished look and gritted his teeth as the curse victims wrestled him to lie facedown on the cobbles. The magician could probably free himself, but he would have to hurt innocent people to do it.

Aliénor rocked on her feet, torn by indecision whether she should help him or keep running.

Mistress Helen strolled down the street then. She wore a white cloak, a little bloody and torn, but the fine tasseled hood seemed to be keeping her dry.

Thomas's cloak. Aliénor's eyes burned, her insides churning.

Ignoring Aliénor, the blood witch crossed to Llewellyn and hurriedly knelt to tap his forehead. He went limp in his captors' arms, and Aliénor recognized the spell Llewellyn had used on her just yesterday.

Mistress Helen gave Llewellyn's wet hair a small pat like he was a child. "I'll play with you later." She straightened and leveled her angry, assessing gaze at Aliénor. "Now, Princess—"

Aliénor whirled around and leapt off the short dock, onto the burned-out remains of the ship that should have carried her to safety. *I just hope I'm right about moving water and her magic.*

It seemed the stories were right, though, for the witch's face immediately crimped with annoyance, and she flung her hands into the air. "Why must you make this so difficult, you little brat?" With narrowed eyes, Mistress Helen flicked a finger out.

Godric, poor Godric, shuffled forward. His eyes were shut like the others', but whereas their faces were all blank, his was scrunched and tense as if his dreams were a torment. His clothes were torn and bloody. Shadows and lines had carved themselves into his face as if he had aged ten years after only a week or so under the witch's power.

Aliénor shuffled back a step, the wounded boat bobbing around her, making her balance chancy. She steadied her grip on her sword, her stomach fluttering. She pitied Godric and feared him in equal measure, but he was not getting his hands on her again.

Godric stood on the very edge of the street now, ready to walk onto the dock and her small boat. The witch glanced back and forth between Godric and the water. At last, she narrowed her eyes and flipped her hand in a gesture almost of dismissal. Godric's body heaved itself off the safety of the road, trying to overleap the gap and land on her boat. Aliénor flinched, bracing for the coming attack.

But as soon as Godric's feet left land, the witch's will seemed to leave him. His body went boneless, and he splashed unconscious into the water, just shy of the boat's edge.

Aliénor rushed to the side, instinctively reaching down to grab him, but the ruthless tide had already carried him too far. As she watched, the lines of his face smoothed out, a small smile twitching on his lips though he still slept. He spun in the coursing river like a leaf carried by the wind. Slowly his heavy clothes soaked up the water and he sank, disappearing under the dark tide of the river. The smile on his face never faltered.

Aliénor flinched, her stomach roiling at this waste of life. "Your power doesn't work here, witch."

"It works well enough." Mistress Helen chuckled, but the tension in her shoulders put the lie to her smile. "Come off the ship, little princess. Or shall I drown someone you *do* care about? Shall I choke this river with dead bodies?" She raised two fingers and flicked them toward the river. Noémi and Violette marched forward and stood swaying at the very edge of the dock, ready to walk to their deaths at the witch's whim.

Aliénor rubbed her hands over her face, all of her shaking with fear and cold and anger. "What do you want?"

"I want you to come with me to awaken King Thomas."

"Why?"

The witch snorted. "So I can take off with him and rule Lyond as his queen. My plan hasn't changed." She flung her hands out to take in the still forms of the accursed sleepers. "You think I want to be queen of the sleeping kingdom? No. Anyway, they'll all be dead in a few days if they don't eat. Drink."

Thomas would be dead in a few days if they didn't lift the curse. Noémi. Violette. Aliénor shook her head. "You'll kill me if I go with you."

"Yes, but only after we've woken King Thomas together. And the city. Are you really so selfish that you refuse to help me?"

Aliénor turned her face up to the rain, letting the cold water pummel her skin. Her feet were numb, her body shuddering with uncontrollable chill. *There has to be a better way.* It was a stubborn thought, perhaps a foolish one, and yet... "If I wake Thomas up, you'll just take control of him again. I'd be saving him just to turn him into your slave."

"Yes, but he'd be *alive*." The witch was impatient, her foot tapping, her voice a brisk snap like a whip.

Aliénor pressed a palm to her own throat, to the bruises there. She could feel her pulse pounding beneath her fingertips, frantic as the tumbling whirl in her mind. "Why did you send Thomas to kill me? Why not just try yourself?"

The witch rolled her eyes. "Never mind. I'll come get you myself." She yanked the sword out of Noémi's hand, and the witch jumped off the dock.

Aliénor scurried back as the boat rocked with the witch landing. The wounded boat seemed to groan under the extra weight, the wooden beams creaking. Water sloshed over the side, splashing across Aliénor's face like a slap.

The witch swung the sword as she landed. Aliénor dodged, and the blade stuck in the wood of the small, half-burned cabin compartment.

The witch tugged and grunted in frustration, trying to free her blade. As she stumbled back, she yanked the spell-knife from the sheath at her belt. She tilted the blade to flash in Aliénor's eyes. "Better this way, eh? No more coaxing."

Aliénor's belly went cold. "Blood magic won't work on open water."

"Are you sure? Care to test your luck?"

No. Very much no. Aliénor tore her own knife out of its sheath.

The witch snorted. "Pretty toy, Princess. I don't think you ever learned to fight with a knife, though, did you? You never *had* to learn."

Aliénor also snatched a broken board up off the deck, hoping she could keep the witch far enough back. As the witch advanced, Aliénor swung her board at Mistress Helen, but the witch ducked and came up slashing with her own knife. Aliénor stumbled away, swinging the board one-handed, trying to hold on to her little knife as the grip grew slippery with water.

The witch looked cocky now, confident. She and Aliénor both knew she only needed to get the shallowest cut in and the fight could be over. "Do you know why I sent your king to kill you, little Aliénor?"

Aliénor dodged away. The witch slashed at her face, and Aliénor wheeled her arms, trying to balance. Aliénor lost her footing and landed on the deck, her rump stinging. She'd dropped the board, and Mistress Helen kicked it away with a snort of contempt. Aliénor scuttled backward as the witch advanced toward her.

Mistress Helen grinned. "I sent King Thomas to kill you because that is the surest way to make him mine. If you were still alive in the world, he'd fight me to get back to you. To be free. But if you're dead, and at his own hand, then my control becomes a refuge for him. He'll never want to be himself again after that, never want to face what he's done. It's the perfect prison."

Aliénor's body tensed, seizing up with anger. With a cry of rage, she hurled herself at Mistress Helen, knocking the other woman to the deck of the little skiff. Aliénor's knife went skittering away. Something cracked beneath them, and they lurched downward together, water suddenly sloshing over both their faces. Aliénor reared up out of the water and slammed the blood witch down hard again. Again.

Mistress Helen spat water and thrashed beneath her, clawing for Aliénor's face. She'd dropped her knife too, and lost it to the river pouring into the boat. "You stupid—"

With a crack, the boat split in half underneath them, and they were both dumped into the chill, rushing water together.

Chapter Twenty-Two

Under the water, tossed by the current, the witch clawed for Aliénor's throat. Chest aching for air, Aliénor shoved back at the woman as the river tossed them along. Aliénor twisted free of the blood witch and kicked toward the surface of the river.

She swam hard for the dock, pawing at the boards, her sodden garments dragging at her all the way. The witch slammed into her back, slipping and grabbing to use Aliénor's body as a boost to heave herself up. Aliénor elbowed the other woman in the gut and slapped her hand over Mistress Helen's face. She pushed hard. Mistress Helen fell back, her eyes wide, and splashed into the water, going under.

Aliénor braced herself against the dock, holding on, watching the water, waiting for the witch to resurface. After a moment, she dared to turn her back and gripped the wooden dock to lever herself up.

The wood cracked, the board breaking lose to bang against her head. She crashed into the river, the water swirling her round and round. Alarm flared inside Aliénor and she struck for the surface, for air.

Something caught at her legs, tugging her back. For one horrified moment, she thought it was the blood witch. But as she felt down around her ankle, she realized her now-tattered skirt had caught on a nail in the side of the dock. She yanked again and again and at last felt the fabric give.

With a voiceless cry of relief, Aliénor hugged the pylons under the dock, holding on to them as she swam through the murky water up to the surface. She caught a trailing rope in the water, used that to drag herself up the rest of the way.

With a gasp, she popped her head out of the water and sucked a deep breath into her quivering lungs. She held grimly onto her rope as the river rushed around her, trying to tug her back into its suffocating embrace. Her arms ached, and her body shivered hard enough to hurt.

Something bumped into her from behind and she startled away, an unwise scream causing her to swallow a mouthful of water.

It was the blood witch, facedown in the river. Aliénor caught at the woman's clothes with one hand as Mistress Helen's limp body rushed by. But Aliénor's hands were too numb and cold-clumsy. The witch's body spun away from her to the center of the river's tide and was soon swept out of sight. Just one more piece of detritus from the storm.

"Princess? Princess Aliénor!" At the sound of Llewellyn's voice, Aliénor's eyes pinched closed with relief.

"*Here*." She tried to scream it, but the word came out only a half-strangled croak. A board banged into her side, then a dead sheep. Her body was going cold, sluggish, her eyes drifting closed. Her fingers wanted to loosen on the rope, let go—

Llewellyn's hands fastened around her arms, and he hauled her up like a landed fish, water sluicing off her clothes and hair. They flopped together onto the dock in an ungraceful tangle of limbs and wet clothes.

After a moment, Llewellyn groaned and pushed himself up onto his elbows. "The witch is dead, then?"

"Drowned, I think. How did you know?"

He tapped his temple. "Her spell lifted off me, and I woke up. And the sleepers are no longer under her control."

"Are they—"

"Still asleep. It's my magic too in this spell, and unfortunately, mine was the stronger. Perhaps, if all else fails, I'll have to—" He broke off and cleared his throat, staring at Aliénor. "Anyway, are you all right?"

She just shook her head and pushed unsteadily to her feet. "I'll decide later. Let's break this damn curse."

The cursed sleepers had all collapsed again, dozing peacefully right in the middle of the road. Aliénor and Llewellyn dragged the ones by the dock under shelter to make sure no one was washed away or drowned in a street puddle. More in-depth help would have to come later. For now, the best thing for everyone would be to break the damn curse.

The nobleman's house lay empty, of course. Discarded blankets and bandages littered the floor, and a few splashes of blood from men who had been forced to stumble out of bed to follow the witch's call.

A note atop the table caught Aliénor's eye, and she staggered over to the small scrap as if towed there by a leash. Her name was scrawled across the folded note. Eyes stinging, already guessing what she would read, she unfolded the paper. He'd written it in Jerdic. For her.

"*Dearest Aliénor, I must leave you now to confer with your cousin.*" A splotch of ink lay just there, as if he had sat thinking with his quill pressed to paper before he could continue writing: "*Last night was the most wonderful night of my life. I hope we can discuss the terms of our mutual surrender again today. I leave my heart here behind with you. Guard it well until we meet again?*"

For some reason, the blood witch had not drafted Thomas into her army of sleeping soldiers. He lay stretched out atop the jacquard quilt, his hands folded neatly upon his chest, his face still and composed like in death. He looked like a king, like the golden splendor of glory and honor personified.

I do not want a carven king. I want a tongue and teeth, pokey elbows, strong hands. I want willing arms and a warm kiss. Aliénor folded up beside his body, her knees giving out. She leaned over Thomas, water from her wet hair dripping onto his face. He did not stir, did not even flinch in his cursed sleep.

Llewellyn brushed her shoulder with his fingertips. "You should change your clothes. Dry off. Eat something."

"No."

"Princess—"

"*No.* No more delays. I put this curse on him. I will not make him wait to be free of it. Let's try it now."

Llewellyn held his empty hands out. A notch of worry had formed between his brows. "I'm not...sure."

Aliénor thumped the bed in frustration. "You're a magician. You drew this poison out of me."

"The spell was weaker then. And I don't want to risk you."

"Risk me?"

He shook his head, half-distracted as if he didn't quite have the words.

Aliénor gripped Llewellyn's arm and forced him to turn toward her. "You have an idea, don't you? What is it?"

The magician just shook his head, looking frazzled. "Kiss him."

She recoiled. "Kiss him?"

"Yes."

"Just *kiss him*? Like a silly fairy tale or something?"

Llewellyn folded his arms, brow furrowing in exasperation. "Look, when you kiss him I'll open a channel up between you two. You follow that down and bring him back to us. Just leave all the fiddly magic bits to me, all right?"

Aliénor swallowed. "Fine."

"If it doesn't work and you get sucked down into the cursed sleep with him—"

"*What?*"

The magician flung up a placating hand. "Never fear. If this fails, I'll just cut my throat and then all the magic will unravel. All right?"

"*No.*" They glared at each other for a long, tense minute. Then Aliénor swabbed water out of her eyes. "I'm not going to fail." She breathed out through her nose and shivered, her wet clothes clinging to her skin. "You're right, though. I should have changed my gown." With that, she closed her eyes and leaned down, pressing her lips to Thomas's mouth.

He was cold against her and still. *It's not working.* She tried to ease back, but then something gripped her hard, drawing her down into darkness and cold. An eerie quiet. She gasped and stilled her instinctive urge to wrench away. *No. I'm not giving up.*

Instead of retreating, Aliénor threw herself toward that reaching darkness, toward the choking black mass boiling behind her eyelids. The magic took hold of her, a hard, angry grip eerily like being choked. She pressed closer to Thomas. She flung her will, her hope out toward the sleeping king. *I love you, Thomas. Come back to me.*

———◆———

Thomas lay in utter darkness, numb, afraid. His legs felt chained, his arms pinned. Drawing breath grew more painful with each moment, as if someone were stacking rocks on top of him and steadily adding to the pile.

"*You left us.*" The voices of those he'd failed echoed all around him. His dead soldiers. His father. His brother, Hugh. His missing nephew, Gabriel. "*You've destroyed the kingdom.*"

Rosamund...

"*You'd replace me with some foreign girl?*"

"No. Not replace. Never replace." His heart had been dead, dust-barren and empty for so long. How could Rosamund begrudge him this new growth with Aliénor? These hopeful green shoots of spring hurt, but they healed him too.

"*The people will never accept her.*"

"*She'll destroy the kingdom.*"

"*It will mean another war with Jerdun.*"

"Thousands more lives lost because you can't control your lust."

He thrashed, trying to free his arms, trying to stop the voices as they swelled and crashed against him like a wave trying to crush him against the shore.

Rosamund stood beside him, her soft hands tracing over his brow. *"Sleep, Thomas.* Sleep. *Isn't that better? Sleep and forget."*

Under her gentle hands, the riot of voices softened to a gentle susurrus of whispers. Easier to ignore. Thomas expelled a tight breath through his teeth. He was so tired...

"Aliénor will be better off without you, anyway."

"She's so young."

"So bright."

"Why let her chain herself to a dried-up old man like you?"

"Sleep, dear Thomas. Just sleep."

Thomas felt his head nodding, his chest aching. He let his eyes flutter closed, let his limbs relax in their restraints. "Yes. You're right."

"No." The voice was soft, faint, but it brought with it a warm glow, a light that reminded him what sunlight felt like. *Aliénor.*

The voices emitted a chorus of hissing, and his eyes startled open again. When he looked around him, he did not see familiar faces. Rosamund was not here. Just a boiling black cloud. A formless evil thing. The cloud churned, but a figure moved behind. As he caught sight of red hair and a pale face in the dark of the cloud, Thomas tugged at his restraints. "Aliénor!"

She drew closer, the black cloud swirling and shifting around her as she pumped her arms, thrashing and swimming toward him even though the inky blackness tried to haul her away.

A firm hand grasped his chin and turned him away. He stared into the face of Rosamund. *"Thomas, you must* sleep. *Just let go. Stop fighting and we can be together."*

He clenched his jaw, his heart aching with missing her.

"Thomas," Aliénor cried out.

Rosamund's fingers dug into the skin of his jaw. "*Sleep and forget, Thomas. Forget your responsibilities. Forget your sorrows. Thomas...*" She leaned down to kiss him.

"No, Thomas, fight!"

He looked back at Aliénor. Her summer-red hair swirled around her as if a great wind buffeted her. She gripped the edge of his platform, her fingers white. Tears streaked her cheeks.

He wanted to dash the tears away, but when he tried, the chains around his wrists clattered.

"*Sleep, Thomas.*"

"No!" Aliénor's nostrils flared with anger. "Thomas, you've fought so hard for other people. To do the right thing, the honorable thing. Fight that hard for yourself now. Fight that hard for *us*."

He turned his face away, tears stinging his eyes.

"*Thomas,*" Rosamund crooned and leaned toward him again. Yet when he looked at her, really looked, her skin was gray, wispy at the edges, like a face formed in a cloud.

He pulled as far away from her as he could. "I will always love you, Rosamund. But I can't linger in the past anymore." He'd done that for fifteen years, held so hard to the memory of her that he hadn't tried to move on at all. "I want more than beautiful memories now. I want a beautiful future."

The apparition hissed and recoiled from him, breaking into the black fog once more.

Aliénor let out a sobbing gasp of relief and flung herself against him. "We have to go."

The chorus of voices erupted again, cruel laughter that sounded eerily like the blood witch, but magnified—as if the whole world were Mistress Helen doubled and doubled again. A whole chorus of cruel, laughing witches.

"*You think you can have that with Aliénor? She'll never forgive you. You choked her, nearly killed her. You've failed at everything. What woman would want you now?*"

Thomas swallowed and pinched his eyes closed with pain. *Of course*. He turned his face away, turned from that grace that he did not deserve.

"Thomas." The voice was stern now and so near. A gentle touch brushed against his cheek, forcing him to turn to her, to see her. And he felt her skin, her warmth. He wondered how that shadow touch could have felt so real to him when he had breath and life standing beside him now.

"It's not real, Thomas." Aliénor's skin glowed faintly lustrous, luminous as a pearl, and the coppery-red waves of her hair danced gracefully around her as if stirred by a warm breeze. The maiden of spring. His beautiful princess with summer-red hair.

"Thomas," she said again. A soft plea, a tender touch of her soul to his own.

"I did hurt you, Aliénor. I failed you."

"It wasn't your fault."

"I'm weak. Foolish. Old."

"I choose you. I want you. Come back to me." She gripped his face in both her hands, her sweet breath stirring against his skin.

"You deserve better."

"Thomas." She was fading, the light of her blinking out, dimming away. "Thomas, *stop*. Stop fighting me. Believe in me. Trust in us."

He let out his breath, and it felt like one of the bands around him had loosened. A warm spring breeze seemed to tease across his face. "Surrender to you?" he whispered.

She smiled, and the whole world brightened around her, pushing the black fog back. "Yes, Thomas. *Yes*. I'll surrender to you if you surrender to me. Remember?"

"Aliénor..."

"Thomas." Her lips traced over his, gently, sweetly. Her mouth opened against his, exhaling warmth and life back into him. He opened himself to her gift, her light. Her life. Pins and needles started along his arms, pain. Light engulfed him, and a tingling warmth that almost hurt. Something pulled him forward, *up*. He felt dizzy, light-headed. "Aliénor?"

"I'm here. Follow me, Thomas. Follow me home."

Aliénor gasped in a deep breath and her chest hurt with it, as if it were the first real breath she'd taken in her life.

The room spun around her, but Llewellyn caught her by the shoulders before she could fall backward off the bed. "It was so dark." She frowned, and rubbed at an ache behind her eyes. "Did it work?" she whispered.

Thomas still lay quiet and unmoving on the bed, breathing deeply, eyes closed.

"My king?" Llewellyn's voice shook.

"Thomas." She leaned toward him, her heart hammering. She traced a hand down his cheek. "Thomas, it's time to wake up."

He still didn't open his eyes, but his mouth crimped in a small smile. "But if I lie here and keep pretending, no one will make me do anything."

Llewellyn barked out a half-hysterical laugh. Aliénor took in a shuddery deep breath, her heart swelling with a love strong enough to burst it. "Maybe you need another kiss, my king?" Catching her breath, holding it, she leaned down and kissed him again.

With a small groan, his mouth opened against hers, and he gasped in a deep breath, like a man swimming up from deep water.

She sat back and smiled at him, combing her fingers through his hair. "Hello."

His eyes opened at last, and his gaze was warm on her face, adoring. "Aliénor."

She bit her lip and traced her thumb over the soft curve of his mouth.

"*Llewellyn!*" A voice from downstairs. Someone calling. Someone else *awake*.

The breath gusted out of Llewellyn. He clasped the king's shoulder in relief, then pushed Aliénor gently down on the bed. Llewellyn allowed no such rest for himself, but rose instead to go to the stairwell.

"Hello?" Llewellyn called down.

"Master Llewellyn!" It was Violette's voice.

Aliénor closed her eyes, almost doubling over with relief. *Praise be.* Violette was awake. Violette was all right.

"Is the princess there?"

Llewellyn laughed. "Yes, yes."

Violette clattered up the stairs, her voice still over-excited as she babbled from the hallway. "Everyone was asleep."

"We know."

"Even the Tiochene outside the walls were asleep. But they're all awake now. All of us too. Noémi's here."

"Oh—"

"They're retreating. The Tiochene. They're fleeing into the wilderness."

Aliénor widened her eyes at that.

Llewellyn grinned. "Scared of our magic, I wager."

Violette stood in the bedroom doorway now, mussed and bloody, but beaming fit to split her face in two. "Anyway, Lord Guillaume urgently wishes to speak with you, Master Llewellyn. He's outside. He wants to get all of us, soldiers, citizens, *all* of us people out of the city as fast as we can before the Tiochene return. Something about joining up with one of the other Jerdic city-states before he attempts to strike back." She bit her lip, looking worried. "I think Lord Guillaume thinks this city is cursed now." Her gaze flicked back and forth between Llewellyn, Thomas, and Aliénor. "He's worried it was the Tiochene who cast the sleeping spell and it backfired on them. *I* wondered...was it you?"

"No, it was Mistress Helen," Aliénor put in before Llewellyn could open his mouth. Guillaume still did not know Llewellyn was a magician, as far as Aliénor was aware. Best not to let her cousin figure that out *now*, of all times.

Llewellyn tugged at the ends of his hair, pacing in place, his brow furrowed in thought. "All right. I'm on my way." With a last sunny look at the king, Llewellyn hurried out the door to clatter down the stairs. Violette trailed behind him, happily rambling on about Lord Guillaume's plans for evacuation and eventual reprisal.

Aliénor shook her head, ignoring the bustle outside the door, and leaned closer to Thomas. "King Thomas."

"Princess Aliénor?" Thomas tilted his head to the side, his expression quizzical.

She brushed her mouth over his, teasing his lips with her own. "I received your note. Would you like to negotiate the terms of our mutual surrender now?"

A grin flashed over his face, and he sat forward to catch her about the waist, pulling her down on top of him. "I would like that." He hesitated, and his gaze darted up to lock with hers. "I would like that *very* much. My queen?"

Aliénor caught her breath. *Mutual surrender. Mutual compromise.* Was that not the way to make a marriage work? Both of them moving together, working together in tandem. A team, a partnership. She cupped his jaw in her hands and leaned down to kiss him again. "Yes," she whispered against his lips. "I say yes, my king."

*

Thank you so much for reading *Enchanting the King*. If you enjoyed it, please consider leaving a review on the retailer's site to help other readers discover it. There are also three more books in the series if you'd like to spend a bit more time with these characters: *The Beauty's Beast, The Apprentice Sorceress* and *The Changeling Child*.

*

Would you like to join my Reader Group and stay up to date on all my news & new releases? Anyone who joins my Reader Group will receive a free short story. You can find the sign up on my website:

www.elidonovan.wordpress.com

Acknowledgments

Many thanks to:

My editor Deb. My copy-editor at the Formatting Fairies. My original cover artist Simone. My graphic designer Najla.

My Viable Paradise writer buddies who brave the perilous word mines with me, especially my beta readers on this project Devin, Nancy, and Nadya.

My supportive family (Mom, Val, Ev & the cats). 2023 update: And my kids for actually going to sleep in a timely manner so I could work on the re-release.

And, of course, so many thanks, all the thanks really, to my handsome husband (who completed SO MANY MISSIONS in Skyrim while I neglected him to finish this book).

Apologies to Eleanor & Henry for the way I have mangled their histories and personalities (again!) for my own nefarious ends.

Also by Eli Donovan

Science Fiction with Romantic Elements (and time travel!)
The Time Traitors Series:
Time Traitors

Time Traitor Files: Agent Nakamura – novelette

Time Trap (*coming soon!*)

*

Standalone SF Romance with some heat
Jacen

Zandro

*

Fairy Tale Retellings (sweet, closed door)
The Fairy Tales of Lyond Series:
The Beauty's Beast

Enchanting the King

The Apprentice Sorceress

The Changeling Child

*

Fairy Tale Retellings with some heat
The Fairy Tales of Jerdun Series:

The Swan's Prince (available in the duology *The Swan Princess Reimagined*)

*

About the Author

Eli Donovan is an author who grew up reading too many Robin McKinley books and knows all the words to every Disney song. Eli lives in Southern California with a husband, kids, and one grumpy elderly cat.

Eli Donovan Website: www.elidonovan.wordpress.com